DARE TO SURRENDER

THE DARE MÉNAGE SERIES
BOOK FIVE

JEANNE ST. JAMES

Editor: Proofreading by the Page
Cover Art: April Martinez
Beta Readers: Author Whitley Cox, Rita Cerdeira, & Krisztina Holló

www.jeannestjames.com

Sign up for my newsletter for insider information, author news, and new releases:
www.jeannestjames.com/newslettersignup

Dirty Angels MC, Blue Avengers MC & Blood Fury MC are registered trademarks of Jeanne St James, Double-J Romance, Inc.

Keep an eye on her website at http://www.jeannestjames.com/ or sign up for her newsletter to learn about her upcoming releases: http://www.jeannestjames.com/newslettersignup

Author Links: Instagram * Facebook * Goodreads Author Page * Newsletter * Jeanne's Review & Book Crew * BookBub * TikTok * YouTube

THE DARE MENAGE SERIES

The Dare Ménage Series:
(All can be read as standalones)

Double Dare
Daring Proposal
Dare to Be Three
A Daring Desire
Dare to Surrender
A Daring Journey

DEDICATION

I don't always do a dedication, but I wanted to do one for this book.

When I began writing Eli, Grant and Olivia's story, I had no idea that Eli would speak French. I usually find things out about my characters at the same point in the story that you readers do. My characters talk to me, and most of the time they laugh in my face if I try to actually plan their story.

So in this story, Eli suddenly starts to speak French and Grant loves it. It's hot, right? The only problem is that I don't speak ANY French. Plus, I needed a good reason for Eli to speak French in the first place! But I digress...

The point of this long-winded dedication is: I wanted to say thank you to my friend Rita Cerdeira who speaks fluent French! (Phew!) She corrected all of Eli's bungled French (or more like mine).

So thank you, Rita. And Eli and Grant thank you, too! <3

CHAPTER 1

Olivia could hear nothing but the pounding of her heart in her ears. She stared at the large gold letters on the wall above the reception desk... *Ward, Jordan, & Holloway.*

The receptionist's lips were moving but Liv had no idea what the woman said.

She needed to turn and hightail it out of there before she got caught. This was a bad idea. One of way too many she'd made in her life.

Her stomach churned, and her mouth felt like it was packed full of cotton.

She closed her eyes for a moment, as a wave of panic washed up and over her. She could fix this herself. She'd been surviving on her own most of her life.

She never needed anyone to save her, and she didn't now.

Right.

She stiffened when she felt something, or someone, large and very warm at her back. She shook her head in an attempt to clear it and finally heard, "Are you okay?"

So, unless the receptionist had a deep, masculine voice, it wasn't a woman. A shiver ran down her spine.

When a large dark hand landed on her arm, she could only stare at it. She blinked. Why was this person touching her?

Then fingers wrapped around her chin, lifting her face and her gaze. She stared into very, very dark eyes. Eyes full of concern and... something else.

She wasn't used to the concern. That look seemed foreign to her. And the other? She had no clue why he would look at her like that.

"What?" she whispered, almost as if trapped in a fog.

"Are you okay?" The man snapped into motion, leading her over to a nearby chair and pushing her gently into it. "Cassie, grab a bottle of water."

From the corner of her eye, she saw the receptionist move at a hurried pace.

"Are you okay?"

Why did he keep asking her that?

"Yes," she murmured, her tongue thick.

"Are you here to see someone in particular?"

Liv watched his dark lips move. They were full and looked nice. And his teeth were really white. Nice people had nice lips, nice voices, and nice teeth.

Why did she care if he was nice?

"Yes."

"Who? Who do you have an appointment with?"

Liv shook her head slowly. "I don't."

"Then who are you here to see?"

She sucked in a shaky breath. "Trey."

"Trey," he echoed softly.

"Yes, Trey Holloway."

He tilted his head, his gaze searching her face. "Does he know you?"

What a weird question. "I hope so. He's my brother."

His dark eyes narrowed, and he only left her long enough to grab the bottle of water from Cassie, the receptionist. He cracked the seal on the lid and opened it, handing the bottle to her. "Drink."

"I'm not thirsty," she said, her tone flat, even though she felt parched.

"Drink anyway."

Liv lifted the bottle to her lips and sipped at the cool water. She blinked again and glanced up at the man towering over her. "Who are you?"

"Eli."

"Eli," Liv repeated, frowning, still feeling as if in a daze.

"Elliott Stone."

That was a nice name for someone with nice features. Some men didn't look right being bald. He did. His head was perfectly smooth and nicely shaped. Bald fit him. "Elliott," she repeated.

"Yes. Let me get Trey for you." He stepped back and turned to leave.

"No!"

He stopped, his back straightening. He was tall. Dark. And oh-so handsome. But, right now, none of that mattered.

Nothing mattered but why she was here.

Though, she should really leave before her brother was dragged into her mess. Especially since she hadn't seen him in sixteen years.

Because of that, he might not be happy with her. She had disappeared without a trace. No calls, no letters, no emails. She had gotten lost. Completely disappeared. And left him behind to deal with what was their nightmare of a childhood.

So, it was a bad idea for her to show up here in her moment of weakness.

"No. I'm just going to leave. I'll catch up with him another time. I thank you for your kindness." She pushed to her feet and beelined toward the lobby elevator.

He snagged her elbow as she passed and swung her around until they came face to face, his eyes dark and searching. "Whoa. No. You're not going anywhere."

She jerked her elbow, but his grip was tight enough that she couldn't pull free. "You can't tell me what to do."

"The hell I can't," he mumbled close to her ear. "You know why? Because I've worked here for a while now and never knew Trey had a sister. And now I'm wondering why I never knew that. So, to satisfy my curiosity, I'll escort you back to his office."

"Get your hand off me," she snapped, still tugging her arm.

"You didn't say please."

Right now, she didn't think he was so nice. "Please," she said with a forced nicety.

"That's better. But no."

She looked in panic toward the receptionist who just gave her a blank stare in return, like the woman was used to seeing large men dragging women through the lobby. Liv couldn't imagine it happened on a regular basis. But she'd seen a lot of crazy shit in her life, so nothing would surprise her.

"Let's go," he said, a determined look on his face.

Liv tried to dig her heels into the nice carpeting, but he was too big and too strong to resist. She hardly got a glimpse of the various offices they passed until he abruptly stopped in front of another woman. A secretary maybe.

"Trey in?"

The woman's eyes bounced to Liv before landing on this bossy Elliott, giving him a big, flirty smile.

Whatever.

"He's not in his office. He's in a meeting."

"A *real* meeting or a *meeting*."

Liv had no idea what he was getting at, but it made her glance up at him. He ignored her.

"Uh. I would hope just a regular meeting since Grant's in with them. Because if it's not a regular meeting, you may have to step in." Then the secretary giggled.

Which was strange. Liv had no idea why what she said was funny.

Elliott frowned, and his already dark face got darker. "Then it's a regular meeting."

"If you say so," she murmured, then gave him another bright smile. "Large conference room."

Elliott, Eli, or whatever, gave the woman a sharp nod and dragged Liv down another hallway to a long room made up by a wall of windows. Several people sat around a long oval conference table and as he approached with his hand firmly on her elbow, all heads swung toward them.

He must have communicated something silently through the glass because a large black man got up and opened the door just as they hit the threshold.

"What's going on?" the large man asked, frowning.

Ignoring him, Elliott dragged her into the room, asking Liv's brother, "This belong to you?"

With wide eyes they stared at each other.

"I think so," Trey murmured, studying her hard.

"You think, or you know?"

Trey Holloway stood and looked at her from head to toe. "Yeah. She's my sister. *Damn.*"

"I found her skulking around the lobby in a state of panic," her captor announced to the room of strangers.

Her gaze shot up to him. "What? I wasn't skulk—"

"Quiet," this Elliott said sharply, cutting her off.

"Eli, you want to let her go?" the fourth man at the end of the table asked, slowly rising to his feet.

"She might run."

"What?" Trey asked, his eyebrows shooting to his hairline.

"She tried to take off."

"Why?"

Eli shrugged his broad shoulders and glanced down at her for a moment before saying, "I don't know. You'll have to ask her."

Liv frowned. "I'm right here. I can hear you and I'm quite capable of answering."

Eli shrugged again and finally released her elbow. As she rubbed it, her gaze drifted over everyone in the room.

Her brother looked good. Mature. Important. But then, he'd been a star quarterback for the Boston Bulldogs and helped them win the Super Bowl Championship a couple of seasons ago.

A woman with long strawberry blonde hair watched her with curious eyes. When she stood, Liv couldn't help but notice the sexy way she was dressed. Pencil skirt, stockings, and heels that were high, not as high as stripper heels, but they made her legs look endless. Liv's gaze landed on her chest. She certainly had plenty there. The woman moved next to Trey and placed a hand on her brother's back.

Liv found that curious.

And when the woman said something softly to her brother, he seemed to snap to attention like he'd just woken up. As he moved forward, Liv thought he was going to grab her into a bear hug, but then he froze and looked at her cautiously.

"Olivia, what are you doing here?"

Coming here was not a good idea. "What? I can't stop in and say hello to my brother?" Her teasing fell flat.

"It's been sixteen years."

And there it was. The one sentence that brought all the guilt she'd been carrying around with her to the forefront. Heat rushed into her cheeks as all eyes pinned on her. "I… uh…"

"Baby, maybe we should clear out and let them have a moment."

Liv spun to the man at her right. He was also tall, but not as tall as Eli. He had a nice tan, and very kind, warm hazel eyes behind glasses that made him look highly intelligent. But she wondered who he called baby, since the only other woman in the room had now clung to the only other black man in the room. The one who seemed to be in charge. Liv found it strange that the woman took liberties like that with both men.

"Grant, they may need me," Eli answered him.

This Grant called Eli "baby?" Elliott Stone did not look like someone who would let another man call him that endearment, especially in a professional setting. Weird.

"I'm sure if they need you, they'll let you know." Grant looked at Trey, who only nodded in answer. "See? We can wait in my office until they're done."

"Yes, but—"

"Eli," the man said firmly to her former captor with an undertone that clearly meant not to question him.

Eli nodded and then sighed. He leaned toward Liv. "We're not done."

Liv pulled all the bravado she could gather and said, "Oh, we're done," matter-of-factly.

His wide lips flattened, and he reluctantly followed the other man, who Liv assumed was another attorney since he wore a suit, out the door. They shut it behind him.

Then there were only four. Her, her brother, and the other two.

"Why now?" Trey asked.

She wondered why the other two didn't excuse themselves. She purposely avoided looking at them when she asked, "Can we speak privately?"

His eyes flicked to the large black man, then the blonde woman before saying, "No. Anything you have to say can be said in front of Rayne and Gryff."

Rayne and Gryff.

"They're my partners," he clarified, then added, "in all things."

In all things? What did that mean?

The man who had to be Gryff said, "We can give you two a few moments alone, T."

"No, stay. I want you to stay," Trey answered. Without turning around, he reached his arm back and they touched hands briefly, then dropped them.

"So again, why and why now?" Trey asked.

"No hug for your baby sister?" Liv asked, which even sounded lame to her ears. She was stalling.

Something flashed behind his eyes. "Really? You disappear at sixteen, show up sixteen years later and I'm supposed to act like it was just yesterday that I saw you? You left me behind."

Liv closed her eyes and inhaled a shaky breath. "I know."

"Not even a peep. Not once. Not when I graduated high school. Not when I went off to college. Not when our *lovely* mother died. Not when I was drafted into the NFL. Not when I won the fucking Super Bowl."

The last part sounded bitter and raw. Liv watched various emotions cross his features. "I'm sorry," she whispered. "I was just trying to survive. I did what I had to do."

"Yeah, so did I."

Liv looked at him in surprise at his tone, wondering what he had to do to survive. Whatever he had to do, it seemed he had come out on the winning end.

Gryff moved forward, laying a hand on Trey's shoulder. "Look, you both did what you had to do. It was your mother who was to blame. T, don't lay that on your sister's shoulders. She was an innocent like you in the whole thing."

Maybe the man was an ally.

"Which one of you is Jordan and which one is Ward?"

The stunning woman came forward with a smile and held out her hand. "I'm Rayne Jordan. And that's Gryffin Ward."

Liv took her hand tentatively, but Rayne shook it firmly and with respect. She raised her gaze from their clasped hands to her face, blinked at how green the other woman's eyes were and then gave her a small smile. "I'm Olivia Holloway."

"I gathered that. Why don't you have a seat?" Rayne swept a hand toward one of the many empty chairs that looked expensive but comfortable.

"I… uh…"

Gryff pulled out a nearby chair and also indicated that she should sit. She sat. Then her brother and his partners moved to the other side of the table and settled across from her.

Liv cleared her throat since she suddenly felt as though she was on trial. "I'm sorry for coming here unexpectedly."

"You're family. No need to apologize," Gryff said, his expression blank.

Family? Yes, to Trey. But…

She slid her gaze to her brother. "Trey."

"Yes?"

"I… uh. I need help."

"Yeah, I didn't think you showed up because you missed me."

Once again, heat crawled up Liv's throat to flood her cheeks. "Sorry, I shouldn't have bothered you."

She rolled back her chair and before she could stand, a loud, deep voice commanded, "Stay."

"Boss," Rayne murmured.

Gryff didn't take his eyes off Liv. "No, she came here for a reason. We need to hear why."

Boss? She thought they were partners.

"Olivia," Gryff started.

"Liv. Please, call me Liv."

"Fine. Liv, no matter what, we're family."

Her eyebrows furrowed. "I don't understand how we're family."

The three across from her looked at each other and then back to her. Trey finally said, "These are my partners, Liv."

"Okay, I get that. I saw your last names in big gold letters over the receptionist's desk."

Trey took a deep breath. "We're committed life partners, too."

Liv blinked, then stared at her brother. Committed life partners. What did that mean?

Oh shit.

"All three of you?"

He nodded.

"Oh."

"So, as much as I'm enjoying this little family reunion, can you tell me why you're coming to me now after all these years?"

"I… uh."

"Oh, for fuck's sake," the large man across from her muttered, his hands flexing on the table.

"Gryff," Rayne said softly. "Give her a chance."

Liv's eyes slid to Rayne, to Gryff, then back to her brother. "I... I shouldn't be here."

Her brother was happy, settled, successful. She didn't need to be dragging him into her mess.

She could do this on her own. She could.

Fuck. She couldn't.

She had no one who she could trust. She had nowhere to go. This was it. She had no choice.

"I need help."

"You said that," Trey said, his eyebrows pulled low. "Legal help?"

"Yes... No..." She shook her head. It was all so freaking confusing. "I don't know."

"You don't know?" Gryff asked, frowning.

"I'm in trouble."

Gryff leaned back in his chair, his arms stretched out, his palms flat on the table in front of him. "No shit."

It was not a good idea to come here. It wasn't. She needed to leave. She had no right to ask her brother for help. She had no right to intrude in his life. He owed her nothing.

"I'm sorry," she whispered, meeting her brother's eyes. He had the exact same eyes as her. The same color hair. They looked so much alike but were complete strangers.

"Don't be sorry," Rayne said softly. "Talk to us. We can help."

"I'm not so sure about that."

"Then why did you come here?" Trey asked.

"Because I have nowhere else to go." The words spilled out of her in a rush. They were true, but she hated to admit it.

"You found a place to go sixteen years ago," her brother said softly, the hurt evident in his voice.

Liv closed her eyes and sucked in a breath. "I had nowhere to go then, either."

"Are you going to get to the point or are you going to continue to jerk our chains?" Gryff finally said.

"Boss," Rayne murmured softly. Her hand slid over to cover one of his.

His eyes dropped to study them then lifted back to Liv. "We can't help you if you don't tell us what the problem is."

She opened her mouth, closed it, then opened it again. Even if they couldn't help, she needed to get this off her chest. She sucked in another breath. "I witnessed a murder."

Deafening silence greeted her from around the table. She stared at her own clasped hands, afraid to see their expressions.

"Just go to the police and tell them what you witnessed," Trey said like he heard that confession every day.

If it was only that simple. "I can't do that."

"Why?" Gryff asked, his deep voice now tinged with suspicion.

"Because of who was involved," she told the table.

"Fuck," Gryff grumbled.

"Who was involved?" Rayne asked softly.

She was afraid to even say his name. "Randall Dean," she whispered, fear shooting through her. If anyone overheard her, found out what she knew, what she saw...

Rayne sucked in a sharp breath, and Gryff made a noise. Liv glanced up at Trey, who was shaking his head, looking confused. "Who?"

Gryff shot Trey a look. "Randall Dean," he repeated, as if that would clear up her brother's confusion.

"I have no fucking clue who that is," Trey answered.

"He was involved?" Gryff asked, leaning forward, his body tense.

"Yes," Liv answered.

"How?"

"He killed her." God, he killed Peggy.

"Who?"

A woman who was making changes to her life, a life she was

trying to improve. Liv knew exactly what that was like. She had been in her shoes once. "A woman I knew."

"How do you know it was him?"

He freaking wrapped his hands around her throat until all the life was squeezed out of her. "I saw him do it."

"Fuck!" Gryff barked to the ceiling. He grabbed the phone on the center of the conference table and jerked it toward him. He picked up the handset, jabbed some numbers and then growled, "Eli, in here, now," then slammed down the phone.

"Holy shit," Rayne murmured. She sent worried eyes Liv's direction. "Are you sure?"

"Yes." Hell yes, she was sure. She'd never forget what she saw. Not ever. That was burned into her brain and would be for the rest of her life.

"So why can't she go to the police?" Trey asked, still confused.

The conference room door was yanked open and her former captor stepped in, closing the door, eyes locked on her. Suddenly the room had so much less oxygen. She was finding it hard to breathe.

"Are you okay?" Rayne asked, concern lacing her voice.

No, no she wasn't.

She had pushed what she saw from her mind, trying only to think about how she could escape, how she could save herself. Once again, how she could survive.

Suddenly, everything was coming crashing down on her all over again.

And having this big man standing next to her, dark, intense eyes pinning her in her chair didn't help.

"Boss," Eli grumbled.

"Sit down," Gryff said.

"I'm fine..."

He needed to sit down. To give her space. "Please," Liv croaked. "Please."

Eli looked at her, his dark eyebrows furrowed. But he finally moved to the chair down from her, leaving an empty seat between them. For that, she was thankful.

Something about his presence overwhelmed her, and she wouldn't be able to talk, to answer questions, with him looming over her.

"What's going on?" Eli asked, his eyes flicking from her to Gryff back to her.

"She saw a Randall Dean kill someone," Trey said from the other end of the table.

Eli's gaze swung his direction. "What?"

"Do you know who he is?" her brother asked.

"Holy fuck," Eli breathed.

"Right," Gryff grunted.

"This is a mess," Rayne added.

Eli held up a hand. "Hold up. We need to rewind, and I need to hear this from the beginning."

"I think we all do," Gryff agreed.

Then all eyes landed on her. *Shit.*

CHAPTER 2

Eli studied Trey Holloway's sister. She looked just like the former Super Bowl champion. He should've seen it from the beginning.

Trey was a pretty boy. Eli had to admit the man was sexy and the former football star certainly knew it. But Olivia was more than pretty, she was beautiful. Stunning, even. But her beauty appeared haunted.

After what he just heard, he could understand the shadows under her eyes, the worried look, the fidgeting.

But the haunted look ran deeper than that.

However, he doubted that had anything to do with the information he just heard. He slid her water bottle toward her. "Take a drink. Take a breath. And start from the beginning."

With a shaky hand, she unscrewed the cap and tipped the plastic bottle to her lips. Eli watched her throat undulate as she swallowed.

And, for fuck's sake, that made him feel something he hadn't felt in ages.

He hadn't had an attraction to a woman in a great long while. Maybe it was because she was a female version of Trey? Trey was hot, sure. But even so...

What was crazy was that as soon as he saw her in the lobby acting like a skittish filly, an overwhelming need to protect her had rushed through him.

He hadn't felt that in a long time, either, because his husband, Grant, definitely could take care of himself.

And when the woman was ready to run, he stopped her. He hadn't wanted her to leave. He would never stop a client, or a potential client, from walking out of the firm. It wasn't his business to do so.

But Olivia Holloway was no client.

And the name that Trey had just thrown out made a chill run down his spine.

Randall Dean.

Fuck.

He turned to Trey. "Randall Dean is a state senator. Very powerful, uber conservative. He's got connections. Most of them questionable."

"He's the one always pushing against women's rights. Like a woman's right to choose. He's even against birth control. Hell, he's the type of man who'd remove a woman's right to vote, if he could. Take away a woman's voice. And equal pay? Forget it. His wife's a freaking scared mouse who's a puppet," Rayne explained to Trey, her voice as cold as ice crystals. "She probably brings him his slippers, a pipe, and a fucking bourbon on the rocks when he walks in the door, while wearing pearls and a dress with an apron over it."

Trey's gaze fell on his sister. "So, you saw him kill someone." Not a question, but a statement.

Eli still needed for Olivia to rewind her story. He needed to hear the details. "Again, Olivia, start from the beginning."

"Liv," she corrected him, twisting the cap back on the water bottle. Then her sky-blue eyes met his and held. No, he was wrong. He may have thought she was skittish and maybe in her current situation it was true, but there was strength hidden behind those worried eyes. She was strong, tough, a survivor.

Like Eli. Like Gryff. Like her brother, Trey.

He knew how she'd grown up because he had investigated Trey a couple years ago and found out about his past, including his mother. Somehow, he'd missed Olivia's existence. Although, he hadn't been looking for that.

But now he was looking right at her.

She might be tough deep down inside, but he needed to coax out the information from her gently. He needed every detail she could remember, and he didn't want her to shut down.

Not if she needed their help. His help. Because he had a feeling this was going to land on his shoulders. And, fuck him, he was going to volunteer to help her, no matter what came out her mouth, no matter how bad of a mess she was in. And with Randall Dean involved, bad might be an understatement.

"How far back do you want me to go?" she asked, studying him.

This was not the time or the place for this woman to be peaking his interest. And he wasn't thinking about her troubles, he was thinking his interest in everything that was her. Everything that made Olivia Holloway who she was.

He wanted to know everything about her. What she had done every second of every minute since she ran from her childhood nightmare, leaving her brother behind.

"First off, how do you know this woman?"

"I met her on the street when she was prostituting."

Jesus Christ. Was Trey's sister prostituting, too? It wouldn't surprise him. Most young runaways ended up doing whatever they had to in an attempt to survive. Including selling their bodies, selling their souls.

Eli shot a quick glance to Trey, but his face was a blank mask. Gryff's appeared the same. His boss would wait to hear more details before judging the situation, but then that was Gryff. Solid and stoic, for the most part. Rayne looked sad. His eyes slid back to Liv.

"Okay…" he said, encouraging her to continue.

"I helped her find a decent apartment and a job. It wasn't anything great, but it was a start."

"Why'd you do that?" Gryff asked, but Eli raised a hand.

"Doesn't matter," Eli told Liv. "That's a story for another time. Let's stick to what's important right now."

"I... uh... I would stop in once a week to check on her. Take her to lunch. Make sure she was staying on track, staying off the street..."

"How did she know Dean?"

Liv shook her head. "He'd been one of her johns."

Rayne made a noise, causing Liv to glance in her direction.

"For how long?" Eli asked.

"I don't know. A long time. Before I met her. He was a regular."

"Mr. Upstanding God-fearing Man. Hypocritical asshole," Rayne grumbled.

Eli shot a look at Rayne and shook his head slightly. She needed to keep her temper under control. He could understand why a lot of women didn't like Dean, he wanted to go back to the fifties when a woman remained under her husband's thumb.

Hell, the man thought gay marriage was an abomination. He was of the "God made Adam and Eve, not Adam and Steve" close-minded variety. Equality was certainly not a word in that man's vocabulary.

"Once she was off the street and no longer prostituting he continued to see her?"

"Yes. I think she held out hope, sort of like in the movie *Pretty Woman*. She expected him to take her away from everything. Hell, even leave his wife. I told her it was never going to happen, that she was fooling herself. He only went to her because he liked..." She grabbed her bottle of water, unscrewed the cap and finished it off.

"Liked?" Eli prodded.

He didn't miss it when she swallowed hard.

She lowered her voice. "He liked certain things. Things he could never ask his wife to do. Things Peggy was willing to do to keep him around, to try to draw him in. But that's the only reason he showed up. He didn't want her. He didn't want a future with her."

"Of course not," Eli murmured.

"What kind of shit was he into that his wife wouldn't do?" Trey asked.

"I don't think that's important—" Eli started.

"She only told me some of it. I stopped her before she could tell me the rest," she told her brother.

"Again, that's not important right now. If and when it is, you can tell us," Eli assured her.

Liv nodded.

He continued to try to keep her on track. "So, the day she was murdered, what did you see? How did you see it? What lead up to it?"

"I stopped over there because I was close by. I had no idea he would be there. She had no idea I was coming. I figured I could treat her to lunch... I..."

She squeezed her eyes shut, the hand still holding the empty water bottle tightened until the plastic bottle crushed between her fingers.

Eli pulled it from her and put it aside, grabbing her hand with his. He could feel her tension as she squeezed his fingers in a death grip.

"I knocked, but she didn't answer. I knocked again. Nothing. But I heard her inside. I even called her name. She wouldn't come to the door and I got worried. I heard thrashing and a voice. I... I thought she was hurt." She stopped, her eyes still shut, her face pale. Her fingers still gripping his. "Fuck," she whispered, then she opened her eyes and looked Eli dead in the face. The haunted look was there, stronger than ever. "I tried the knob. It wasn't locked. Why didn't he lock the door?"

"I don't know," Eli murmured. "What did you see?"

"She was on the floor."

"Where was he?"

"On top of her."

"Having sex?"

She shook her head. "No."

"Then what?"

"He had his hands around her neck." *Fuck*.

"Was she fighting?"

"No. Her face was purple. She wasn't fighting him at all. I think she was already dead."

"Jesus," came from Gryff across the table.

"Piece of holy-roller shit," Rayne murmured.

"Why do you think he killed her?" Eli asked softly. She probably didn't know. It could have been a simple lover's quarrel where one lover was totally unstable. Though, she surprised him with her answer.

"I know why he killed her," Liv said in a monotone voice.

"Why?"

"She was pregnant. He wanted her to have an abortion."

Rayne sucked in a breath and Liv turned her attention toward her.

"She refused. She wanted the baby. Thought it would bring them together."

"Well, that fucking backfired, didn't it?" Trey said, running a hand through his dirty blond hair in an agitated manner.

"Trey," Rayne whispered.

Trey turned his attention to Rayne. "Well, it did," he stated. "But I still don't understand why the police aren't involved."

"I'm sure they're involved," Gryff said.

"Then why can't she come forward?" Trey asked, still not understanding the gravity of the situation.

"Did he see you?" Eli asked Olivia.

"Yes."

Fuck. This was worse than he thought. "What did he do?"

"I don't know because I ran."

Eli nodded calmly, though he felt anything but. She witnessed a powerful politician killing a woman who was carrying his child. A *married* politician killing his former prostitute lover whom he wanted to have an abortion, something he was so publicly outspoken against and was trying to make illegal. And he was into some sort of kink. Talk about being ripe for blackmail.

"Peggy told me once he has the police in his pocket. He's powerful. He knows who I am since she talked about me. He knows I saw him. I figure by now he knows where my apartment is. I can't go back there. I couldn't go to the police because I don't know who to trust."

"Police aren't the only ones in his pocket," Eli told Gryff and Rayne.

"Right," Gryff answered. "This is a problem."

"A big one," Rayne added.

"Now what?" Trey asked. "What can we do?"

Eli smoothed a hand over his bald head. He had to think about this. Should they go to the feds? Should he go to the DA?

Jesus. The problem was Eli had no idea who Dean had in his pocket. He was smart and ruthless. He wasn't going to let a woman take him down. Not a former prostitute, not Olivia.

"You did the right thing by avoiding your apartment," he finally said.

"I have nowhere to go. I stayed in a motel for a couple of nights, but I can't afford..." she drifted off.

"I can pay," Trey said.

"No. She shouldn't be left alone," Gryff said. "She could come stay with us. She needs protection in the meantime while we figure this all out."

"Or at least until his ass gets caught and thrown in jail," Rayne added. "I'm sure they collected evidence at the crime scene. They have to have his DNA."

"That woman's apartment is full of his DNA, Rayne," Gryff reminded her.

"Right. So that should put him at the top of the suspect list," she returned.

Gryff snorted. "So you'd think. Again, depends on who's in his pocket."

"Shit," Rayne whispered.

"I don't want to be a burden," Liv said. "I can stay at a motel. Hell, I can leave the state."

"No. You can't. You've just showed up in my life again, you're not taking off," Trey said quickly but with determination. "I'm the only family you have. You can stay with us."

"No," Eli cut in. "She can't." All eyes turned his way. Grant was going to kill him. "She can stay with us."

"What? Why?" Trey asked, surprised.

"If he finds out she's your sister—or maybe he already knows—where's the first place he's going to look?"

"Fuck," Gryff grunted.

"Right," Eli said, nodding. "And Trey, you're not hard to find. You're too well known in the area. She can come stay with Grant and me temporarily until things cool down or he gets caught. Or we figure out what authorities we can trust with her information."

Eli felt her heavy gaze on him. He turned his head and met it head on.

"Why would you want to do that?"

He had no fucking clue. He had no valid reason to invite a woman he didn't know to come stay in the house he shared with Grant. And without even running it past his husband first. He had no idea why he wanted to protect this woman, to make sure she remained safe.

"Eli," came a gruff voice from across the table. He slid his eyes to his boss who lifted his chin toward the door. "A word."

He pushed from his chair and left the conference room with Gryff on his heels. As soon as his boss shut the door behind them, he turned and, keeping his voice low, he asked, "Why are you doing this?"

Good question. "She needs help."

"Yes, but she's not your responsibility. You have no obligation to step in in that manner, to put you and Grant out there like that. However, I do want you involved since you are our P.I. and you might have ideas on how to handle this sticky situation. Though, as expected, we'll pay you for that."

Eli shook his head. Before he could respond, Gryff continued, "But what we don't expect you do to is go beyond what your job entails. Especially for Trey's sister who's a stranger to us all. Even him. I mean, we don't even know if what she's saying is the truth."

No, she spoke the truth. His gut instinct would tell him otherwise. And he had good instincts, it's what made him one of the best P.I.'s in the business. It was also one reason why Gryff poached him from another firm. "I believe her."

"And I'm taking her at face value right now, too. But she's had a questionable past... And sometimes people with that type of history become experts at lying."

"Boss, we have the space, we're both capable of keeping an eye on her, keeping her safe and we have an excellent security system. It's not that big of a deal."

Gryff stared at him for a few moments. He was trying to read Eli. See what his motivation was.

Eli kept his face neutral.

"We could put her up in a hotel," Gryff suggested.

"She might not be safe there." And that was the truth. Hotel security wasn't top-notch, and it wasn't like they could give them a heads up. Olivia would need an alias and need to stay locked in her room. It was more hassle than it was worth.

"She could stay at Grae's," Gryff said next.

"You want to drag your brother and his family into it?"

The corners of Gryff's lips turned down. "Not really, but if I have to, I will."

"Gryff, we got it. We'll be fine. You treat us well and we

appreciate our jobs. We don't have to hide who we are while working here. We'd be glad to help."

Gryff nodded and squeezed Eli's arm. "I hear you. We're lucky to have both of you. But you might want to clear this with Grant first."

"Yeah, I need to go break the news to him."

"So, you're just telling him and not asking," Gryff said, clearly fighting back a smile.

Eli smirked. "Grant thinks he wears the pants in the relationship. But I wear them, too."

"Okay. I'll go in and talk to Liv and you go do what you have to do. Just don't let it screw up your smooth relationship."

"The one as smooth as yours?" Eli joked.

Gryff barked out a laugh, whacked Eli on the back, then went back into the conference room, closing the door.

"What?" Grant Lane watched his husband pace in front of his desk. He removed his glasses and scrubbed a hand down his face.

Eli's long legs ate up the length of the room in just a few strides. With his constant going back and forth, he reminded Grant of one of those shooting galleries at the state fair. And with what Eli just told him, he was about to start pinging him with a freaking BB gun.

"Why the hell would you invite her to stay in our home?" This couldn't be happening.

He loved Eli. He did. But he really had a serious dislike for him at the moment.

"Grant..." Eli started, rubbing a hand over his bald head.

"Eli..."

"I know I should've run this past you first..."

"No shit," Grant murmured.

"But I can't shake this need to help her. And it's Trey's sister..."

"So fucking what? Trey has more money than all of us combined.

He can figure out how to keep her safe. Gryff is smart. Hell, so is Rayne. They can figure it out themselves. We're not a motel for runaways."

"She's thirty-two, Grant. Not sixteen."

"Right. She ran away at sixteen and now she's on the run at thirty-two. I see a pattern."

Eli stopped pacing and faced Grant, his face way too serious for Grant's liking. "Both situations were and are beyond her control."

Grant shook his head. "I don't understand why you're defending her. I don't understand why you're even taking a personal interest in her. You met her like..." He looked at his watch. "An hour ago? If that."

With a sigh, he got up from his office chair and came around his desk to step in front of Eli. Even though he was only two inches shorter than his husband's six-three, he had to look up as he stepped into him. He reached up and smoothed fingers along Eli's tight jaw.

"What's really going on, big man?" he asked softly.

"Nothing."

"Bullshit. I've known you way too long for you to get away with a lie like that." He placed a palm on Eli's chest. The man's heartbeat thumped at a wild pace. "Tell me," he murmured.

Eli's dark brown eyes hit his and his lips parted. "I love you, *mon amour*. You know that."

Shit. And he was pulling out the French, which was Grant's weakness. "I know."

"I mean... you're my *âme sœur*, my soulmate."

Shit. He wasn't playing fair. "I know." Grant's heart started to race as fast as Eli's.

"I..." Eli's gaze shifted away from him.

Grant tried to swallow but his Adam's apple got caught. He finally forced it down. "What the hell is going on, Eli?"

"Fuck," Eli muttered. "I just need to help her. *We* need to help her."

"Why?"

"I don't know why, Grant. I fucking don't know. I just know I need to... I have this... I... *fuck*." He blew out a breath. "The second I saw her, I just felt the need to take care of her. Like she belonged to me. To us, even. It's fucked up. I don't know how to explain it."

"To us," Grant repeated. "Somehow I don't have that burning desire, Eli. I met her briefly. I understand getting the urge to help someone who needs it. You're a caring, loving man. I mean, that's one of the reasons why I fell for you. But still... She's not a stray puppy that you bring home."

Eli pulled away from him and moved to the windows, turning his back on Grant.

"And, honestly, do you really want to bring someone into our home, into our life, someone you have this strange urge to protect and possibly bring turmoil into our relationship and our marriage? Do you want to risk it?"

Grant's heart skipped a beat as he watched Eli turn and his face go through a gamut of emotions.

"Yes. I need to do this."

"Jesus, Eli," Grant whispered. He dragged his fingers through his hair and dropped his head to stare at the floor for a moment. Finally, he looked up. "I don't understand."

"I know. I'm not sure I do, either."

"Why the hell would I agree to this?"

"*Parce que tu m'aimes.*"

Because you love me. Grant let out a bitter laugh. "I love *us*, too."

"It's just for a short while, *mon amour*. Just until we figure this out. We hide her. We keep her safe. That's all I'm asking."

"That's not all you're asking, Elliott. That's bullshit. And what are we figuring out? I have a feeling your meaning's different from mine."

Fear crawled through Grant. If Eli was gay and not bisexual like Grant was, he wouldn't care if a woman came to stay with them. It would be inconvenient, sure. But there was something about this woman, who neither of them knew *at all*, that was affecting his husband. He couldn't wrap his head around why. Maybe he needed to get to know her. Watch their dynamic together. Maybe it was just a big brother thing Eli was feeling.

But he doubted it. There was no way Eli bonded with a stranger in such a short amount of time.

Although, that's what happened to the two of them. An instant connection.

Shit.

"I just don't want this to be the end of us," Grant said softly.

"It won't be. I promise."

I promise. "I trust you, big man."

And he did. He trusted Elliott one hundred percent. He never had any reason not to. And he hoped that didn't change any time soon.

With a sigh, he finally conceded. "Let's help Trey's sister."

He might have just agreed to the biggest mistake of his life.

CHAPTER 3

Liv wandered through the living room, her fingers brushing along the edges of the dust-free furniture and the expensive knickknacks. Which probably weren't knickknacks at all. They were most likely expensive pieces of art. She jerked her hand away. She didn't need to break anything and certainly couldn't afford to replace anything, either.

The house was quiet. Not a dog, not a cat, not a pet in sight. No children. Nothing.

It seemed to be a huge house for only two men. Two men who were not only lovers, but were married.

If being a senior associate attorney and a private investigator for Gryff's firm allowed them to purchase this house, she wondered how big the house was that her brother lived in. After all, he was not only a Super Bowl champion with endorsement deals, he was a partner in a prestigious, well-known law firm.

He'd come a long way from their shitty beginnings. But then, so had she, just not as far and definitely not financially.

She had never lived in a place so nice, so clean, so... not her. She had to remind herself this was only temporary until they got her out of this mess. Or she ended up dead and buried so Randall Dean could keep his secrets.

Eli and Gryff's reactions to the senator's name cemented her suspicions and the limited knowledge she had on the politician. He was corrupt and powerful. A scary combination.

While Olivia Holloway was a nobody and no match for someone like him.

She sighed and made her way into the kitchen, which was huge. A chef's kitchen that any cook would love to have, and she loved to cook. She taught herself when she went out on her own. Since she couldn't afford to buy meals at restaurants, she scrounged for ingredients and learned to put together somewhat satisfying dishes. Bruised fruits and vegetables. Dented cans. Open boxes. Day old bread. Anything she could get cheaply, or even free, to transform into something she was proud to eat.

Hell, at sixteen and seventeen she ate better than when she lived with her neglectful, alcoholic mother.

One day, she hoped to have a chance to sit down with Trey and learn how he survived and flourished. At least during those tough years, he'd had football. She had nothing. And that's one reason why she left. If she would've encouraged him to come along, he would've given up his future as a football star. He may never had graduated high school, either. Forget college. Forget the NFL.

"Liv," she heard from across the expansive kitchen. Her nostrils flared as she inhaled the smells of whatever Grant was cooking at the stove.

The man had looked hot in his suit when she saw him earlier in the day at the firm. Now he wore a worn pair of Levi's, a soft-looking mauve T-shirt, and was barefoot. His glasses were gone, too.

He still looked boiling hot. Too bad he was gay.

And married, she reminded herself.

Eli came into the room, wearing long, loose black shorts, no shirt, and was barefoot, too. From what she could see, a sheen of sweat covered his torso as he leaned into Grant and pressed his mouth to his husband's ear.

Whatever he whispered made Grant turn his head enough so that their lips met for a quick kiss.

A rush of warmth ran through Liv and she hadn't expected that reaction. Two men sharing a kiss made her want to squirm and not in a bad way. She hoped they did it again and took it deeper.

Unfortunately, they didn't.

"How was your workout?" Grant asked.

Eli peered into the skillet at whatever Grant was stirring. "Good. Starving. Dinner soon?"

Grant ran his gaze slowly over Eli, opened his mouth, seemed to catch himself, then peeked over at Liv. She could only imagine his thoughts were dirty and he stopped himself from saying them out loud in front of a guest.

She wouldn't blame him one bit. As Eli turned toward her, her gaze swept over his chest, too. His deeply dark-toned skin shined like ebony. His muscles were well-defined. His pecs, his arms, even his neck were corded. His stomach had definition, as well.

A tingling and another rush of warm wetness was felt between her thighs.

Again, too bad such hot, beautiful male specimens were gay. It was a loss for women everywhere. But at least she got to appreciate the view.

Eli's lips curled up as he caught her gawking at him. "Hungry, Liv?"

Oh, yes, she was.

"Grant's a good cook. His food won't kill you. Mine? No guarantees," the man teased, his dark eyes crinkling at the corners.

"I appreciate you allowing me to stay here. You certainly didn't have to do that. It's very generous of you... both."

"It'll be a nice change of pace."

"Yes, because apparently, I bore my big man," Grant said as he pulled the skillet off the stove and turned off the burner.

"*Tu ne m'ennuies jamais, mon amour*," Eli murmured.

"Mmm hmm," Grant murmured back, then he twisted toward Liv. "You speak French, Liv?"

"No."

Grant placed a hand on Eli's stomach. "Then, baby, no French, please, unless we're in private."

What a shame. It sounded perfect coming from Eli's dark, full lips, especially with that hint of an accent he had that she couldn't place. "It's a beautiful language."

"That it is," Grant agreed.

"Maybe I can teach you," Eli suggested. "I've taught Grant all of the important stuff." He smiled wickedly at her.

Was he flirting? Impossible.

"Eli, set the table?"

Liv jumped forward. "I can help. I need to earn my keep."

She didn't miss the slide of Eli's eyes from her to Grant. And Grant didn't, either. Something went unspoken between them. Something intimate. Liv's breath shallowed and her pulse raced.

"You're our guest," Eli stated.

"I want to help," she said more firmly.

His answer was a cocked eyebrow, then he smiled. "Okay, I'll show you where everything is."

As he moved around the kitchen opening cabinets and drawers, Liv stuck to his side. And when he reached over her to get something on an upper shelf, his arm brushed hers and she shivered.

Holy shit, Liv, get yourself together. They're married. They're happy. And you're only here because you're in a mess. Don't make more of one.

"Liv," Eli murmured.

Her gaze lifted to meet his. "I..."

Shit. Her nipples were painfully pebbled, and she could feel his searing heat. What the fuck was going on?

"I..." she started again and swallowed hard.

Grant cleared his throat, breaking the connection between Eli and her. "Table, Eli," he reminded him.

Eli blinked. "Right." He grabbed the stuff for the place settings and moved away.

"So, Liv, what do you do for a living?" Grant asked.

"I work at a halfway house."

Grant's head spun toward her and she could also feel Eli's curious gaze.

"Oh, as a counselor?"

She shook her head. "No. One day maybe. Once I finish my degree."

"You're working on getting your college degree?" The question came from the table area.

She glanced over at Eli. "Yes. Slowly. I only take one class at a time. I've been working on it for a while. I sort of started late."

"Why's that?" Grant asked.

Because I'm poor and had to struggle in life just to get my GED so I could get a half-decent job, which I still don't have at thirty-two years old.

She pushed that out of her head.

Eli finished setting the table and moved closer to her to lean back against the counter, crossing his arms over his chest. "What do you do there?"

"I'm just an aide for now."

"An aide," he repeated like he was tasting the word on his tongue. "That can't pay much."

"It doesn't pay shit. That's why I'm only taking one course at a time. Would I like to go to school full-time and get my degree as soon as possible? Yes. Maybe one day when I meet my sugar daddy." She laughed, but it fell flat.

Once again the men's eyes met, held for a moment, then fell back onto her.

"Where do you go to school?" Eli asked.

"Just at the community college. I do classes online. Luckily. Otherwise, this whole mess would be screwing that up, too."

"Right. Not a good idea to go onto campus right now," Eli stated.

"Or to work," Grant added.

Shit. "I can't afford to lose my job, even if it doesn't pay squat. I won't be able to pay my rent or continue with school... Shit! I'm so screwed. I don't even have my laptop since it's at my apartment. How am I going to do my course work?" The reality of this whole situation swept over her like an avalanche. "Randall Dean is really fucking up my life."

Eli made a noise and she looked up at him. "Right. The laptop we can deal with. The job we can deal with. Keeping you off the grid is the most important thing right now," he reminded her.

"I know, but I have stuff on my laptop..." Her eyes widened when she remembered just what she had on there. "Shit!" She pressed her hands over her face and groaned.

"What?"

"I had texts, pictures."

"Compromising texts and pictures?" Grant asked, surprised.

Eli frowned. "Of you?"

She dropped her arms. "No! No. Shit! I forgot. Peggy gave me the memory card from her cellphone. I had downloaded it onto my laptop. It had texts between Randall and her. And photos of the two of them! That might be my only evidence against him. She said to hold onto them if things went badly between them."

"The laptop is in your apartment?" Eli asked.

"Yes."

"What did you do with the chip? Give it back to her?"

"No, I didn't. I was going to. But I hid it and forgot about it."

"She never asked for it back?"

"No. Maybe she didn't need it. I don't know." Liv chewed her bottom lip. "It's in my apartment, too. Fuck. I need to go back there."

"No, you're not going back there. Not now. He could have someone watching it."

"But I need—"

"No, Olivia. You can't go back. You were right in not going back after witnessing what you did. We'll figure a way to get in and out without getting seen."

"We will?" Grant asked, his eyebrows had climbed up his forehead.

Eli's gaze flicked to him then back to Liv. "I will."

"Eli..." Grant breathed.

"I'll figure it out."

"I don't want to put you in any danger, either. Either one of you," Liv said. "I truly appreciate you helping as it is by letting me stay here. But that's enough. Actually, it's too much. You don't even know me."

"We know your brother."

"*I* don't even know my brother," she said, then ground the heels of her palms into her eyes, groaning. "What a fucking mess."

"We'll deal with it," Eli said firmly.

She was glad someone was confident, because she sure wasn't.

Eli continued, "Well, being on house arrest will give you time to get to know him."

"House arrest?"

"Sorry, bad joke. But it'll be similar. For now, you need to stay here and not go anywhere. We have a great security system. After dinner, I'll show you how to use it. Though, I'd prefer that you not even go outside right now. At least until we get an idea on what's going on."

Who knew how long that would be and she had nothing but the clothes on her back. "But I don't even have anything to wear."

"We'll get Rayne to help out with that."

Great. From how she saw the woman dressed, her wardrobe was so out of her league. "I can't afford to buy new clothes."

"It's covered."

"By who?"

"Trey, Rayne, Gryff, whomever. It's not going to be a problem, they can afford it."

"I can't ask that..." She didn't want to be a burden and she might not be able to pay them back.

"Olivia, it'll be fine," Eli reassured her.

She was glad someone thought so.

CHAPTER 4

"Eli, I don't want you going to that apartment," Grant said.

Eli watched his husband slip off his glasses and slide them onto the nightstand on his side of the bed.

"*Mon amour*, I'm dark. I can slip in and out at night without anyone noticing."

"That's not even funny."

Eli sighed. "I know. Sorry."

"It's dangerous."

Grant climbed onto the bed and moved until he was pressed to Eli's side. Eli put down the book he was reading and combed his fingers through Grant's hair. "Thank you," he murmured.

Grant's hazel eyes tipped up to his. "For what?"

"For agreeing to this."

"Believe it or not, I like her."

"I know. I do, too."

"And she's not cocky like Trey," Grant added.

"He's changed."

"True, but he still has his moments."

"Mmm hmm," Eli murmured, letting his fingers trace over Grant's jawline, down his neck and over his collarbone.

Grant's hand slid over Eli's stomach and up to his chest, stopping over his heart. "You want her," he said softly.

Eli refrained from answering. Instead he took his time gathering his thoughts. He didn't want to start a fight and he didn't want to hurt the man he loved, either.

He definitely wanted Olivia. During dinner and afterward, he couldn't deny the attraction. And when she stood close to him while he taught her how to use the security system, her scent, her closeness had made his body react in a way it usually only did for Grant.

"Yes, but that doesn't mean I'm going to act on it. I'm happily married, remember?" He wiggled his ring finger, which was encircled by a wide, engraved gold band. He was also strong enough to resist following every whim or desire.

"You've never cheated on me." Grant's fingers curled into Eli's skin.

Eli sucked in a breath. "Of course not. And I don't plan on starting. I would never do anything that you don't agree with."

"So... you're asking," Grant stated softly.

Eli remained quiet. He wanted to, yes.

Grant continued, "I figured there was more to it."

"I'm not asking. I'll let you decide how and when things progress."

Eli waited for Grant to stiffen or push away and get pissed. But, surprisingly, he didn't. It was a good sign.

"We don't even know if she's interested," Grant said softly.

"True."

"She's attracted to you, though."

"You, too. It was hard to miss."

"So, what are you saying?"

Eli shook his head. "I don't know. I mean.... Her life's a freaking mess right now and she's in real danger. Shouldn't this be the last thing on my mind? Hell, on *our* minds?"

"Her safety should be our first priority."

Eli didn't need that little reminder. He knew that. "I never thought I'd be attracted to a woman again. It's been a long time."

"Me, too."

Eli glanced down at his husband whose head now laid in his lap. His cock twitched at the thought of Grant's mouth being so close. All he had to do was pull down his shorts just enough...

But those two words his husband had just said bounced around his brain. "Are you attracted to her?"

Grant let his hand slide back down Eli's sternum and over his abs to his lower belly. Eli's cock began to rise.

Grant sighed. "Surprisingly, I am. Though, I shouldn't be. She *does* remind me of Trey and that man's hot as hell."

Eli chuckled. "Agreed."

"But it's been so long since I've been with a woman."

It had been for them both. That's because they'd been a couple for a long time. Over ten years.

"Okay, well... We could always explore this..." Eli let the last hang.

Grant's fingers slipped under the elastic band of Eli's shorts and tugged them down slightly.

Now Eli's cock was fully at attention, making his loose shorts tent in his lap.

"You're tempting me, big man," Grant murmured.

Eli didn't know if he was tempting Grant with the idea of Olivia or with his erection. "Hmm, yes. That's my evil plan."

Grant smiled up at him. "Nothing wrong with having dessert twice."

Eli agreed. "No, there isn't."

"If I do this for you, I get to top you."

"Ah, doing some negotiating, counselor?"

"I'm an expert at it."

"You certainly are."

"Will you accept the deal?" Grant asked, the corners of his lips curved, his fist gripping Eli's cock tightly.

Eli rocked his hips upward. "I think those are acceptable terms. Wait. Are we talking about Olivia or you giving me head?"

"A blowjob. If you want to negotiate in regard to Olivia, it's going to take more than just one night of topping."

"Hmm. I was afraid of that."

Grant tugged Eli's shorts down even farther, until his cock sprung free. Grant squeezed the root with his fingers and his warm, wet tongue circled the crown, sweeping away the sole bead of precum.

Eli dug his hands into Grant's hair. It wasn't long enough to get a good purchase, but it wasn't too short, either. Eli loved the man's hair, especially since he had none of his own.

Grant shifted, getting in a better position to take Eli fully into his mouth and when he did, Eli's eyelids lowered, and he tilted his head back, staring up at the ceiling for a moment, letting the sensation of Grant's warm, wet mouth swirl over him.

Oh fuck. Grant was great at giving head. He tipped his eyes back down, watching his partner rise and fall on his cock as he sucked hard, then soft, letting his tongue roam the length and circle the crown.

"*J'ai hâte de t'avoir,*" Eli groaned.

Grant lifted his head just enough to say, "Uh-uh. I get to top tonight."

"Why did I ever teach you French?"

Grant chuckled but it was muffled when he took Eli back between his lips. Eli's hips rose slightly, not getting enough of his husband's mouth. Warm, long fingers cupped his sac, then played along the crease, pressing, teasing until he wormed a finger farther down.

Grant lifted his head again, whispering, "That's mine tonight."

"It's yours every night, *mon amour.*"

Grant cocked an eyebrow. "Yeah?"

Eli chuckled. "You know what I mean."

Then Grant lowered his head again and when he made an

"mmm" sound around Eli's cock the vibrations made his balls tighten.

Fuck, he was going to come in Grant's mouth if he didn't let up.

"*Mon amour...*"

"Hmm?"

"Fuck... I'm going to come."

Another *mmm* vibrated around his length.

"Not yet. I don't want to come yet..." Eli breathed, his eyes rolling back in his head as Grant's tongue traced the thick veins, teased the spot where his sac met his cock, then swirled his tongue over the head once more.

Grant was good with his mouth, whether giving a closing argument in the courtroom or wrapping it around Eli's length. Or even simply kissing.

He was happy to have such an intelligent, caring lover. And he couldn't screw that up.

He wouldn't.

But he still needed to explore this pull with Olivia. And for a moment, he imagined it was her sucking him, stroking the delicate skin of his sac, and squeezing his balls gently but firmly.

Holy fuck. His eyes popped open and he hadn't even realized he'd closed them with his little fantasy. He stared down at his husband who was giving his all to pleasure him, to bring him to the peak and...

His hands flexed in Grant's hair as he thrust up and came into his mouth, down his throat, Grant's eyes never leaving Eli's as his pulsing cock released every last drop. His lover took all of it like he always did.

Grant released him and gave him a soft smile. "You always taste so good."

"Because you feed me well, *mon amour*. You know that makes a difference."

"So you say. Now, my turn." His eyes glittered with anticipation.

"How do you want me?" Eli asked, his heart, which had started to slow down after coming, began to race all over again.

"Mmm. Love that question."

Eli chuckled, running a thumb over Grant's bottom lip. His husband pushed up and pressed his lips to Eli's, who parted his mouth and let Grant slip in his tongue, giving him the control. But not for long. Eli's fought back and their tongues tangled and sparred, which drew a moan from both of them. Grant's hard length pressed against Eli's thigh and he couldn't wait to feel it against him and inside him.

As much as Eli loved to top Grant, he also loved when Grant topped him. It gave him a sense of completeness, as if the two of them were one. Partners, lovers, two halves of a whole.

"Finish taking off your shorts," Grant murmured against Eli's lips, his breath coming faster than normal. "Then take off my bottoms."

"Ah, not only are you going to top, you're going to be bossy, too."

"Just a little bit."

"When you're bossy, there's nothing *little bit* about it, *mon Napoléon*."

"But it turns you on."

"That it does. And me speaking French does the same for you."

"That it does," Grant echoed. The amusement in his voice quickly disappeared. "Now... shorts off."

When Grant rolled away, Eli lifted his hips and yanked his shorts the rest of the way off his legs before tossing them over the side of the bed.

Then he tackled Grant with a growl, knocking him flat on his back, shoving his fingers into the waistband of his pajama bottoms and pushing them down until his husband's cock sprang forward.

With a quick lick to the crown, Eli finished pushing the cotton drawstring pants down his legs and ripped them off his feet. He tossed those aside, too.

He slid his body slowly back up Grant's, making sure they

remained skin to skin. When they were finally face to face, Eli dropped another kiss on the other man's lips, sliding his hands down Grant's arms to snag his wrists. Before Eli got a chance to pin them above Grant's head, his lover spun, taking Eli with him and with a whoosh of breath, Eli found himself on his back looking up at his husband.

"Naughty boy," Grant teased, the corners of his eyes crinkling. He tilted his hips, thrusting his cock along Eli's inner thigh. "Tonight's my night."

"Can't blame a guy for trying," Eli said, fighting back a smile.

"Back or belly?"

Grant was giving Eli a choice. A difficult one because he liked it both ways. So why not do both? *Les deux.*

"Mmm." Grant lifted his weight off Eli and slid to his side. "On your belly to start. Let me grab the lube."

Warmth radiated from Eli's stomach into his chest and down into his groin. If he hadn't just orgasmed, he'd be rock hard at Grant's words.

His lover never failed to turn him on.

While Grant dug in the nightstand drawer, Eli rolled onto his stomach and a quiver ran through him at the thought of what was about to happen. He turned his head to watch Grant pop open the cap on the tube of lube and squeeze a generous amount onto his palm. Then he fisted his cock, spreading the lube up and down his length.

"Think she'll hear us?" Grant asked, stroking himself so slowly, so methodically that Eli couldn't tear his gaze away.

"She's at the other end of the hall."

"Still..."

"Keep your wailing to a minimum," Eli suggested with a smirk.

"Me? It's not me... Well, okay, sometimes it is. And when I sink into that tight hole of yours, it may very well be me tonight."

"Want me to gag you?"

Grant laughed. "No, I'll try to be quiet."

"I think you have spread it around enough, *mon amour*."

Grant's gaze dropped to his cock. "So I have. It feels good, but your ass will feel much better."

"Yes, make me yours."

"Gladly." Grant walked on his knees in between Eli's spread legs. "Show me what you're offering."

Eli reached back and spread his cheeks. "*Quelque chose juste pour toi.*"

Something just for you.

"Yes, me and only me, big man. Don't forget that," Grant murmured as he dripped the lube down Eli's crease.

When Grant circled his anus, working the lube around his entrance and dipping his finger ever so slightly into his hole, a shudder went through Eli at the anticipation.

"You're being a tease," Eli growled.

"And you're being impatient. Now I'm tempted to make you wait and spank your beautiful black ass."

"Yes," Eli hissed. "You could do that. But I think you don't want to wait, either."

"Ah, but you know anticipation is half the fun."

And that was true, too. But he doubted Grant would wait.

"Next time," Grant murmured, moving over him.

Eli's lungs emptied, his body tremored slightly and his grip on his ass cheeks tightened as he felt the smooth, bulbous head of Grant's cock at his entrance.

He sucked in a breath as Grant pushed just slightly. "Relax, baby. Let me in."

When Eli blew out the breath he was holding, Grant tilted his hips and pushed past the tight ring, entering him oh-so slowly.

Eli released his cheeks and tangled his fingers into the sheets, closing his eyes as Grant filled him. And Eli took him all, every inch before Grant stilled.

"Baby," Grant groaned. "Fuck... This is..."

"*Exquis,*" Eli moaned.

"Yes, exquisite. That's the perfect way to describe it."

"I can never get enough of you," Eli managed to get out.

"And I you, baby. Never," Grant breathed, then he leaned over and laid kisses down the line of Eli's spine.

When Grant began to move, Eli moved with him, lifting his hips, meeting him stroke for stroke.

Exquisite was right. The pressure, the feeling of Grant's cock against his prostate, it was certainly that. Grant ground against him and Eli cried out. His own cock was slowly coming awake again, too.

Grant was one of the best male lovers he ever had, and he was lucky to have found him. For them to have found each other.

"On your back, big man," Grant demanded. "Not sure how long I'm going to last. And I want to watch your face when I come."

As soon as Grant pulled out, Eli rolled to his back.

Grant tapped Eli's thigh. "Knees to chest."

As soon as Eli complied, Grant's entry was anything but slow this time. With a hard thrust, he took Eli, leaning over, staring down into Eli's face.

His lips were parted, his eyes unfocused and his breathing ragged as he slammed Eli hard over and over.

Eli kept his knees bent and open to accommodate Grant's body between them. He stared up into his lover's eyes.

"That's it, *mon amour*, give me everything you have."

Grant grimaced and blew out a shaky breath. "Take everything I'm giving you."

"I am. I want more," Eli moaned.

A groan bubbled up from the back of Grant's throat and he fucked Eli harder and faster, their flesh slapping together.

"More, *mon amour*."

"Eli," Grant breathed in protest, his pace hiccupping.

Eli reached between them, grabbing his own cock, which was fully erect once more. He stroked himself at the same rapid pace Grant fucked him.

"Will you come again?" Grant asked, his voice a bit strangled.

"Yes."

"With me?"

"Yes."

"Tell me when. I can't hold off much longer," Grant warned.

He wasn't going to have to, but those words couldn't escape Eli's lips. He was breathing too hard, his hand moving frantically so he could come at the same time his husband spilled into him.

He wanted them to come together, too.

"Like that..." Eli panted. "Yes, like that... *Fuck*... Grant."

"Baby, I'm going to come."

"Me, too. Kiss me."

Grant leaned in farther and Eli met him halfway, their mouths slamming together, their tongues finding one another as both of them stiffened, and Eli couldn't ignore the strong pulsations as Grant came deep inside him. Grant swallowed Eli's groan as he came again, his warm cum shooting up and landing on his own belly.

Eli dropped his legs, and with a sigh, Grant dropped his weight onto him, not caring about the mess since they would both shower shortly.

"Stay in me as long as possible, *mon cher mari*," Eli murmured, pressing a kiss to Grant's cheek.

"You don't know how much I love you," Grant said softly into his ear.

"I do, *mon amour*. And I feel the same way."

CHAPTER 5

Eli's heart almost thumped right out of his chest as his eyes popped open and he stared at nothing but darkness.

"What the fuck," he grumbled.

Grant shifted next to him and sat up. "What the hell was that?"

"I don't know," Eli answered softly, listening more carefully.

"Maybe—"

"Shh," Eli hushed him.

Then they heard it. A piercing scream. One that set every hair on his body on end. He jackknifed out of bed and, snagging his shorts from the floor, pulled them on with one tug. Grant did the same.

By the time Eli hit the bedroom door, Grant was on his heels. "What do you—"

Another scream, not as loud, but just as disturbing because this time it sounded like a "No!"

Ice rushed through Eli's veins as he yanked the door open and ran down the hall to the spare bedroom. He tried the knob, but found it locked.

She locked her bedroom door!

Raising his bare foot, he kicked near the knob and the door latch broke free with minimal damage. He pushed into the room, Grant at his back. Eli rushed to the bed as Grant flipped the switch, lighting up the room.

Olivia sat up in bed, blinking at them, her mouth open in an *O*. "What's going on?" Her voice was strained, her face pale, a sheen of sweat covered her forehead.

"You were screaming," Eli said, sitting on the edge of the bed and pressing the back of his hand against her forehead. "What happened?"

She blinked again. "I... I don't know!"

"A nightmare?" Grant asked as he approached the bed on the other side.

Her gaze slid to him. "Yes... maybe. I don't remember."

Grant laid a hand on her arm. "You're shaking."

Liv stared down at his hand, then looked back up at him.

"You don't remember anything?" Eli asked, brushing the hair off her damp forehead.

She averted her eyes and said nothing.

"You do remember."

"Baby, she saw someone murdered. I'd have nightmares, too."

Eli glanced at his husband. He was right. That would be enough to affect anyone's sleep.

"You scared us," Grant admitted.

"Sorry."

"Nothing to be sorry about. We just wanted to make sure you're okay."

"Your door's broken," she stated the obvious.

Eli fought back his smile. "It can be fixed."

She shook her head. "I really don't want to be a burden."

"You're not," Eli said quickly. "Now that we know you're okay, we can get back to sleep. You *are* okay, right?"

Grant reached out and brushed a knuckle over her cheek. "You'll be able to go back to sleep?"

After a long hesitation, Olivia answered, "Sure."

His eyes met Grant's over the bed. She was lying.

"Okay." Eli pushed to his feet but before he could straighten, Olivia reached out and grabbed his arm.

"Wait..."

He tipped his gaze down to her and waited.

"I..."

And waited.

"I've never needed anyone. I've always been on my own since the day I left... Trey behind... I don't know how to ask..."

"For help?" Grant finished for her.

"I honestly don't know what I'm asking for... I'm not sure what I need. But..."

"But what?" Eli prodded.

Olivia shook her head then closed her eyes. "I can't ask this of you."

"What?" he encouraged softly.

"Just ask, Liv," Grant said just as softly. "If we can help, we will."

"Can you stay?" Eli almost didn't hear her; it was almost as if it was said on a breath. "Just for a little while... please."

Eli met Grant's gaze and realized his husband was studying him, watching Eli's reaction carefully.

Then without dropping his gaze from Eli, Grant said, "This bed's too small for the three of us. But if you want to come sleep with us, you're welcome to."

No one said a word for a few long moments. Finally, Eli broke his gaze from Grant's and swallowed hard as he studied Olivia, who, at the moment, looked like a little girl in their spare bed, swallowed up by one of Grant's T-shirts, her hair in disarray, her blue eyes wide and shiny.

This was not a good idea.

It wasn't.

He realized Grant was only inviting her into their bed to sleep. But it was a step he hadn't expected to take, especially this soon.

And he didn't want Olivia to think they were taking advantage of her vulnerability. Because they weren't.

Right?

"Again, I don't want to be a burden," she said, color slowly returning to her cheeks.

"How could it be a burden to have a beautiful woman snuggled between us?" Grant asked.

Eli frowned. What was Grant doing? The man hadn't been thrilled with the idea of bringing Olivia into the house in the first place and now, only a few hours later, he was encouraging her to come share their bed with them?

Why?

"And I couldn't be any safer sleeping between two gay men, right?" she said, her voice hopeful.

Oh fuck.

"Uh..." Eli started, trying to harness his racing thoughts.

"Right," Grant said quickly, offering his hand to Oliva. She took it and Eli watched as his husband helped her out of bed.

"Grant," Eli started again until Grant shot him a look. Eli remained frozen in place as he watched him escort Olivia out of her room and down the hallway.

"Oh fuck," Eli whispered. The thought of the woman climbing into bed with them, even just to sleep, had the blood rushing in his ears and his heart pounding against his chest. And that blood was also pumping hard right down to his cock. He adjusted himself in his shorts and slowly followed them down the hall back to their bedroom.

When he entered the master bedroom, Olivia was already crawling on their California king-sized bed on her hands and knees to the center. Grant's T-shirt rode up her thighs and clung to her ass.

Oh fuck.

Grant had moved to the far side of the bed, the side he slept on, and pulled back the covers, encouraging her to settle in the middle.

Oh Jesus fuck.

"Grant," Eli said, his voice cracking.

Grant shot him a *you-wanted-this-now-you-got-it* look. Though, his voice didn't match the look. "Baby, come to bed." Then he *patted* the bed.

Eli cocked a brow at him and Grant cocked one back. Then Eli's *pain-in-the-ass* husband plumped his pillow after handing one of his to Olivia, and settled onto his back with a sigh.

"Eli," came the low warning.

Eli unfroze his feet and carefully climbed into bed, making sure he didn't accidentally knock Olivia with his now-raging erection.

Their bed was big, but it wasn't that big. It was still a snug fit with three adults, especially two of them being men over six-feet tall.

Eli turned his head to Olivia, studying her profile as she stared up at the ceiling. "Do you need another pillow?"

"I'm fine, thank you."

"I'll take your extra one," Grant said, holding out his hand.

Eli gave it up with a frown. He really wanted to whack Grant over the head with it for pulling this bullshit.

"Light, Eli."

Eli reached over and turned off the lamp, then laid stiffly in the bed until sleep finally claimed him an hour later.

She needed to get the super to turn down the heat in her building. The radiators were way too hot. Liv blinked her eyes open.

Oh shit.

She wasn't in her apartment.

She wasn't in her own bed.

She wasn't even in Eli and Grant's spare bedroom.

She was smack in between them.

No. No, she wasn't even that.

She was curled into Grant's side, her bare thigh over his, her hand rising and falling with each breath as it laid on his stomach. His arm curled around her shoulders, her head rested on his upper arm.

Something jammed up against her back and ass. Something hot, large and very firm.

Eli's breath was slow and steady, blowing a strand of her hair enough that it tickled her ear. His arm snaked around her hip, his erection pressed into the crack of her ass. The large T-shirt she wore to bed was pushed up around her waist and her panties were all cockeyed. Nothing was between her ass crack and Eli's searing hot erection, except the thin, silky fabric of his shorts.

Her breathing shallowed and her nipples pebbled.

Holy shit.

She hadn't expected to wake up to this. Yes, she climbed into bed with two men she'd only just met. But it wasn't for sex. It was for comfort. Something she never had most of her life.

Amazingly, she'd never slept so well.

Any nightmares that had haunted her the last few nights had been chased away. At least, temporarily.

She felt safe and secure between the two men. Which was strange. That wasn't like her. She usually didn't trust anyone this quickly and it took her a while to warm up to most people.

She tended to be more on the cautious side when first meeting someone, building up that hard, protective shell around her until she knew she could let her guard down. Which wasn't often.

There weren't too many people she trusted. And now with what was going on with this Randall Dean, she had to be even more careful about who she could trust.

But after the initial run-in with the law firm's P.I. and after she saw how much her brother trusted him, relied on him, as well as Eli's husband, she quickly let her instincts take over. And, if she was honest with herself, she was relieved they offered to help her.

Because, besides Eli, Grant, Trey, Rayne and Gryff, she had no one else. Though, now that she thought about it, having those five in her life, if they remained there, made her luckier than most.

Some people didn't even have one other person to rely on. Not one. She'd lived like that herself for a long, long time.

She never should have stayed out of her brother's life for so long. That was something she'd have to live with. And Trey would, too.

But that wasn't her most immediate problem. Oh no. It was early morning, she had a beautiful black man pressed to her back, his cock ready for action and an equally beautiful man practically pinned beneath her. And...

She slid her hand down just enough she could feel where the fabric of his PJ bottoms began to tent. Yep. He sported morning wood, too.

Shit.

Once again, she thought, too bad they were gay. Because, honestly, she wanted to slide her hand down even further and wrap her fingers around him.

Liv released a shuddered breath.

This was just crazy.

She had no idea what time it was, but even so, she needed to extract herself from between the two of them before they woke up. She didn't need to be caught in the middle of an intimate moment between the married couple. They didn't want her. They wanted each other. And she was happy for them. Yes, she was.

So she needed to return to her room, climb into her own bed, albeit a temporary one, and see if she could catch some more sleep. She hadn't gotten much since Peggy's murder.

She'd hardly eaten, also. Last night what Grant made was the first actual meal she could stomach in a while. Hiding out, the worry had eaten at her insides, so food and sleep had been at a minimum.

She wondered if she could slip from between them carefully. Holding her breath, she slowly removed her thigh and hand off Grant and lifted her head. Then she carefully lifted Eli's arm from over her hip, settling it back on his own leg. With care, she wiggled herself down the bed from in between them. Eli groaned and shifted into the empty space she left behind, curling against Grant.

She finally took a breath when she no longer touched any of their body parts and, when her feet hit the floor, she pushed up and snuck out of the room, softly closing their bedroom door behind her.

She paused for a quick bathroom break on her way back down the hallway to her room. Not long after, she climbed back into the spare bed, snuggling deeply under the covers.

Then she laid there wide awake. Her nipples still ached, and her pussy kept clenching in need. She hadn't felt like that in a long time. It had been years since she'd trusted anyone enough to date or even just sleep with someone. She'd never had a one-night stand or even slept with a stranger. Hell, she never slept with someone after the first date.

No. She'd been very selective who she allowed to get close to her.

"They're gay," she whispered, hoping her body would get the hint. She slipped a hand under the large T-shirt Grant had lent her and then let her fingers do the walking down under her panties. She was wet, that was for sure. Her back bowed as soon as she touched her own clit. She was super sensitive and ready, too.

She shoved the T-shirt up with her other hand and found her nipple still peaked into a tight bud. Pressing it with a fingertip, she snagged it between her thumb and forefinger and pinched hard.

She gasped, and her hips tilted. Her breathing shallowed and she swallowed hard before her mouth parted. Rolling the nipple between her fingers, she moaned and closed her eyes. She could only imagine that one of the men, or, hell, both, was doing it for her. But they wouldn't, they never would, so she was on her own.

Her finger slipped between her slick folds, stroking between them from bottom to top, circling her clit, then sliding back down. Over and over, her hips moving slightly with each stroke. She teased herself with one hand while the other continued to caress her breast, cupping, squeezing, pinching, pulling.

Fuck. She wanted Eli's mouth on one, Grant's on the other. She wanted to watch them kiss again. Behind her closed eyelids, she pictured them doing just that while in the kitchen, only in her mind, they did take it deeper, harder. She imagined them touching each other, groaning, stroking each other's cocks.

She sank her teeth into her bottom lip as she finally slipped two fingers inside herself. Crying out, her hips jumped off the bed.

She was so ready, so ripe for contact, that it wouldn't take much for her to orgasm. And her fantasy of the two men together made her even more wet, more wanting.

She desired to be sandwiched between the two, their hands exploring, their mouths brushing her most sensitive places. Their cocks ready to enter her. She was open to them, ready to feel their lengths, their girths deep inside her.

She pushed her fingers deeper and faster, her thumb sliding over her clit.

"Oh, fuck me," she groaned.

And then it happened. Her toes curled, the ripples ran through her, radiating from her core outward. Her pussy throbbed around her slick fingers, her head was thrown back, and a ragged cry escaped her as she came hard.

With a groan, Grant came hard into Eli's mouth. Between Eli sucking him and hearing Liv's long wail from down the hall, he couldn't hold back any longer.

After a moment, Eli lifted his head, gazing up Grant's naked body. "I want to go to her."

So did he. They had both been awake, feigning sleep, when Liv snuck out of the bed a little while ago. Both had raging hard-ons when she did so. And both knew it was way too soon to take it any further than what they had already. Which was letting her sleep between them.

As soon as Liv closed the bedroom door behind her, Eli had made his move, pushing down Grant's PJ bottoms and taking him into his mouth.

And, of course, Grant didn't fight him off. He needed a release and Eli was eager to give it to him.

Though now, Eli was still hard as a rock. And probably expecting to top him this morning.

"I know," Grant finally said. "I do, too."

"So you want her." Eli made it a statement instead of a question.

"Yes."

"I wasn't sure what you were pulling last night when you invited her into our bed."

"I wanted to see if I was as interested as you."

"And you are?"

"Yes."

Eli smiled. "So what are we going to do about it?"

Well, that was an easy fix but the "easy fix" would end up complicating matters more than they already were. "We need to take it slow, Eli. I mean, her situation isn't ideal."

"Right."

"And we have no condoms at all in the house. We haven't for years."

"Right," Eli said again.

Grant smoothed a hand over Eli's head. "That's if it gets that far. But we should be prepared if it does."

"It sounded like she just took care of herself, so I'm assuming waking up between us turned her on."

"Clearly it sounded like that. But a fantasy and reality are two different things."

"Right." Eli glanced toward the closed bedroom door. "Do you think she's fantasizing about being with us?"

"Do you?"

"I hope so."

"Me, too, baby."

Eli smiled up at him. "This is crazy."

"I know."

"I'll go pick up the condoms at lunchtime today."

"Get a big box," Grant suggested with a smile.

Eli chuckled as he grabbed his erection and squeezed it. "So now, let's work on our immediate problem."

"Which is?" Grant teased him.

"What I'm holding in my hand."

"A beautiful cock, that's for sure."

"*Merci, mon amour.*"

"Yes, well, you're going to be thanking me after you stick that beautiful thing inside of me, big man."

"Certainly will." Eli moved up Grant's body and laid a light kiss on his lips.

"That's all I get?"

"No, *mon cher mari*, you get all of me."

"Mmm. I look forward to it."

"Then pass the lube."

Grant laughed and passed the lube to his *mari*, his husband.

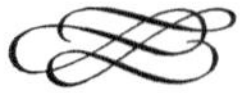

CHAPTER 6

Liv watched Trey pace the kitchen.

"You lived that close and never said a word? Never found me? Never called? Never came to a game?"

"I couldn't afford to go to an NFL game, Trey."

He waved a hand her direction. "I'm just saying..."

"I know what you're saying," she said softly. "I was sixteen. I had no money, I did what I had to do, Trey."

He stopped his pacing and spun on his heel to face her. "So did I."

"I would like to talk about it."

"Now?"

"When you're ready."

"Olivia..."

"Liv," she corrected him.

He groaned and ran an agitated hand through his hair. "I'm older than you, I actually should have taken care of you. I was supposed to be the man of the family."

Liv closed her eyes for a moment, then shook her head. "That's ridiculous. You were a teenager like I was. We're only eleven months apart." She rose from her chair and approached him, laying a hand on his arm. "I didn't want to be a burden to you."

"But you should've told me you were running away."

"You had football. That was your way out of our situation."

"You had…"

"Nothing."

"No. You had me."

She shook her head. "No. Again, you were doing well in football, even as a freshman you were playing Varsity. Your coach was sure you'd get a scholarship to college. Why would I want you to go with me? You had that. You had someone looking out for you."

"Yeah," he snorted.

"What does that mean?"

"He looked out for me."

The cynicism in his voice chilled her. She waited. Trey stood frozen, his body stiff under her hand.

"What happened?"

"Nothing," Trey said too quickly.

"Tell me," Liv said softly.

"Nothing I didn't want to happen."

Liv's heart suddenly thumped heavily in her chest. "What does that mean?"

"I did what I had to do and so did you. Can we drop it for now?"

"Trey…"

"Seriously, Liv, you've been out of my life for the past sixteen years. Don't come back now and act concerned about the things I went through."

"A little harsh there, Trey," came a low, deep voice from behind Liv. She looked over her shoulder to see Eli walking into the kitchen, carrying a bag from a pharmacy chain, his dark eyes pinned on her brother.

Trey stared at Eli for a moment, then moved away from Liv. His Adam's apple bounced as he swallowed hard. "I made out just fine, Liv. I'm doing fine. I'm not struggling. I have Rayne and

Gryff in my life. I'm loved. I'm wanted. I'm successful. I now have it all."

What he said didn't come off as cocky at all, it came off more as bitter. Liv didn't think Trey had it all. He had a past that haunted him, as did she. And only she could understand it since she lived through most of it with him.

"How are things going here?" Trey asked Eli, sounding desperate to change the subject.

"Great. Olivia is making herself at home, right?" His dark eyes turned toward her.

"Liv," she reminded him.

He ignored her correction. "Grant made us a great meal last night and probably will again as soon as he gets his ass home."

"I'm sorry I was busy today at the office and didn't get to ask..." Trey started. "Did you find out anything?"

Liv didn't miss Eli's eyes sliding to her then quickly back to Trey. "No. Not yet."

Trey nodded. "I brought some clothes for Liv. Some basics Rayne picked up. But maybe she should call Rayne and give her a better idea of what she needs."

"Well then, tell your sister that and not me," Eli suggested.

Trey glanced at her.

"I'll do that. Thanks," she responded. "Hopefully, I won't be here long, so I won't need much. But I do need my laptop."

"I can buy you a laptop," Trey said.

"I have documents for school on mine."

Trey's eyebrows furrowed. "School?"

"Yes, she's attending community college online," Eli volunteered.

She quickly added, "Just one course at a time."

"Why only one?"

"I have a job... or did. I'm sure I'm going to lose it since I went AWOL. But even with it, I can't afford to take more than one at a time."

"Next semester you can go full-time. I'll cover it."

"Trey..." she whispered.

Her brother lifted his hand. "I got it. It's the least I can do."

She shook her head. "I don't want hand-outs. I've been fine on my own for a long time."

Eli shot her a frown. "You're no longer on your own, Olivia. Accept his generosity. He has more money than he knows how to spend."

"Gryff won't let me spend it how I want to."

Eli laughed. "Well, yeah, you need to invest it wisely and stop buying the stupid shit you do."

"A Maserati isn't stupid."

Eli tilted his head. "True. I'm with you on that one. But some of the other stuff..."

"I earn it."

"That's true, too." Eli turned to Liv. "So, please, let him help pay for your education. It's either that or another ten-thousand-dollar massage chair."

A what? Her brother spent ten thousand dollars on a chair?

"It's sweet," Trey insisted.

"A complete waste of money."

"Okay, *Gryff*," Trey mocked.

Eli laughed and shook his head. "I'm sure Gryff wasn't pleased when that was delivered."

"He didn't even notice it for two weeks."

Eli laughed again. "Right. Then you had to have hid it in the basement because it's hard to miss that atrocity."

"I have Rayne sit on my lap when—" Trey's eyes flicked to Liv. "Never mind."

"Yes, that's for the best," Eli agreed. "I'm sure your *sister* doesn't need to hear about her *brother's* sexual exploits."

"Yes, I'll pass on that, thank you very much," Liv agreed.

Grant entered the kitchen, coming up behind Liv and putting his hands on her shoulders. "I thought I heard a stud muffin in the kitchen."

"Which one is the stud muffin?" Liv asked him.

"Me," both Eli and Trey said at the same time.

Grant laughed and squeezed Liv's shoulders. "You two can fight it out while I make dinner. Any requests?"

"Steak," Eli suggested.

"Filet or strip?"

Liv hadn't had steak in a long time and her mouth watered at the thought. The only beef she'd bought in the last few years was cheap hamburger. It must be nice to have a choice of premium cuts.

"Liv?" Grant asked.

"Oh, I... Don't waste a steak on me."

All eyes fell on her.

"What?" Trey whispered, his eyes wide.

"Nonsense," Grant said, recovering first. "Your choice. Filet mignon or New York strip?"

"I... Which doesn't cost as much?"

"Liv," Grant practically breathed. She tried not to wince at the sorrow in his voice.

"Filets, please, *mon amour*," Eli cut in, taking charge.

"Perfect," Grant murmured then turned to Trey. "You staying?"

"No. We have reservations at that," he waved his hand in the air, "golden fork place."

"La Fourchette D'Or?" Eli asked, clearly impressed.

"Yeah, whatever. Gryff made the reservations."

"Are you celebrating something?" Grant asked over his shoulder. "Nothing was said at the office. It's not your anniversary, is it?"

Trey shrugged. "Probably. I guess I'll find out when I get there."

Eli chuckled and shook his head. He watched Grant as his husband moved around the kitchen, pulling stuff out of the fridge and cabinets. "They probably don't tell him, so he doesn't buy more ten-thousand-dollar chairs."

"I love that chair."

"Unless it sucks you, fucks you, and has your babies, it's not worth ten G's, *mon ami*," Eli said.

"Hmm. Gryff said something similar about my Maserati."

Eli grinned. "He would. What time is your reservation?"

Trey looked at his cellphone. "Fuck! Like in twenty minutes."

Grant turned and put his hands on his hips. "You know it's like forty minutes from here, right?"

"Fuck! I gotta go," he shouted then ran up to Liv and encircled her in his arms.

Liv's spine stiffened as her brother hugged her tight and pressed a kiss to her cheek. "Gotta go, sis. Love you." And then he was gone.

She remained frozen where she stood as she watched his retreating back. Even after he disappeared from view she couldn't make herself move.

Eli stepped up to her and with a finger under her chin, closed her gaping mouth. "Sisters and brothers do tend to hug and tell each other they love one another. At least after the teenage sibling rivalry passes."

"I... I guess so. I just never..."

"I know," Eli said softly. "It's been a long time. From what I discovered about your mother, you didn't get any love or affection from her. And your father died before you were born."

Liv looked at him in shock. "Yes."

"You two only had each other."

"Yes," she repeated, then closed her eyes. "And I left him."

"Olivia..." Eli murmured.

She opened her eyes.

"It's done, over. Move on. You're here. Your brother's back in your life. Embrace it."

Liv glanced over her shoulder in the direction where he went. "I'll try."

Eli gave her a soft smile. "That's all he could ask for."

"Now," Grant announced loudly. "Steaks and what else?"

"We'll get Trey to buy her a new laptop," Grant said, his head in Eli's lap. They lounged on the couch watching Thursday night football on the big screen in the family room, which sat off the kitchen.

"*Mon amour*, you heard her. She has her school work on the one she has. *And*, not only that, she may have incriminating files that could finger Randall in the murder. We *need* those files."

"I don't like it."

"I know you don't. But we don't have a choice," Eli reminded him. He raked his fingers through Grant's dark brown hair, careful not to knock his glasses of his face. He loved when Grant wore his glasses, which he had to do while watching TV.

"What's she doing right now?"

"She's upstairs reading. She found a book in the study and I think it's an excuse to stay out of our way. She's still worried about being a 'burden' and being an interruption in our life."

Grant snorted, trailing his hand over Eli's thigh. "Nonsense."

"*Je suis d'accord.*" Of course, he agreed. He wanted to know more about Olivia and at dinner, she hardly spoke about herself, instead asking generic questions about their relationship, about the firm and their positions there. He'd like for her to volunteer more about her past and what she went through. He really didn't want to have to investigate her himself, he'd rather it come from her.

"Did you get condoms?"

"I did." He certainly did. Grant and he hadn't worn condoms with each other in years. They had been together for the last ten, married for the last two and every year they'd gotten tested, even though each was sure the other was faithful. However, they had no idea about Olivia's past and... And what?

Eli sighed. Why couldn't he get Olivia joining him and Grant in their bed out of his head?

If she knew, she might be shocked or very uncomfortable at the least. She might even want to leave.

Though, she did take matters into her hands this morning after leaving their bed. All day he'd thought about her touching herself and making herself come. And all day, he fought an erection. At one point he was so hard, he locked himself in his office and played videos of kittens on his computer until he got himself back under control. He didn't even like cats.

He still thought his reaction to her was crazy.

"Eli..."

"Hmm?"

"I want to fuck her."

Maybe it wasn't so crazy since he wasn't the only one in that frame of mind. Still, hearing that coming out of his husband's mouth was a bit jarring. Welcome, but unexpected.

Seriously, who got excited when their spouse announces they want to fuck someone else?

Grant continued, "Because we're actually considering this, I can't get her out of my head."

"Me neither," Eli murmured, running a hand across Grant's broad chest. He brushed a thumb over one of his nipples, then the other, making Grant's hand tighten on his thigh.

Eli shifted on the couch because just like that, he sported a hard-on once more.

Grant shook with laughter. "You're poking me in the head."

Eli tipped his eyes down to his husband. "Sorry."

"Who are you fantasizing about poking? Me or Liv?"

"*Les deux*." Because, yes, he wanted both of them.

"I still worry, baby. Our relationship is strong, yes. But..." Grant paused and frowned. "I still worry."

"*Tu seras toujours mon cher mari. Je t'aimerai toute ma vie.*"

"You'll always be my husband and I'll love you forever, too," Grant returned. He pushed himself from Eli's lap to a seat and leaned into him. "And you know your French makes me as horny as all hell."

Eli's lips curled. "I know."

"You never play fair."

"You love it," Eli teased.

"I do," Grant agreed, tracing the outer edge of Eli's ear with his fingertip. "So before I get busy seducing you, can we finish this discussion on the laptop?"

"We'll get Trey to buy her a new one no matter what. I'm sure hers is dated and slow and, not to mention, it's evidence. I still need to grab her old one, *mon amour*, and I know you don't like that. But it has to be done. Trey can get her something new and pay for extra classes whenever her next semester starts. She may not like being given these things. But, honestly," Eli shook his head, "she's going to have to get over it. She has a rich brother who does love her, no matter what happened in their past."

"Telling her to 'get over it' is easier said than done, big man."

"I know, but if she's been struggling with that shit job to pay for one course a semester, then she realizes education is important. Though I doubt she even graduated high school, she probably had enough gumption to get her GED. I think she's much stronger than she appears."

"She's determined, that's for sure. Who the hell can make it on their own at sixteen?"

"*Mon amour*, we still don't know the details of what she had to do to 'make it.'"

"True."

"That's what makes me wonder about this relationship with that prostitute. Why was she helping her off the street? Was she in the same boat in the past and someone helped her escape that rat race? Runaways tend to sell their bodies to survive out on the street. It's unfortunate, but true."

Grant grimaced. "Jesus. Do you think she did that? Trey will flip."

"I don't want to think about her being forced to do that."

"Me neither, but..."

"But… let's drop that for now, please, *mon amour*. At least until we know for sure."

"Yes. It's an unpleasant thought."

"Tomorrow I'll get Trey to pick her up a new laptop and I'll go retrieve her old one."

Grant gripped Eli's face in his hands and turned him to face him. "Please be careful."

"Always, *mon cher mari*. Now, are you going to kiss me or are we going back to watching football?"

Instead of answering, Grant pressed his mouth against his and Eli parted his lips, letting him in to explore. He closed his eyes and melted into the kiss, his body heating up, his cock twitching in his shorts. One hand automatically wrapped around the back of Grant's head, pulling them tighter together. The other dropped to his lap and once he adjusted himself to a more comfortable position, he traced his own cock through the silky fabric of his shorts. His balls were tight, and he wanted to take Grant right there on the couch.

"If we fuck on the couch, do you think she'll come down and catch us?" Grant asked against his lips.

"We could only hope. Maybe she'd join us on her own. But, honestly, I don't think we'll see her for the rest of the night."

"She's used to being by herself."

"I think so."

"Baby, that hurts my heart," Grant said softly.

"I know, *mon amour*. Mine, too."

"Well, she has all of us now."

Eli grabbed Grant's chin, turning his face to hold his gaze. "Grant, tell me the truth. Are you okay with this, if something happens between us?"

Grant took a deep breath before answering. "Surprisingly, I am. If, and that's a big if, it's the three of us. Not just you and her. She's only going to be here a short time, if it's her choice to join us during that time, I have no problem with it. I think it will be fun to explore our wild side. We're getting to be a boring married couple."

"We are so not boring." Eli laughed.

"Yes, we are. It's Thursday night. We're lying on the couch watching football and we'll go to bed, then go to work tomorrow. We do the same thing every Thursday night. Not that I have to remind you, but we have a pattern for almost every night of the week."

"I love spending time with you doing things like this."

"I do, too. I just don't want our relationship to become complacent. Maybe this will give it an extra spark and then once she's safe and leaves, we can go back to our boring selves."

Right. Once she leaves. She just got here, Eli thought. "So we've tackled the laptop issue and our boring relationship issue, can we now get to the most important issue of all?"

"Your hard cock, big man?"

"My hard cock," Eli agreed. He bucked his hips off the couch and pulled his loose shorts off, laying them over the arm of the couch.

"Who gets the top?"

Eli smirked. "We should fight it out."

"How?"

Eli arched an eyebrow at him as Grant was pulling off his jeans and yanking his T-shirt over his head. "Sword fight?"

Grant froze, his head still stuck in his tee. "What?" came his muffled question.

Eli grabbed the tee and helped him pull it over his head and he tossed it aside. "Just kidding. Leave your glasses on."

"Why?"

"It's fucking hot." Eli ran his hand over Grant's jaw, the bristles of his tightly trimmed beard tickling his fingers.

"They steam up."

"If they do, take them off then." Putting a stern look on his face, Eli said with an extra deep voice, "Not a moment sooner."

Grant's brows rose. "Oh, someone is taking charge tonight."

"Yes."

"That means?"

"Yes, it does."

Grant sighed. "Fine. You can tag me tonight. But tomorrow you're mine."

"We'll see."

"Oh no, we won't. I'm telling you... Fuck. We need lube."

"The bag's in the kitchen. I bought another tube when I got the condoms."

Relief crossed Grant's face. "I'll grab it." Then his naked ass was up and gone. Eli chuckled as he was back in seconds, the bag in his hand. He opened it and peered inside. "You *did* get the large box."

"I always do what my lover bids."

Grant snorted and glanced up at him. "Uh-huh." He pulled out the lube. "Oh, and the big tube, too."

"Can never have enough lube."

"Not in this household."

Eli laughed and patted his thigh with one hand while stroking his cock with the other. "Come sit."

Grant dropped the bag on the other end of the couch and moved closer, popping the cap on the lube. "Be generous, please."

Eli took the tube from him. "Always." Squirting a healthy amount on his palm he spread it over his length slowly, squeezing the crown with every upstroke.

Grants eyes never left him. "I'm ready," he murmured, his own cock hard and ready, sticking straight out from his lean body.

Eli studied his husband. Grant took good care of himself. They both did. He fed them well to keep them healthy and even after ten years, Grant never failed to get him hard.

And now, he couldn't wait for his life partner to sit on his lap. *"Moi aussi."*

Grant moved over to him, planted both hands on Eli's shoulders and then straddled his lap. "Tell me how much you love me in French."

Eli opened his mouth to tell him.

"Wait!" Grant shifted. "Hold it steady. Okay, now tell me."

"*Je t'aime à l'infini*," Eli groaned as Grant lowered himself onto his cock. Another little shift and Grant pushed himself past the tight ring and they both sighed as he slid the rest of the way down.

Grant wrapped his hand around the back of Eli's neck and ran his other hand down his chest, tweaking one of his nipples. "God, you feel so good inside me," he breathed.

Eli's breath caught. "I'm not going to argue that fact with you, counselor."

The corner of Grant's lips curled up. "Yes, I don't like to lose arguments."

"You're the best at them. And riding my cock, too." Eli's fingers dug into Grant's narrow, but muscular hips. "Jesus, Grant," he groaned.

Grant leaned over and swiped at both of Eli's nipples with his tongue then sucked one hard. He moved to the other one and scraped his teeth over the small hard tip. Eli arched his back wanting more. He'd debated getting nipple rings because he loved his nipples being played with, but he never got around to it. Though, every time Grant teased his nipples, he considered it again.

Then his husband nipped him hard on one of his pecs, hard enough to leave an indentation.

Eli leaned his head back against the couch, but kept his eyes on Grant as the man moved slowly up and down his length, his canal squeezing him tight.

"We are so not boring, *mon amour*," he teased, then sucked in a sharp breath when Grant pressed his mouth to his ear.

"I love your cock in me, big man. So hard, so hot, so thick. So deep. Every time you fuck me, I become yours all over again, Elliott."

Those words whispered in his ear made him shudder and his balls tighten. He could come in seconds, but he wanted it to last a lot longer than that.

Eli reached for the tube of lube and cracked it open, squirting more on his palm. With one hand, he fisted Grant's erection, while his other traced along the man's jaw, down his neck, over his shoulder, exploring and appreciating everything that was Grant. Everything that was the man he'd made a life with. Who he took to bed every night. Who he worked side by side with every day.

Who he cuddled on the couch with to watch football. Or sappy movies. Or sometimes even hot porn.

He could not get enough of the man who slid up and down his length, squeezing him tight, nipping along his shoulders, scraping his teeth down his neck.

The faster Grant rode him, the faster Eli fisted his cock. And when Grant took his mouth, he groaned and came deep in his ass. Seconds later, cum shot up between them as Grant's cock pulsed within his hand.

Grant released his mouth and pressed his forehead to his. After a few calming breaths, he murmured, "I don't want to move."

"Then don't."

"We're going to have to move eventually."

"We have a few moments."

"If that," Grant said.

Which was true. The older they got, the quicker they lost their erections after coming. They couldn't keep that connection afterward as long as they used to.

But they shouldn't complain, at least they could still function and please each other in all ways.

A sound caught their attention and they looked toward the entranceway to the kitchen.

Eli had been wrong. Olivia did leave her room and he had no idea how long she'd been standing there watching them.

CHAPTER 7

Liv's heart pounded in her chest so hard she could feel it all the way up into her neck and down into her stomach. Her thighs trembled. Her hands shook. Her throat was dry.

She'd been frozen in that spot for way too long. She'd never seen two men having sex before and she could honestly say what Grant and Eli did was absolutely beautiful. The two of them had moved together like it had been choreographed. They were so connected to each other that neither knew she was there.

Nothing had existed for them but... *them*.

The voice in her head kept telling her to leave, go back up to her room, leave them to their privacy, their intimacy, but she couldn't. She couldn't help but watch them.

Heat had bloomed through her whole body, her breasts ached and felt as if they had actually swelled with the need for attention, her panties were soaked.

After watching them finish, she really needed to go back upstairs to her room and make herself come again. She'd never wanted sex so much in her whole life until these last two days.

She should be worried about her safety and working on getting her life back on track as soon as possible and not longing for the attention of two men. Who were gay, for crissake.

Two married men who were clearly in love with each other and, obviously, had a healthy sexual appetite for one another.

But, *God*, she yearned for something like what they had. For someone to love and care for her deeply. Someone to be intimate with and share secrets, jokes, and even just the boring everyday goings-on in life.

She never realized how badly she wanted all of that until now. Until watching them. The way they interacted while in the kitchen at dinner time, the way they were last night when they busted into her room worried about her, the way they were right now... It wasn't just sex. Hell no, it wasn't. It was so much more than that.

And here she was, gawking at them like they were a circus side show.

She needed to give them their privacy and then get out of their house, even if it wasn't safe for her anywhere else. She couldn't intrude on their lives any more than she had already.

"Olivia."

Eli's low, deep voice washed over her, and she shuddered.

Funny how neither of them had moved. They didn't jump apart embarrassed with being caught in the act. Neither rushed to cover their nudity. And they hadn't even separated; they still remained connected intimately. But they watched her as if her watching them was completely normal.

So strange.

"Liv," Grant called to her, his voice huskier than normal.

She had seen everything they had just done, and she should be embarrassed. *They* should be embarrassed. But they weren't. She wasn't, either. She was... fascinated. Intrigued.

And the reason floored her.

She wanted to join them. She wanted to be a part of what they had with each other. Even if it was for just one night. She wanted to be included in that cocoon of love and passion, of sexual exploration and satisfaction. Even if it was just for one hour.

She'd take anything they gave her. She just wanted to feel a part of them. Of something worthwhile.

But they would never go for that. They would never understand her need to belong. To be actually wanted and included.

Her chest tightened, her muscles froze. And she was paralyzed in place.

"Olivia," Eli said again. "How much did you see?"

"Everything." Her voice didn't sound normal. It was different, sounding more hollow than usual.

"Olivia, come here."

She shook her head woodenly. She felt like a puppet on a string waiting for someone to make her body move.

"Liv, please," Grant said softly. "Talk to us." After a moment, he turned his head to Eli. "Baby, I'm going to get off you. We need to clean up. I think Liv's in shock."

"No," she heard herself say. "I'm not in shock."

"Then what?" Grant asked her.

"More like awe."

"Awe?" Eli echoed.

"Have you ever seen men having sex before?"

"No."

"Does it disgust you?" Grant asked carefully.

Liv shook her head. More to get it out of a fog. "No. Not at all. It was beautiful. You two are... beautiful."

Eli and Grant glanced at each other quickly, something went unsaid between them, then they turned their attention back to her.

"You could make it more beautiful," Grant suggested.

"What do you mean?"

Eli finally spoke up, "You could be with us. You could join us."

She shook her head again. "Why would you want that?"

"Why wouldn't we?" Eli asked her.

"Because you love each other."

"You being with us, sharing us, wouldn't stop us from loving each other."

"You're also gay. I thought..."

"We're..." Eli sighed. "We've both been with women before. You could call us bisexual if you need to label us. But I've never only been attracted to men. And it's the same with Grant. We love each other because of who we are, what's inside, not because of our gender."

Suddenly the fog lifted from her brain. What Eli said made perfect sense. You love someone for who they were, not what they were.

"So you like women, too?"

Eli gave her a soft smile. "We like you, Olivia. Both of us do."

"You want me to have sex with you?"

"Do you?"

Liv took a tentative step into the room, drumming up the courage to confess her desire. "The truth is, I'd love to experience what you two have. Even just once."

"We can make that happen," Grant said, shifting off Eli's lap with a groan. "But right now, I need to go clean up." He tapped Eli's shoulder. "You do, too."

Eli turned his attention back to Liv. "Why don't you go and wait for us upstairs?"

Liv's heart began to race. Was this really going to happen? The men letting her join them? This was way beyond her wildest imagination.

"In your bedroom?" Her voice trembled with... excitement. Anticipation. And a little bit of fear of the unknown.

Her limited sexual encounters in her past had never been anything worth repeating. And there'd been no one she wanted to continue any kind of relationship with. She never had that "spark" that she read about in so many of the romance novels she devoured with anyone. She'd always wanted that connection, that special something. And at thirty-two she was beginning to wonder if she'd ever find it.

Not that she had looked very hard. Again, her cautiousness with meeting new people tended to hold her back when it came to socializing and meeting men. She always figured if it was meant to be, it would happen. Like fate would intervene…

"Yes, in our bedroom. If that's what you want, Olivia. Make sure it is first. If it isn't, go to your room instead. We'll understand completely if you don't join us. You'll still be welcome to stay here as long as necessary. So, please, don't feel pressured."

She didn't feel pressured at all. And she had no doubt what she wanted. She didn't need to think about it at all. She wasn't going to change her mind. Hell no, she wasn't.

"I'll be upstairs," she whispered. Heat licked up her chest and into her cheeks, her pussy clenched hard at the thought of climbing into their bed, waiting for them to come join *her*. And not the other way around.

She glanced down at the large T-shirt she'd worn to lounge in her bed while reading. It wouldn't do at all. She needed to hurry upstairs and change. With a last look toward the couch at the two men who looked poised to move once she left, she did just that.

Having cleaned up in the downstairs bathroom, and after Eli pulled on his shorts and Grant his PJ bottoms, they moved down the hall toward their open bedroom door. Eli grabbed Grant's arm and pulled him to a halt.

"*Mon amour*," he began. With a little shove, he pushed Grant's back against the wall and stepped close, both hands gripping his face, and he pressed his forehead to his husband's.

Grant blinked slowly. "Yeah?"

"I know I keep asking this, but this is your last chance to back out. Are you *sure* you want to do this?"

"Eli..." Grant breathed, then reached a hand between their pinned bodies to run fingers over Eli's erection. "You're looking forward to this. Your body doesn't lie." Then he grabbed Eli's wrist, pulled his hand from his face and pushed it between the two of them until he pressed it against his own erection. "Mine doesn't, either."

"It's not our bodies' reaction I'm worried about." Eli tapped a finger against Grant's temple. "It's up here."

"Have you had a threesome before? I can't believe I've never asked you that before."

"Yes, a long time before I met you, but it wasn't with anyone I loved."

"Do you think that will make a difference?"

"I don't know."

"Are you worried about my reaction or your own?" Grant asked.

The man was way too intuitive. Eli hardly ever got away with hiding his feelings and Grant never hesitated to call him out on them.

When Eli didn't answer, Grant continued, "Let's treat this as just sex. One night with someone who will soon extract herself from our lives. Let's just enjoy the brief time we have. I mean, maybe it'll be awkward and won't work at all and we'll all end up laughing about it in the morning."

Eli highly doubted that. If they stepped into that room together and they find Olivia in their bed, Eli had this feeling it was going to become more than just sex. He still had this weird pull toward the woman that he couldn't explain.

Maybe after spending more time with her, he'd find out it was nothing, that he'd only imagined it.

"Okay then," Eli finally said. He dropped his mouth to Grant's and kissed him long and deep. His tongue swirled around finding Grant's and when the other man groaned he swallowed it, combining it with his own.

They were certainly both primed again in anticipation for who was waiting in their bed. And they knew she was in there since the spare bedroom door was wide open and the room was dark. While in contrast, the light was on in theirs. A good sign.

"Ready, *mon amour*?" Eli tried to keep the quiver from his voice.

"Yes, baby, I'm ready."

Eli grabbed his hand and tugged Grant away from the wall. He didn't release it until they stepped into the bedroom and were greeted by something they hadn't quite expected.

Olivia sat up in the center of their bed, her back to the headboard, her dark blonde hair loose around her shoulders. Her cheeks were flushed, and her nipples were as hard as diamonds beneath what she wore.

And that's what caught him off guard: what she wore. It was a maroon silky nightgown, long enough to cover her legs down to her ankles. But even with her sitting on the bed, he could see it clung to every one of her curves. The neckline plunged, emphasizing the smooth, milky white skin of her breasts. They filled the silk and lace triangle shaped cups perfectly. Spaghetti straps held up the weight of those breasts and Eli had a difficult time ripping his gaze away from the rapid rise and fall of her chest.

She was either very excited or very nervous.

Or perhaps a bit of both.

"Baby," Grant breathed next to him.

Yes, he felt the same way. He swallowed down the lump in his throat before asking, "What are you wearing?" Like he couldn't see it with his own two eyes.

She ran a finger over one of the thin straps and down over the fabric covering her breast. "Rayne sent this over."

He would have to thank Rayne tomorrow for the perfect gift. Not the gift to Olivia, but to him and Grant. Because what waited for them in their bed certainly was one. "You were wearing Grant's T-shirt earlier."

His brain must be addled. He was asking stupid questions. He was surprised he wasn't stuttering or tongue-tied.

Her hand continued on a path down her side and smoothed the silky fabric over her hip and thigh. "I normally don't wear anything like this. His T-shirt was comfortable. This is... not really made for comfort. But I thought you might appreciate it more than a worn tee."

Eli definitely appreciated it. He snuck a glance at Grant. No doubt he did, too.

"We do. You look stunning in it. It's not only perfect for your coloring, it emphasizes your curves perfectly. Rayne did well picking out your size."

"Well, Rayne certainly knows how to dress for attention," Grant murmured.

"That she does, *mon amour*."

His own attention was drawn to Olivia's fingers trailing back up her thigh, back up her belly and then it blazed a path between her full breasts.

Eli wondered if she even knew what she was doing, if she had skills of seduction. Then it hit him, maybe she *had* been a prostitute.

Fuck.

He finally released Grant's hand and approached the bed. "Olivia, have you had a threesome before?"

Grant moved up to him, placing a warm hand on his lower back.

Her blue eyes widened. "No. Is that going to make a difference?"

Oh, hell no, it wasn't.

"No, I just..." Fuck. How did he approach this issue? "I'm not sure how experienced you are..." He trailed off before he stuck his foot in his mouth. Last thing he wanted right now was to piss her off and watch her storm back to her room. "Have you..."

"I think what my husband's trying to ask you, Liv, is if you ever sold yourself to men."

Olivia's mouth dropped open.

Grant quickly lifted a hand. "Sorry for being so blunt. But we're well aware of some of the things teenage runaways have to do to survive living on their own. We understand it's out of desperation and would never hold that against you. I'm going to safely assume he's asking out of concern for you, rather than us. He wants to make sure that you having two men at the same time isn't going to overwhelm you. Because, having two at once can be. Believe me, I've done it myself. I was young and thought it'd be exciting. It actually turned out to be a nightmare. But then, I just wasn't with the right people and that makes all the difference. We simply don't want this to turn into something uncomfortable for you. We want this to be a beautiful experience for you. And for us," he added.

"Jesus, counselor, this isn't a closing argument." Though, Eli was relieved that Grant turned Eli's concern with Olivia's past into something more positive than negative.

"And this is no time to beat around the bush, Elliott," Grant said sharply, and turned his gaze back to Olivia. "So, how much experience with men have you had?"

The flush in Olivia's cheeks darkened and Eli braced himself for the worst possible answer.

"I never sold myself," she whispered. "I've only been with three men."

"In your entire life?" Grant asked, clearly surprised.

Her hand, formerly seductive, now covered her throat. Probably in horror at their lack of manners. "Yes, is *that* going to make a difference?"

Eli felt Grant's body relax next to him. And so did his. "No," Eli jumped in. "Not at all. Like Grant so bluntly put it, we were just more concerned for you." That was the story Grant told, so Eli was sticking to it.

Eli plucked the bag from the pharmacy out of Grant's hand and placed it on the nightstand. Turning his back to Olivia, he whispered fiercely, *"Bien joué. J'aurai pu tout gâcher."* Because Grant could have messed this all up for sure.

Grant surprised him when he answered in French, *"Tu voulais le savoir."*

Of course Eli wanted to know. He was sure Grant did, too. But at least he was trying to be more tactful about it.

No matter what, it was water under the bridge and Olivia hadn't stormed out of their room insulted or in anger.

"So now what?" she asked, drawing their attention back to her.

"Now," Grant began, moving around to his side of the bed, "we make you forget that you've even been with those three men. Now, we make it so you only remember your time with us."

"Is that possible?" Olivia asked, her eyes getting heated, her hand back in motion, running over the maroon silk of her long nightgown.

"I don't know," Grant said with a grin. "But it sounded good."

"That it did, *mon amour*." Eli yanked off his shorts and climbed onto the bed. "But we will try our best for that to happen. That I promise you, *ma chérie*."

The mattress dipped as Grant climbed onto the bed after stripping off his loose cotton pants. While both naked and on their knees, their gaze met above Olivia.

"Come here, big man. Kiss me." Grant's voice was gruff, his erection long and hard, a drop of precum glistening on the end.

Eli wanted to lick it away. But instead, he did what his lover asked and leaned forward to let Grant take his mouth. Eli took charge by taking the kiss deeper, digging his hands into Grant's hair, holding him close, tangling their tongues.

They only broke the kiss when they both had to gasp for breath. Who knew having a woman in their bed watching them would be such an aphrodisiac. When he finally broke Grant's intense gaze, he looked over at Olivia, who was still pressed against the headboard. But now the flush in her cheeks raged due to excitement and nothing else. Her eyes, hidden partially by heavy eyelids, sparkled. Her thumbs circled her nipples. Not only were the tips visible through the silky fabric but so were the outlines of her areolas.

"Does us kissing make you wet, Olivia?" Eli asked, his breath a bit ragged. They hardly started, and he was already struggling to keep himself under control.

"Yes," she hissed, her eyes dropping to where their cocks met over top of her.

"We're going to kiss again, and this time please do what you will. Join us, touch us. Whatever you'd like to do. We'll let you make the first move. But we want you to only do what you feel comfortable with."

"If there's anything you want from us, ask. If you want us to stop, tell us," Grant added.

"I want to touch you," she whispered.

Eli smiled and turned to Grant. "Kiss me, *mon amour. Laisse-la nous explorer comme elle veut.*" Yes, let her explore us as she wants. Her pace, her will.

"Fuck, baby. With Liv in our bed and you speaking French, I think I may very well implode."

"Not yet," Eli chuckled, wrapped a hand around the back of Grant's neck and pulled him close, taking his husband's mouth as if he owned it. Because he did. Grant's mouth was his.

But he was willing to share.

CHAPTER 8

Grant started when a hand wrapped around his cock, a thumb brushing over the crown to spread the bead of precum that had been hanging precariously from the tip. They were not Eli's fingers that held him. Hell no, they weren't. Liv's hands were smaller, softer, and it made him groan again into Eli's mouth as she stroked him from root to tip.

It had been a long, long time since a woman had touched him. Even before meeting Eli, it had been a while. He'd always preferred men, but he had always found himself attracted to some women, too. And he loved fucking both. Sinking into a woman's wet heat or sliding into a tight ass, either way, it all felt good—and right —to him.

But, of course, he hadn't been with anybody else since the day he met Eli. The moment he met him, he knew he wanted to spend the rest of his life with this man. He thought it crazy at the time, and, when he thought back, he still considered it crazy. But he'd seen Eli sitting outside of a courtroom that Grant had been about to enter with his client. Their eyes had met, and Eli gave him a broad smile that shot lightning down his spine. He'd been caught so off guard at his reaction that he almost screwed up his opening argument.

The whole time he was defending his client, he cursed himself for not getting the man's number since he'd probably never see him again.

But he was wrong. When he left the courtroom, Elliott Stone, Certified Private Investigator and one premium hot piece of ass, was leaning against the wall opposite the courtroom doors, his arms crossed across his broad chest, his eyes dark and intense, his smile turned wicked in the sense that it held a promise of things to come.

The man did not move a muscle. Instead, he made Grant approach him. Which he did, asked the handsome dark man to join him for a drink and then...

Later that night he had the best sex of his life.

Within two weeks, they were living together and not even a month later, he talked Gryff into poaching Eli from the firm he worked for.

Though it didn't take much convincing.

Just like it didn't take much convincing from Eli to have Liv join them in bed.

And now the woman was stroking not only his cock, but Eli's, too. When a warm, wet mouth sucked on his sac, he jerked and broke the deep kiss he shared with his husband.

"Fuck," he groaned, pressing his forehead to Eli's.

They needed a game plan. They should have discussed it when they were cleaning up earlier in the bathroom, but they weren't sure if Liv would change her mind.

She didn't and now he had no idea who got to fuck whom.

The last time Grant had a threesome, he felt like the third wheel. The two other men had spent more time on each other and Grant ended up feeling excluded. It was not a fun or pleasant experience and then he found out later that the two ended up dating afterward. So their attraction to each other had been stronger than their attraction to Grant. He didn't want anyone to feel left out tonight. Because with a threesome, it could easily happen.

Liv shifted so her head was between them and, pressing both of their cocks together length to length, she began to lick the crowns as if she was enjoying a chocolate and vanilla swirl ice cream cone.

His eyes met Eli's. "Holy fuck," he mouthed.

Eli's lips twitched but he said nothing, only reached down to dig his hand into her dark blonde hair. Grant did the same, entwining his fingers into her long tresses as she ran the tip of her tongue over their lengths and in between them.

Holy fuck.

Tipping his eyes down to her was a mistake on his part. Seeing all of her hair between them, her being dressed in that sexy nightgown, and then her mouth on them both took him right to the edge.

He closed his eyes and tried to think other thoughts. Anything that would help make him last longer. He wanted to fuck her and if he came now, he might not get that chance.

This might be a once and done thing and it would kill him if Eli got to fuck her and he didn't. He didn't want to miss the opportunity to sink himself into a wet, soft woman.

With permission from his husband, of course.

That was the most important part. And he was sure it was the same for Eli. They were getting to do something neither had done in a long time and each had a pass to do it.

Liv would get to benefit, too. Or at least he hoped so. He did consider Eli and himself to be good lovers. He could only hope she thought so, too.

But right now, he had to think of anything but what Liv was doing with her lips and tongue.

"*Mon amour.*" Eli's voice was strained, broken. And Grant could understand why. "*D'un côté, elle est tellement innocente. Mais d'un autre, pas de tout.*"

In one way, she's quite innocent. In another, she's so very not.

He was quite right. Grant was glad for his brain having to work at translating Eli's French. Doing so had pulled him back from that dangerous edge enough so that he could gather his wits.

Eli had taught him enough French that he understood most of what he said. But to speak it, Grant wasn't the best. They rarely had a conversation in French, unless they were somewhere where they wanted to keep what they were saying private. Like at work.

It didn't help that Eli's French turned him on. He could listen to his husband's deep, rich voice speaking that beautiful, romantic language all day.

When Liv squeezed his sac, Grant closed his eyes and whispered, *"Ont doit décider qui fait quoi à qui."*

Because, yes, they needed to decide who would do what to whom. And they need to decide that soon.

"Tu veux que je prenne les rênnes?"

Eli asked if he should take the lead. And, yes, maybe that was for the best. Eli wanted this, maybe he should lead and Grant could just go along for the ride. "Yes, please."

"Olivia," Eli murmured. He placed a hand under her chin and disengaged her from the unbearable pleasure she was doing with her mouth. "Olivia, on your back."

"Wait," Grant said quickly. "On your knees first. Let's remove that nightgown."

Eli shot him a look and Grant shot him one back that said, "Sorry."

When Liv rose to her knees, who was taking the lead no longer mattered. They both grabbed handfuls of that silky maroon nightgown and slowly worked it up Liv's body, over her curves and then over her head, leaving her completely naked between them.

No panties, not even a thong.

Grant was pleased to find her pussy wasn't bare, a patch of dark blonde hair covered her mound. Not wild and out of control, no. Trimmed short and neat, similar to his beard. And, once again, surprise washed over him at the desire to press his face there, to inhale her scent and savor her taste.

"J'ai faim," Eli murmured.

Grant was hungry, too. But... "No more French, baby. Liv needs to understand what we're saying."

Her eyes slid from Eli to him. "I don't mind. I love hearing it."

"I do, too. But for now, we want to make sure you understand our plans for everything we're going to do to you."

"And what are you going to do to me?" she asked, her voice husky.

"What do you want done?"

"Everything," she whispered.

Everything was what she desired from these two. The contrast between them was startling. Eli so dark, Grant light. It was like having the best of both worlds and tonight it was all for her.

Being naked in front of two men should be a bit intimidating but it wasn't. With these men, it felt right, even after only knowing them for two days.

Just two days. Hard to believe, but true.

She moved onto her back and watched them share a kiss again, both still on their knees facing each other, stroking each other's cocks.

Then they separated and turned their attention to her and when they did, her breath hitched, her heart raced, and her nipples ached for their touch.

"Tonight is your night, Olivia. We'll do everything to please you," Eli murmured, sliding his hands down her legs and gently urging them to open wider.

His gruff announcement made a shudder run through her. How did she get to be so lucky? Her whole life she'd never been spoiled. Not once. And tonight they were going to do just that.

Eli moved in between her legs, his face so near her sensitive flesh that she could feel his warm breath wash over her. She bent and widened her legs to accommodate his broad body and then... his mouth was there. Right where she wanted it. Licking, sucking, nipping, the tip of his tongue, circling, flicking, teasing.

She cried out, her fingers clenching the bedsheets, her hips bucking under his onslaught.

Grant moved up and took one of her nipples into his mouth, doing the same to it as Eli did to her clit. His hand cupped her other breast, squeezing, kneading, then his fingers pulled, tweaked and rolled her puckered nipple. The more he tugged and sucked, and the more Eli's mouth drove her to the point of ecstasy, the more the warmth bloomed from her core to every part of her body.

Her lips parted, her neck arched, and she released a long, low moan. Her eyes closed when she bucked against Eli's mouth even harder as his fingers entered her slick pussy, curving, searching, finding that spot.

Grant nipped a trail along her skin from one breast to the other, taking the other nipple into his mouth, sucking hard, scraping the tip with his teeth, while his fingers rolled the nipple his mouth had previously been on.

Then it hit her. An orgasm like she'd never had before crashed through her. Her body bowed off the bed, almost bucking the men off, but they held, they continued, as the intense ripples rolled through her, curling her toes, tightening every muscle in her body, and she cried out nonsense, complete utter nonsense since she couldn't form a solid thought.

She didn't want to, either. Complete satisfaction rushed through her as the waves ebbed and waned, her body relaxing, melting back into the bed. Eli and Grant still held on, but slowed their onslaught. Now they leisurely licked, gently kissed, softly brushed their fingers along her heated skin.

Her eyes popped open and the breath rushed out of her as she stared up at the ceiling for a moment, her heartbeat slowing only slightly. They had both stilled and she sensed that they waited.

Tilting her head to glance down her body, she noticed they had their eyes tipped to her, wearing smiles.

"Wow," Grant murmured, softly sliding a thumb across one of her sensitive nipples.

"*Si réactif*," Eli said, his voice husky, his eyes heated. "So responsive," he repeated in English, she figured for her benefit.

"I've never..." Her brain was still muddled. "Not like that..."

Grant slid his hand around her throat and pressed his lips against hers. "Your pulse is ready to leap out of your neck." Then he kissed her, sweeping his tongue deep into the recesses of her mouth. His fingers tightened as he kissed her harder, more roughly.

Liv groaned, her hands coming up to dig into his hair, pulling him closer, wanting more of his demanding mouth, and the thrill of his hand snug on her throat, large, strong, able to easily crush it, made her pussy pulse intensely.

"*Mon amour*, careful," came the low warning.

Grant broke away, his lips just a hairsbreadth from hers as his breathing came fast, ragged, his eyes unfocused as he gazed down at her. "That was beautiful. Your body's reaction was just..."

"*Magnifique*," Eli finished for him.

"Yes," Grant agreed.

Liv noticed that the men's gaze held each other's for an intense moment, and once again, she had the feeling that they could communicate without words.

Grant suddenly moved, slipping behind her to lean up against the headboard, spreading his legs and tucking his hands under her armpits, he pulled her up until she leaned against him, her back to his front. His fingers traced her shoulders, down her arms and back up, sliding along the curves of her breasts and over her nipples then down her belly, until they dipped inside her quickly.

"So wet," he murmured into her ear. She shivered as his deep voice filled her head with naughty ideas. "Eli's going to take you first. Then me. Are you okay with that?"

"Yes," she hissed, the anticipation making her blood rush through her as his fingers trailed back up her body, exploring.

For a moment, Liv became distracted with Eli's movements. He reached over to the nightstand to grab the bag. He removed a tube of lube and what looked like a box of condoms. A large box.

"Just to be honest, we normally don't use protection, Liv. We've been together a long time and we're monogamous. But we will with you. We don't want you to worry."

She nodded as she watched Eli rip open a package and roll a condom over his dark length, his eyes never leaving her. He watched as Grant's hands roamed her body, touching and teasing.

"Did you like my hand on your throat?" Grant whispered.

Surprisingly, she did. It was nothing she'd experienced before, but she wanted him to do it again. "Yes."

"I did, too," he murmured against her ear, his tongue tracing the outer shell before sucking her earlobe into his mouth.

She gasped. She never would have expected something as simple as that would be so exhilarating. Liv kept her gaze pinned to Eli as he walked on his knees back between her legs.

"I'm going to pull you up onto my lap," Grant warned before doing just that. His cock was hard against her back, his precum like hot silk against her skin. "Maybe the next time we're in this position, my cock will be taking your ass while Eli's fucking you. Would you like that?"

Would she? She didn't know. It didn't seem feasible to take two men at once. Neither were small men and she'd never even had anal sex before, so to do something so extreme seemed impossible.

"We're not going to worry about that right now, Olivia," Eli said, his eyes dark and hooded as he stroked his own cock. "Right now we just want to please you."

"You already have," she said on a breath.

He smiled and once again stared at Grant over her shoulder.

"Mon amour et ma chérie, are you ready?"

She was so very much ready. She understood the appeal of Eli speaking French while they were being intimate because it made what they were doing even more beautiful.

Reaching an arm behind her, she wrapped her hand around the

back of Grant's neck and with the other she reached out to place a palm on Eli's chest over his heart. The beats were rapid and strong, his chest rising and falling more quickly than normal.

"It's been a long time for me..."

Eli shifted until the head of his cock pressed against her slick folds, then he pushed just enough to separate them. "How long?"

"Years," she got out before her eyes rolled back as he pressed a little further. Not enough to enter her, but he was right there. He wrapped his hands around the back of her thighs and raised them a little.

"How many years?" he asked quietly, his eyes catching hers.

"Almost a dozen," she confessed softly. She wondered if she should be embarrassed. Who went that long without sex?

His eyes flicked up to Grant and then back to her. When he said, "Thank you for this gift," he surged forward, taking her completely. Filling her, stretching her until she could take no more of him.

Grant's breathing came quickly against her ear, his hands moving faster over her body, twisting her nipples, squeezing her breasts firmly, one hand snaking down her belly until his fingers brushed where she and Eli were so deeply connected. His finger circled her clit, making her clench tighter around Eli, which made the breath hiss out of him.

"*Tellement serré, mon amour.*"

"He says you're very tight," Grant groaned in her ear. "I feel how wet you are, too. I can't wait to be inside you."

Liv trembled at his words because the thought of both men taking their turn with her excited her to the point where she was having trouble catching her breath.

It didn't help when Eli leaned forward and the men kissed each other over her shoulder. She could hear their groans and moans in her ear. When she turned her head slightly, Eli moved to her and took her mouth next. He didn't have to coax her to open her lips. She shoved her tongue into his mouth instead, groaning low in her throat. She gripped his cheek and tilted her head to take the kiss deeper.

Liv had to break away to gasp when he began to thrust harder, faster and deeper. Grant pinched her nipple and her clit at the same time making her jerk wildly against his hand and Eli's cock.

Eli grunted as he thrust deep once more, pushing her over the edge she teetered on. And she welcomed the fall, her body losing control of itself as she twitched with the intense climax that ran through her. The back of her head pressed against Grant's collarbone and he slid his fingers around her throat once more, squeezing gently as the waves of orgasm subsided.

He pressed his lips to her cheek, murmuring, "My turn to make you come."

But Eli hadn't come, only she had...

"Elliott," Grant said firmly as if he was in charge, though his voice was tight, strained. "Now... please."

With a nod, and after dropping a quick kiss on Liv's lips, he slipped from her and moved away.

She was surprised at the sense of loss she felt. Even when she knew that Grant would soon be taking his place.

After removing his own condom, Eli grabbed another, ripping it open as Grant moved from behind her, also giving her a quick kiss on the mouth.

He moved closer to Eli, pressing his mouth to the darker man's ear. Liv felt a twinge of something she didn't recognize when she realized they were sharing an intimate moment or a secret.

Eli rolled the condom onto Grant and then kissed him once more. When they moved apart, Grant grabbed her ankles and pulled her flat onto her back. Eli moved to her head, curling his hand around it and lifting it enough to tuck two pillows underneath, giving her a perfect view of Grant settling between her thighs. Grant tasted her and sucked at her clit for a heartbeat or two, then moved over top of her, his cock now perched at her entrance.

"Fuck me," Liv begged before she could stop herself.

Grant smiled. "I plan to. Eli..."

Eli moved to straddle her, facing the headboard, his knees right above her shoulders. His long, hard length inches from her face. He ran a finger over her cheek then over her lips, tucking his thumb into her mouth. She tentatively touched the tip of her tongue to his digit, then wrapped her lips around him and sucked. His eyes hooded as he watched her suck his thumb, and her tongue swirled around it as he moved it in and out.

Grant's weight lowered and with a single hard thrust, he was deep inside her. She sighed around Eli's thumb as Grant began to move slowly, keeping a steady pace. Almost as big as Eli but not quite, he still stretched her enough that she felt very full of him. The tilt of his hips was perfect, the head of his cock sliding over the spot that made her squirm beneath him.

"Yes," she hissed once Eli freed her mouth. "That's it. Oh, right there," she groaned.

Grant's hands were on her breasts, kneading and squeezing them and then she felt his hot mouth, sucking in a nipple, tugging on the tip with his lips.

She tried to arch her back, but he had enough weight on her to pin her to the bed, and it didn't help that Eli straddled her neck.

"Open up, *ma chérie*. Take me into your mouth." He tapped her lips with the head of his cock and she parted them as he pushed forward. "Take all of me."

She didn't think she could, but she was willing to try.

The taste of his precum was salty on her tongue, but she loved it. She swirled her tongue around the smooth crown, then around the edge before working her way down. It was hard to concentrate on what she was doing with Eli, with what Grant did to her. When she groaned around his cock, Eli dug his fingers into her hair and pulled hard. Then he yanked even harder, making her scalp scream.

She loved it. Like Grant's hand on her throat, she loved the sensation of Eli taking control and guiding her head with her hair.

"Tap my leg if it gets to be too much, *ma chérie*."

It wasn't. It wasn't too much. It wasn't enough. She wished she could take him deeper. She wished she could take Grant deeper, too. She couldn't get enough of either of them. Eli thrusting into her mouth, Grant thrusting into her slick pussy.

A tear slid down Liv's cheek when Eli hit the back of her throat. She relaxed it as much as she could, wanting to take even more. With a hand on his sac, she squeezed his balls tightly and a thrill went through her when he groaned and closed his eyes, throwing his head back.

Grant's rhythm hiccupped as he leaned forward and said, "Bend over, baby, I want to eat you while she does, too."

In a flash, Eli was on his hands and knees over Liv, his cock drilling harder down her throat. She couldn't see what Grant was doing to Eli, but she could only imagine when Eli stiffened above her and stilled, his breath coming in ragged bursts.

"Grant," he cried out. "Fuck... fuck... fuck."

With everything that Grant did to Eli, he never once forgot about Liv. His hips rolled forward and back, his cock stroking inside her deeply while Eli continued to fist her hair, pulling it tight. Tears leaked out even faster now, but she wasn't going to tap his leg. She wanted to give him as much pleasure as she was getting from the both of them.

"Mon amour, je jouis," Eli cried out, his body becoming solid above her as he spilled down her throat. "Ah, fuck," he breathed. He quickly slipped from her mouth, and, brushing a thumb over her lips, asked, "Are you close?"

"Yes."

Then he was twisting away from her, still straddling her body, but now facing Grant. He suddenly dropped his head and put his mouth where they were connected, sucking her clit as Grant pumped into her.

Her back bowed and she cried out, gripping his calves, digging her fingers into his flesh as another intense climax rolled over and through her.

"That's it, honey, squeeze me tight. Holy fuck... Eli..."

Eli rose to his knees and roughly grabbed the back of Grant's head pulling him into a fierce kiss as the man thrust once more and then stilled, his groan muffled as it spilled into Eli's mouth.

Grant's cock twitched and pulsated deep inside her as he reached his own climax.

Then a few moments later, they broke away from each other and fell to the bed, one on each side of her, still catching their breath. As was she.

"Thank you, *mon amour et ma chérie.*" Eli rolled to his side to study Liv and Grant, sweat glistening his brow. "That was fucking awesome."

Grant barked out a laugh and roll to his side, too. "Yes, I have to agree with that. Liv, what's your opinion?"

She smiled up at both men. "That was fucking awesome," she echoed.

CHAPTER 9

Eli moved under the cover of darkness along the side of the brick building. He pulled his collar up higher and his baseball cap lower as he stepped to the entrance and quickly walked in the front door.

Which he noticed had no security at all. No keycard, no lock, no system for the residents to buzz visitors in. The place was a complete dump. The front door's glass panel had a long, diagonal crack in it, the red outdoor carpeting on the steps was frayed and worn almost down to the concrete underneath it.

"Jesus fucking Christ," he muttered as he stepped inside, which was even worse. Filthy cracked and missing tiles, peeling puke green paint, a burned out light and the hallway carried a heavy odor of piss. How could Olivia live here?

How could anyone live here?

She lived in what looked like squalor, while her brother lived high on the hog in a mansion in the best part of town.

And, of course, she lived on the third floor in a building with no elevator.

With another curse, he bound up the first flight of steps then had much less energy for the second. Well, it *was* four in the morning and it was difficult to muster up the energy this early. Especially after he and Grant fucked Olivia once more after recovering from the first round last night.

All three had finally fallen asleep just after one a.m. totally exhausted. And here he was, trying to get a jump on grabbing her laptop while it was still dark. He didn't want to wait until tonight since he figured it was safer to do it at a less orthodox time. And, anyway, tonight he planned a repeat of last night, except he was going to encourage them to start a lot earlier in the evening.

Once he hit the third-floor landing, he paused and listened to see if anyone was following him. Greeted by complete silence, he released a breath of relief. He surveyed the hallway and the three apartment doors. Unfortunately, this floor was no better than the first. If it was up to him, the building would be condemned, and he hadn't even seen her apartment yet.

He approached apartment number ten. The zero hung upside down by one screw, and the number one was completely missing. Pulling the key from his pocket, he inserted it into the deadbolt, but the door creaked open a crack before he even had a chance to turn the key.

Fuck.

The locks had been broken.

Someone had already been in her apartment and he doubted it was the super. Cautiously, he opened the door. The apartment was completely dark as he took a single step inside and halted, listening carefully once again. He didn't want to turn on the lights in case someone watched outside from the street.

He pulled his small, but powerful, LED flashlight from his pocket and twisted it on. Keeping it low, he shined it over the floor and froze.

The place was trashed, and he doubted Olivia kept her apartment in that condition. He took two more steps deeper into the living room and things crunched beneath his feet.

Everything had been tossed. The beam of light crossed the old worn couch against the wall. The cushions had been overturned and slashed. The old analog TV smashed. He turned the other direction and shined the light into the small galley kitchen. Every cabinet hung open, every mismatched plate or glass Olivia owned was scattered across the linoleum in pieces.

Whoever did this had to have made a lot of noise. He wondered if any of the neighbors had called the police. Or if it had been the police on Randall Dean's payroll that had actually done the "search."

Either way, Olivia was right, Dean knew who she was and where she lived. She was a liability for the senator. An inconvenience of epic proportion that needed to be dealt with.

Not only was Olivia correct, but so was he for making her come stay at their house.

She told him her laptop had been left charging in her bedroom, but he knew it wouldn't be there. Regardless, he went into her bedroom, the narrow, bright beam of light leading the way.

Her mattress and box spring had been overturned and tossed to the center of the small room. Both had been sliced open similar to the couch cushions. Her dresser was knocked over and her clothes scattered across the floor. Of course, there was no laptop. Not even the remnants of a destroyed one. Someone took it.

He stepped closer to the closet which hung wide open. Clothes and a few pairs of shoes laid in a heap on the bottom of the tiny closet.

Even with everything a mess, he could tell Olivia didn't have much. Her apartment was sparse for the most part and only included the basics. Or had, anyway.

He doubted she'd ever be able to come back to this apartment again. As soon as the super saw the condition, he figured there would be an eviction notice plastered to the door.

That was fine with him. She deserved so much better than this place. If Trey didn't step up and help her, then he and Grant would.

He needed to get out of there, but he needed to find the memory chip first. He didn't know if Dean knew it existed, but he hoped not.

They wanted her laptop and they wanted her. They might not have known there was any incriminating evidence on her computer, either. But once they accessed the hard drive, they definitely would.

Then the hunt for Olivia would be even more intense.

They needed to keep her safe.

And to do that he needed to find that fucking chip.

He reached into the closet, his hand feeling around the inside edge of the wall. He slid his hand up and down until he finally felt it.

A small piece of Duct tape. Eli ripped it off the wall and turned the flashlight on it, flipping the grey tape over.

He blew out a relieved breath. It was there, still stuck to the backside of the tape.

Thank fuck.

Peeling it off, he balled the tape up into a tight wad and dropped it amongst the mess, then pushed the chip deep into the coin pocket of his jeans.

Then he got out of there, making sure he still wasn't spotted or followed.

Sticking to the shadows, he jogged the two blocks back to his blacked-out Land Rover and sped all the way back to the office to see what secrets that tiny chip held.

"Trey, sit the fuck down," Gryff barked at this lover. "Your pacing is driving me mental."

"I can't help that I'm worried," Olivia's brother snapped back.

"We're all fucking worried," Gryff growled.

"Boys," Rayne murmured in her soft way that had both men's eyes landing on her instantly. "Trey, sit down. Boss, calm down."

Eli fought back a smirk at the control the woman had over both of her partners. He was pretty sure if they wanted sex with her tonight, they needed to stay out of the doghouse. One way of doing that was by paying attention to what she said. And spoiling her.

Oh, did they love to spoil her. Not that he blamed them. He could imagine getting locked out of Rayne Jordan's bedroom because she was pissed would be a punishment of devastating proportions.

Gryff's mouth closed. Even though he leaned against the wall, his body was still tight, his arms crossed over his chest, his face dark. And it was more than his skin tone. Eli could see the concern clearly in his boss's face.

But they were all concerned.

Grant stood behind him as Eli leaned back in his office chair, rubbing a hand over his smooth head. Trey sighed finally and settled in one of the chairs facing Eli's wide desk.

Rayne was already settled in the other one, her gorgeous legs in sexy stockings crossed. Eli did his best not to ogle his bosses. Whether it was Gryff, who was smoking hot in a dominant way, Trey who was smoking hot in a professional athlete way, or Rayne, who was just smoking hot, especially how she dressed and carried herself.

And all three of them had intelligence to spare. Though, sometimes he wondered about Trey. He might be smart, but the man could do stupid things.

But then, like Eli, Trey had no father to raise him or give him guidance. At least, Eli had a good, caring mother. Trey and Olivia hadn't even had that much.

"Eli," came softly from behind him. "Are you going to keep us all on pins and needles?"

Eli glanced over his shoulder at his husband. "No. I was just waiting for Trey to settle the hell down, so he'd pay attention."

"I'm paying attention," Trey grumped as he crossed his arms over his chest, too.

"Good. Let me start by saying this, Olivia's not going back to that apartment ever. You'd be appalled to see it, not because it was trashed but because it's a slum house. I'm going to lay it out for you, Trey, what you need to do for your sister and you need to listen carefully." His eyes slid to Rayne then Gryff. "Though, I'm sure if you forget, you'll have someone to remind you and ride your ass." He finally did smirk. "And not in the way you enjoy, mind you."

"Since when did you become boss here? If I remember correctly—"

"Trey," Rayne cut him off with a soft voice.

Trey shut up immediately, but not without a frown. He ran a hand through his longish dark blond hair, messing it up even more than it already was.

"Until this is over and until you find her a safer place to live, she'll remain with us," Eli announced.

He didn't miss Gryff's brows raise in surprise. His boss's gaze landed behind him, most likely on Grant. "You don't mind?"

After last night, Eli highly doubted Grant minded. But now was not the time to point that out. He doubted Trey, Gryff and possibly even Rayne would be thrilled to know that Olivia was now sleeping in their bed. Or, at least, did last night. And if it was up to him, she would remain there during the duration of her stay.

"No, I don't mind at all," Grant said carefully behind him.

Eli was tempted to turn around to see if Grant struggled to keep a blank expression.

"Okay, so she's safe at your house for now. She can't go back to her apartment because Dean knows she lives there, they took her laptop, so they know, or will know, that she has incriminating evidence against the asshole. And you have the backup memory chip in your possession," Trey summarized. "Can we get on with what needs to happen next? What our options are?"

Rayne reached over, grabbed her lover's hand and squeezed.

Eli understood Trey's impatience, so he tried not to let that get under his skin. Even though the man was hot and the type that, years ago, Eli would've picked up at a club, taken home, and fucked him until they passed out... he was glad he didn't live with the man. Sometimes the former star quarterback acted like an immature child. And more often than not, Gryff or Rayne had to step in to remind him of that. They had a lot more patience than Eli did. Okay, maybe Rayne had more patience than Gryff.

Eli sighed. "I went through the chip. Unfortunately, there's not a lot on it, but what there is may point the finger at Dean between the at least half dozen texts and the dozen pictures of Dean caught in compromising... *situations*."

"So, what's his kink?" Trey asked.

"I will preface this by saying, I have nothing against kink as long as it's between two consenting adults. His taste is certainly not mine... or Grant's. And I really doubt it's yours, either. But..." He paused. "What he was into isn't illegal in any sense of the word. However, as an uber conservative who spouts pious nonsense and who wants to control women as well as their choices, I'm sure if these photos got out, he'd be finished. It would prove what a hypocrite he is. And the texts do prove, at least in theory, that this Peggy was pregnant. She claimed it was his and he insisted on her 'taking care of it,' which were his words, but they were not the only way he said it. In one text, he came right out and used the word abortion, which he's on a campaign to ban."

"Very hypocritical of the *good* senator," Rayne said bitterly.

"Yeah, well, we all know he's a piece of shit," Grant chimed in. "Even other people in his own party know that. But he does have a rabid evangelical following who treats him as though he's the second coming of Christ."

"Well, they'd be appalled at what his true nature is," Eli confirmed.

"So, what's his kink?" Trey asked again.

"I... uh..." Eli started, trying to gather his thoughts.

"Fuck," Gryff muttered from across the room.

"I don't know the extent of it. Only what I saw in the photos and read in a couple of the texts. But nothing was said in detail. I think Olivia may know a little more, but she did say she told Peggy she didn't want to know. And I'm not sure knowing details will help us. Just the general fact of him wanting to hide his kink from the public, as well as Peggy being a prostitute who was carrying his child, as well as his demand for her to get an abortion is enough to create a reasonable suspicion that he was indeed the murderer."

"Jesus, Eli, what the fuck is the man's kink?" Trey asked, his voice raised.

"Trey!" Rayne snapped.

"Well, the man's avoiding the answer."

"It's not that I'm avoiding it, it's—"

"Elliott," came the low warning behind him.

Eli took a deep breath and let it spill out, "Dean's into paraphilic infantilism."

"What the fuck is that?" Trey asked loudly, releasing Rayne's hand and leaning forward in his seat. "And that's not illegal?"

"No. It's nothing more than wanting to be treated like an infant."

"An infant," Gryff repeated.

Eli's eyes landed on his boss. "Right. He wore diapers, drank from bottles, sucked his thumb or a pacifier. Peggy played the role of his 'mother.' He'd 'nurse' from her, if you get my meaning. Though, there *is* one text where he wanted her to find a woman who was lactating. And he did offer a pretty penny for that service if she could find one."

"Did she?"

Eli shook his head. "I don't know. Again, my information's limited right now to the text and photos that Peggy thought to save. I'm sure she had more prior to becoming pregnant and realizing that things might not go her way."

"I'm not sure that wearing a diaper and nursing on a bottle would have looked good on his campaign posters or on future campaign posters," Rayne mentioned with a smile. "That fucker's finished."

"Rayne, we need to concentrate on Liv and only exposing the fucker to keep her safe and make sure Peggy gets justice. We shouldn't concentrate on his religious or political views," Gryff reminded her. "Being a hypocrite isn't illegal. It's immoral, yes, but murder is illegal. Let's remember that."

"Right," Rayne said with a sparkle in her eye. "Oh, there will be justice."

"For women everywhere," Grant added softly behind him.

Rayne's gaze lifted to above Eli's shoulder, so he could only imagine that she and Grant were sharing a knowing look at the satisfied smile that Rayne wore. He sighed again.

"Okay, so now what?" Trey asked. "We know he's fucked up; we know he murdered this Peggy woman. So..."

"So, I need to talk to some people, keep my ear to the ground and see what the man's up to. And you have assignments, too," Eli told Trey.

"Like what?"

"This is where Rayne and Gryff will have to keep you on track."

"I don't need a babysitter, for fuck's sake."

Eli shrugged, purposely not looking at Gryff who would probably refute what Trey just said.

"You need to go get her a burner phone. We need to dispose of her cell."

The one she had, they turned off the GPS and the power before throwing into the safe in Gryff's office after hearing that Dean was after her. That one had to go. There was no way Dean was going to use that to track Olivia down. And it was an outdated phone anyway. But right now, a burner would work.

"Program all of our numbers into it and that's it. Then I need you to get her a new laptop since she needs it to continue with school."

"We have a spare one here," Gryff cut in.

"No. Trey's going to get her a new one. Top of the line and loaded." His gaze hit Trey. "She needs something that will get her through her school work and her degree."

"Which is what?" Gryff asked.

Good question. He had no idea, but he planned to find out. "I don't know. I don't care if she isn't taking graphic design, but get her one powerful enough and with enough memory as if she is."

"Damn, you're bossy," Trey grumbled.

Eli cocked an eyebrow at him. "This is your sister. I saw her apartment. She was living in squalor. She deserves a lot better, do you not agree, Mr. Super Bowl Champion?"

Trey frowned. "Of course."

"Eli, it wasn't Trey's fault—"

Eli lifted his hand, stopping Grant. "I know it wasn't. But Trey shouldn't have any problem stepping up and helping to take care of his younger sister. Right, Trey?"

"Right."

He turned his attention to Rayne, who had her lips rolled under in an attempt to keep a straight face. Though her sparkling green eyes gave her amusement away. "Rayne."

"Should I start calling you Boss, too?"

"Don't you dare," Gryff growled behind her.

Rayne finally gave up and laughed. "Okay, Eli, what do you need from me?"

"Gift cards for clothes. I'll have her buy her own online and let her get what she wants. And though you have a great sense of style, I doubt she'll be comfortable wearing your type of clothes. Though, the nightgown..."

Eli stopped, the memory of Olivia waiting for them in bed wearing that maroon number sweeping through his mind.

"*On te remercie pour cela.*" He and Grant certainly thanked Rayne for that purchase.

Rayne winked at him. "*Avec plaisir. Ce n'était rien.*"

He disagreed. Though she said it was nothing, Eli wondered what was swirling in that mind of hers.

Trey's head spun toward Rayne. "Wait. Did you buy her a sexy nightgown? And, what the fuck? When did you learn to speak French? Is he teaching you French?"

"Just a little," Rayne murmured. "And yes, I bought her something to wear to bed."

"How sexy is it? Because I can't imagine you buying some dowdy Amish-style flannel nightgown. And if it's anything like the ones you have at home..." Trey asked, scowling in her direction.

"Very," Rayne said honestly with a small smile. "But it covers her to her ankles, big brother, so don't worry."

"What was wrong with the baggy T-shirt she borrowed from Grant?"

"Nothing, but the woman probably never owned anything impractical like that, so I got it for her." She lifted one shoulder slightly like it was no big deal.

"Rayne," Gryff said, his voice low.

Without looking at Gryff, she waved a hand over her shoulder at him, dismissing his verbal warning.

"She doesn't need to wear anything sexy while she's in their house." Trey pinned his glare on Eli. "Don't get any ideas. And don't even think about touching her." His eyes flicked up to Grant behind him. "You, either. Neither of you. She's off limits."

Eli raised his gaze to Gryff who hadn't moved a muscle since he came into the office. He still leaned back against the wall, arms crossed over his chest. But now he seemed to be amused at Trey's protective older brother attitude.

However, Trey might blow a gasket if he found out that he and Grant slept with his sister, so he needed an ally if that ever came to light. More than just Rayne, who he now had no doubt was doing some scheming. But the woman had performed a miracle to get Trey and Gryff together. It almost didn't happen, but she was one determined woman. And look at them now...

Okay, maybe not that exact moment, since Trey was a bit butt hurt with Rayne's mild meddling.

But Eli had seen it before, it would just take one touch or one whisper from Rayne and Trey would be over it. At least, until the next time.

Gryff pushed away from the wall and clapped his hands together once. "Okay, so let's recap. Eli, do what you do best. We'll leave it in your capable hands. Whatever you need from us, just let us know. T, you're on the new burner phone and laptop. Rayne, gift cards to clothing retailers who are not Victoria's Secret. Got me?"

Rayne smiled, though Gryff was behind her so he couldn't see her. Which Eli thought might be for the best. "Got you, Boss," she said finally.

"Eli will follow me to my office to grab Liv's cellphone to get rid of it." Gryff turned his dark eyes to Eli. "What about her logging into the school's website? Will someone be able to track her IP address?"

"I don't know. I'll work on that."

Grant laid a hand on Eli's shoulder. "You have enough to worry about, big man. I'll work on that. I'm finishing up a brief, but as soon as I'm done, I'll do a little research."

"Thanks, *mon amour.*"

"Okay, I think we have everything covered for now," Eli said and pushed out of his office chair. Grant's hand slipping from his shoulder to slide down and settle on his lower back.

Before everyone could remove themselves from Eli's office, his cellphone rang. Eli picked it up and said, "It's Olivia calling from the house number."

Everyone froze mid-motion to turn their attention to him.

He swiped his finger across the screen and put it to his ear. "Olivia."

CHAPTER 10

Olivia's words flowed like honey into his ear. "Eli, I called my work to tell them I had a family emergency."

"Did you call them from this line?" He had told her if she was going to make any calls, especially to her building's super or work, then she could only use the land line until another phone was obtained. At least Eli had the house number blocked from any caller ID.

"Yes, I did what you said... And..."

"What?" Eli sucked in a breath to brace himself.

"They said someone had been there looking for me. Not just once. But every day since Peggy's murder."

Fuck. "What did you tell them?"

"That I had to rush out of state."

"Good thinking. To where?"

"Chicago."

He breathed a little easier. "Good."

"I told them I had family there."

"Whoever's looking for you might not believe that story," he warned softly.

"I said I had a distant relative who was extremely sick."

Her story might throw them off the path but not for long.

"Are you going to lose your job?" Eli asked. Not that he cared. It didn't pay enough for her to even live decently. They needed to find her something better.

"I don't know." She paused, then said in a shaky whisper, "Eli, I can't afford to lose my job."

"That job wasn't paying you shit."

"But it's all I have."

Eli closed his eyes for a moment at the desperation in her voice. *Damn it.* His desire to take care of her bubbled to the surface like an erupting volcano. He needed to cool it. She was an independent woman and had been taking care of herself for a long time. She'd balk at someone insisting on doing things for her. They had to do that slowly and with care. Get her used to the idea that she was no longer on her own. That she had people around her now that wanted to help, who wanted to be supportive.

She didn't have to struggle anymore. Not if it was up to him.

He opened his eyes and his gaze landed on her brother who was watching him intently. Stepping in to take care of Olivia might not only alienate her but also Trey. He had to be careful.

And though Grant's tune had changed quickly, he still wasn't sure his husband was on board fully with how he'd like their relationship to develop with Olivia.

Hell, he wasn't even sure how he'd like it to go. He had an idea, though. But it was way too early to even consider it. They'd known her for barely three days.

Three days. Things had moved quickly with Grant when he met him, but not this fast. However, Eli had always been the kind of man who, when he knew what he wanted, went after it.

He also had a good gut instinct.

Right now, his gut was screaming that Olivia's temporary move-in shouldn't be so temporary.

"Eli," Grant murmured.

Eli realized that he was still on the phone with Olivia and neither were saying a word.

Fuck.

"Don't worry about your job right now. We'll deal with that later."

"But—"

"We'll discuss it when we get home." And even then, he hoped they could put off that discussion for a later date. They needed to deal with other stuff tonight other than her crappy job.

"What time will you be home?"

Home. He liked hearing that word come from her lips. "As long as I don't get tied up, about five. Grant should be home around then, too, if not sooner."

"Okay," she said softly into his ear. "I'll make sure dinner is ready at six."

His chest tightened. "Olivia, you don't have to do that."

"Yes, I do. I need to do *something*. I need to keep busy. And I'm a good cook, I promise."

"As good as Grant?"

Olivia laughed, and it pulled a smile from Eli. "Yes, just as good. But I'll let you be the judge of that."

"Okay. Keep the doors locked, the curtains closed, and the alarm activated."

"I will."

"See you later."

"Bye, Eli," she said on a breath.

His phone went dark. His heart had squeezed at her final words and he had no idea why. Just her saying goodbye to him affected him in a way he couldn't explain.

Grant curled his fingers around Eli's waist and squeezed. It was a good reminder that he still had an office full of people.

Gryff cleared his throat. "Okay, you all have your assignments. Eli, follow me to my office so I can grab her cellphone and you can dispose of it."

Eli gave Gryff a sharp nod. He laid a hand over Grant's and squeezed back as he turned his head toward the other man. *"Je t'aime,"* he murmured. Because he did. He loved Grant to the ends of the earth and back.

"Me, too," Grant whispered, then broke away, leaving the office.

"I'll go with you two," Trey said to Gryff.

"No. You need to go get the stuff Eli told you."

Trey frowned. Rayne grabbed Trey's hand and lifted it to her lips to kiss it. "Come on, *mon amour*, let's go shopping. Maybe I'll practice my French on you while we do it."

Trey smiled and jerked their clasped hands until she fell against him. She laughed and offered him her mouth. He accepted and dropped a deep, messy kiss on her. Then he tugged her toward the office door, stopping in front of Gryff.

"Boss man," Trey said, looking up at Gryff. "Give me some sugar before we go."

Gryff rolled his eyes and gave him a fake scowl, but wrapped his large hand around the back of Trey's head and pulled him close enough to give him a thorough kiss. When he released Trey, he did the same to Rayne.

Eli watched the three of them interact and swallowed hard. This is what he and Grant could have. But did they need it? Did they need to add a third person into their relationship? It may completely change the dynamics and he didn't want to mess up a good thing, either. Hell, not a good thing. A *great* thing.

He envied what Gryff, Rayne and Trey had with each other. The three were not afraid to show it. They never hid their affection for one another. There had been many a time where one of their office doors was closed and it wasn't hard to figure out what was going on behind it. In fact, Gryff had installed locks on his and Rayne's offices shortly after the three of them hooked up. Eli was pretty sure that Trey's office now had a lock on it, too. While no one else's in the firm did.

Very telling.

Gryff might pretend Trey was a pain in his ass, but he loved the man. That was clear.

Once again, Eli realized how lucky he and Grant were to work in an environment where their relationship didn't have to remain a secret, where they weren't ostracized or judged for their sexual orientation. And even better, Gryff, Rayne and Trey, who were of a like mind, were their friends outside of work, also.

They even sometimes hung out with Gryff's brother, Grae, who lived with and loved Paige and Connor. Actually, Grae didn't live with *them*. The married couple had moved into Grae's large house and they've been happy together ever since.

"Coming?" Gryff's deep voice broke into his thoughts and Eli realized Trey and Rayne had left.

"Yes."

Eli followed his boss through the halls of the large firm back to where the partners' offices were. He greeted Gryff's secretary, Dani, as they passed. Once he stepped into the big boss's office, Gryff shut the door behind him, then moved to the center of the room.

The man planted his hands on his hips, turned to face Eli directly and growled, "What the fuck is going on?"

Eli blinked in surprise. "What?"

"You heard me. What's Rayne up to? Is there something going on that I should know about, that I need to prepare for? Especially with Trey?"

"No."

"Bullshit," Gryff barked, staring at the floor shaking his head. Then he lifted it and caught Eli's gaze. "Liv's safety and getting her out of this mess is a priority, Eli. Not you adding a third to your bed."

"I—"

Gryff held up a hand, stopping him. "Don't bullshit me. You're not the only one around here that's good at sniffing things out." He turned on his heel, shrugged off his suit jacket and threw it onto a nearby chair, then grabbed the knot in his tie and tugged it loose.

The man then removed his cufflinks, tossed them onto his desk blotter before beginning to roll up his sleeves.

Jesus, was Gryff getting ready for a throw down?

"Boss," Eli murmured.

"What?" Gryff rolled up his white dress shirt sleeves until Eli could see the tail of his dragon tattoo peeking out near his elbow.

Eli knew the man had the large inked piece over his shoulders and across his back. Trey had let it slip one day and Eli sometimes got a glance of the tail that came down low on his arm. But he'd never seen the whole thing. He doubted many people had.

"Are you going to hit me or something?

Gryff looked at him in surprise. "What? No! For fuck's sake, Eli, why would I hit you?"

"For fucking Trey's sister."

Gryff froze, his narrowed eyes pinning Eli in place.

Oh, shit.

Oh, fuck.

Gryff didn't know. Eli mistakenly thought the man knew and that's why he was leading the conversation about Olivia in that direction. He thought maybe Olivia had told...

Fuck! Why the hell would she tell Rayne?

She wouldn't. Even if she would, she probably wouldn't have had the opportunity yet since it only happened last night.

Eli groaned. He just fucked up big time.

"I'm sorry?" Gryff growled. "Did you say you fucked Liv?"

"Gryff," Eli began.

"That's not an answer. But I'll take that as a yes. Does Grant know?"

"Uh..."

Gryff lifted his palms out. "Wait." He shook his head. "Wait." He turned and stared out of the long line of windows behind his desk for a moment. Then two. It was hard to miss the muscles in the man's jaw popping. "What the fuck," came the soft mutter. Then he turned and pinned his gaze on Eli again. "Was it both of you?"

"I've never cheated on my husband."

"So, you didn't have sex with Liv." There wasn't one indication of a question in that sentence.

"Uh... Shit," Eli whispered.

"Fuck!" Gryff shouted to the ceiling. "You both had sex with her!"

"Gryff," Eli tried again.

"No." He shook his head. "No. Fuck. I'm assuming she was willing. Fuck! Of course, she was. You and Grant wouldn't force... Oh, fuck me," he groaned. "We need to keep this quiet. Keep it from Trey. At least for now." Gryff blew out a loud breath and rubbed his hands over his face. "How did this happen?" came muffled from behind his fingers.

"She caught us..."

He dropped his hands and his eyebrows shot up his forehead. "In your bedroom?"

"No..."

When his eyebrows dropped low, Gryff appeared more menacing than normal. "Where?"

Shit. "On the couch."

"You have a house guest and you're fucking on the couch?"

Eli winced at his shout. And here he was, just thinking about how much he appreciated working for Gryff and this firm and now he was afraid he would lose his job.

Even worse, maybe Grant would, too.

Then there would be three unemployed people living in a house that had a monthly mortgage payment that cost more than his first Toyota.

"We didn't think that—"

Gryff raised his hand again. "Stop right there. You didn't think. Period."

"You're right. We didn't. No... *I* didn't. I'll take the blame."

"Did you pressure her?"

"What? No! We'd never do that."

"You know what surprises me? That Grant was okay with it."

Eli kept his mouth shut since he didn't think Gryff wanted a response.

"You know, I wondered why you offered to take Liv in so quickly."

"That's not why... I... Fuck!" Eli took a breath and started again, "Gryff, there's something about her. Something that drew me from the first moment I saw her in the lobby. I'm sorry. I didn't expect all of this. I know she just came into your lives, back into Trey's life... Hell, into our life. And it's sudden. It just... happened."

Gryff just stared at him quietly, his face revealing nothing. And the longer he stared, the more Eli gathered his courage to make it clear to Gryff that their intent wasn't to take advantage of Trey's sister.

But he never got a chance because suddenly Gryff jerked forward, making Eli take a quick step back. Though he was an inch taller than Gryff's six-foot-two, his boss outweighed him by at least twenty pounds and it was all solid muscle. Gryff could thump Eli into the ground if he wanted to. He really hoped his boss didn't want to. Eli could hold his own, but he was sure Gryff would get the upper hand eventually.

Luckily, Gryff only headed across the room to move the painting on the wall, revealing his built-in safe. He punched in a code and pressed his thumb to the ID pad and the safe unlocked with a loud click. Within seconds, Gryff had the cellphone in his hand and had the safe locked and concealed once more. He turned and unexpectedly tossed the phone to Eli, who caught it. But barely.

"Do what you have to do with that thing. Make sure it's never found again. Now get out of my office. I need to think about what I just discovered and whether I'm going to tell Rayne or not. Though, she'd probably buy balloons, flowers and streamers."

Eli wanted to laugh because he could picture Rayne doing that, but he figured now was not the best time to laugh at his boss's sarcasm.

He was just glad to be leaving Gryff's office in one piece.

~

Grant leaned back against the counter and watched Liv move around his kitchen. It was nice to have someone else prepare dinner for once. If dinner was left up to Eli, they ended up with take-out. Which was a nice change but not for every night.

When he got home, he'd gone upstairs to change into a soft pair of worn jeans and an old T-shirt, then barefooted it back downstairs to watch Liv putt around the kitchen.

Whatever she was making smelled really good and he hoped it tasted like it smelled. She wore a pair of skin-tight black yoga pants and a loose sexy top that looked like a wide-necked sweatshirt and fell off her left shoulder, proving that she wasn't wearing a bra. And that wasn't the only way he could tell. Every time she moved or reached for something, her breasts bobbed under the cotton and her nipples pressed hard through the soft fabric.

He fought the urge to grab her, push her loose top up and latch his mouth on one of her nipples to suck it hard. But he was afraid if he did, he'd end up bending her over the counter and fucking her from behind.

The last thing he needed right now was Eli walking in and catching them fucking without him.

He had no idea how his husband would react, other than be surprised... maybe. It was best that he didn't find out. No, he needed to wait to touch Liv until Eli was home and could join them.

Which was only fair because he wasn't sure how he would feel if the tables were turned and he came home to find Eli and Liv fucking without him.

Though, the thought of watching Eli fucking Liv made his cock go from being semi-erect to steel hard, pressing uncomfortably against the zipper of his jeans.

"Liv," came out of his mouth in a gruff manner before he could stop it.

Standing at the stove, she turned her head to glance at him over her shoulder. Her long dark blonde hair fell loose down her back and over her shoulders as her sky-blue eyes stared at him in question.

He cleared his throat. "Are those the clothes that Rayne brought over yesterday?"

"Yes. Why?"

His eyes skirted down her back and settled on her perfectly shaped ass gripped tightly in the stretchy material. Fuck him. Those pants hugged every curve she had.

This was crazy. He never wanted a woman so badly. He could only guess it was because he got a taste of her and his appetite was whetted. Though, he'd had plenty of women when he was younger, none had captured his attention enough for him to go back for seconds.

For some reason, he couldn't get enough of Olivia Holloway.

This was all Eli's fault. He was the one who was interested in her in the first place, he was the one who put the thoughts into his head. Now it was Grant who felt like he was drowning.

He needed to come up for air because he loved Eli more than anything and he didn't need his sexual desires screwing that up. He wanted nothing or nobody to ever come between them.

Liv had no idea the power she currently held over the two of them. They were both like stud dogs panting over a bitch in heat.

Maybe it was just because it had been so long since either one of them had been with a woman and they had needed to experience it once again. At first, he thought being with Liv last night would only remind him why he preferred men.

But he'd been wrong. And that worried him.

How he got from leaning back against the counter, to encircling Liv in his arms, pressing his cock against that round ass of hers, licking her neck and brushing his thumbs over her tight nipples, he'd never know. One minute he was lost in his thoughts, the next he was molesting their guest.

Though, it wasn't really *molesting* since she was gasping, whimpering and encouraging his actions. She should really be discouraging him instead. At least until after dinner and most definitely until after Eli came home.

But, holy hell, he suddenly felt the same draw to the woman that Eli must have felt immediately when he found her at the office.

Now he kind of understood. Only kind of, since he was still struggling to understand his own reaction.

"I want to fuck you," he whispered against the skin of her neck, his hand slid up from her breast and he pressed it to her throat.

"Yes," she hissed.

"We can't. Not right now. We have to wait." Though he made no move to back away.

"Why?"

"Because it's not smart. Not only because this is new, but it's not fair to Eli. He needs to be included. If the three of us are going to have sex, it needs to be the three of us together, not separately. At least in the beginning..."

"The beginning," she repeated softly.

When she repeated that, it hit Grant what he'd said. He made it sound as though this would continue. At least for a while. Like this wouldn't end as soon as they got her mess straightened out and Randall Dean was behind bars for murder.

Because he was sure as soon as that happened, she'd be moving out and moving on. She'd get a degree, a better job, have a better place to live and get back to her independent self.

"I agree." The low, deep voice came from the entranceway from the hall to the kitchen.

Grant stilled but didn't move away from Liv. He didn't want to appear guilty, like he was doing anything wrong. He turned his head to give his husband a welcoming smile.

"Sorry that you caught us in a compromising position." He kept his voice light.

Eli moved farther into the room, carrying packages. One was from a big-box electronic store and the other from a well-known computer store. Trey must have come through. Or at least Rayne had kept the man on track.

"I can't blame you, *mon amour. Elle est irrésistible, non?*"

Yes, she certainly was irresistible. But Grant was relieved to see that Eli didn't seem angry at all. He decided to answer in French. "*Désolé, la tentation de la plier sur le comptoir et de l'avoir est presque trop forte.*" He decided to confess his desire to bend Liv over the counter and fuck her. They needed to remain completely open with each other if this was going to work.

"*Mais tu ne l'as pas fait.*"

But you didn't, Grant translated in his head.

Eli continued, "That's all that matters. *Mon amour,* if we are going to teach Olivia French, we need to follow it with English when we speak it. Agreed?"

"Yes, agreed. Do you want to learn French, Liv?" Grant asked as he extracted himself from her and stepped away.

"Yes, I'd love to. I'm not sure how much I'll pick up in the next few days, but, hey, just learning a few words would be cool."

Grant's eyes slid to Eli and the darker man tilted his head in response. Eli placed the packages on the kitchen table and moved up to him, grabbing his T-shirt and pulling Grant to him. Then Eli's mouth hit his, giving him a deep, cock-hardening kiss. Though, Grant was already hard from Liv.

"I didn't give you that," Eli murmured against his lips.

"No."

Eli stared him in the eyes for a moment then moved away and over to Liv. He brushed a hand over her long hair, then, with a hand to her back, leaned into her, peering over her shoulder. "What are you making?"

"I make a mean Lemon Chicken."

"Mmm. Smells great and so do you." Eli nuzzled Liv's neck, then slid the hand from her back down until he cupped her ass. "*Ça te dérange que je te touche?* Do you mind me touching you?"

"You're asking a little too late, aren't you?"

Eli chuckled. "*Oui, c'est vrai.* Yes, it's true. *Pardon.* You can smack me if you want for being so rude."

Smiling, Liv reached up and traced her fingers over his jaw. "I'll forgive you. You two can touch me more after we eat."

When Eli glanced his way, Grant shot him a smile.

"I'll let you get back to it. I'll set up your gifts from Trey."

As he walked back toward Grant, Liv spun around. "What gifts? I don't want gifts."

"Stuff you needed, Liv. Don't worry, he's not trying to buy your love."

"He doesn't need to do that anyway. I do love my brother."

"I know you do," Grant answered softly. "It's a temporary cellphone since you can't use yours anymore. Yours was trackable, so Eli got rid of it. And in the other package is a laptop for you so you can do your schoolwork."

"What happened to mine?" She glanced at Eli. "Didn't you find it at my apartment?"

Eli sighed and rubbed a hand over his eyes. "I didn't, Olivia. I'm sorry." He glanced at Grant quickly before continuing. "Your place was trashed. They didn't only look for you at the halfway house, they broke into your apartment. They took your laptop. Everything else was pretty much destroyed."

"Everything?" she whispered, her eyes wide and now shiny.

Shit. Grant steeled himself in case she started crying. Everything she probably owned and worked hard for had been in that apartment. He could see it being a major loss.

"Yes, unfortunately. Some clothes might be salvageable but we're not going back there. It isn't worth it right now."

Liv quickly brushed a hand over her eyes, sweeping away any evidence of her being upset. "Did they get the memory chip?"

"No. I found it."

She sighed with relief. "Okay, well that's good, right?"

Eli hesitated.

"Right?" she asked again.

"Yes, but you downloaded it to your computer, correct?"

She nodded. "Yes."

"Then, when they break into your hard drive, they will know exactly what you know."

"And that's bad."

"It is," Eli confirmed.

"They're going to want to find me now more than ever."

"That's my feeling," Eli said.

"We'll deal with it," Grant added.

Her gaze landed on him, held for a moment, then suddenly her spine straightened, her eyes cleared, and she went back to the stove. "That's right. I'll deal with it like everything else that's been thrown at me my whole life. I have no choice but to deal with it."

"No, Liv, *we'll* deal with it. All of us," Grant corrected her. "You're no longer alone. We are all here for you."

Liv nodded but kept fussing with the chicken in the skillet.

"Did you hear Grant, Olivia?"

"Yes," she said firmly, still keeping her back to them. "I'll have to thank Trey for the laptop. Hopefully, I'll be able to catch up on my course tomorrow."

Grant and Eli looked at each other for a second, then Eli went to set up her new laptop.

CHAPTER 11

Liv didn't think she could get any wetter. Grant laid flat on his back while she straddled his head as his tongue stroked between her folds and teased her clit. When the tip of his tongue circled and flicked, she ground her hips harder onto his face. And when he sucked her hard, she just about hit the ceiling.

Eli made a noise and her eyes met his. He was sliding in and out of Grant at a pace that was slow and steady. His gaze ran over her face, then down to her breasts where Grant's fingers twisted and tweaked her aching, pebbled nipples.

Eli's dark fingers dug into Grant's hips as he continued to thrust, his eyes intense as he watched Grant pleasure her.

Reaching out, she ran a finger over his full lips and when he parted them, she slipped it inside. Taking advantage of that, he sucked and swirled his tongue around her digit. She never realized a man sucking her finger could be so erotic.

She slipped her wet finger from his mouth and he said gruffly, *"Je veux te voir jouir sur son visage.* I want to watch you come on his face."

She agreed with Grant; Eli's use of French during sex was the cherry on the sundae.

"*Touche toi*," he said.

This time she didn't need him to repeat his command in English. She could figure out what he wanted her to do. After slipping her finger back between his lips just for a second to get it wet, she pressed it to her clit while Grant fucked her with his tongue.

Sensations flooded over her in a rush, making her arch her back and push her breasts into Grant's hand as he squeezed them roughly. She focused on where the two men connected, Eli's dark cock sliding in and out of Grant from tip to root. He groaned into her pussy and the vibrations made her grind against his mouth even harder with a gasp.

She was beginning to really appreciate it when Grant got rough. He seemed to be holding back, though, and she didn't want him to.

Not at all.

When his hand climbed up to her neck, she took over squeezing her breast, tugging on her own nipple roughly as Grant's fingers curled around her throat and tightened.

A shiver ran up her spine as he constricted her air just enough to make it exciting.

"Tighter," she whispered, and Grant complied, his fingers squeezing just a little more. Not enough to cause pain, but enough to take her to that very edge. She held Eli's gaze as she said, "I'm going to come."

Then she exploded, her body stiffening and twitching over Grant. She cried out as the thrill of him tightly holding her neck turned into an intense orgasm that made her want to collapse into a blissful pile. But she couldn't. They were far from done yet.

Shifting slightly to let Grant breathe, she leaned over and licked away the salty beads of precum that clung to the tip of his cock. He was hard and ready as Eli continued to fuck him at his—she was sure—maddening slow pace. After a kiss and another quick lick to the end of Grant's cock, she rose and brushed a bead of sweat off Eli's forehead with her thumb.

She realized that Eli's pace had to be driving both men crazy.

Though, with Grant's mouth busy, he hadn't had a chance to complain.

An idea came over her as she stroked Grant's erection, his hips rising and falling along with both her movements and Eli's. After laying a kiss on Eli's mouth, she murmured, "I'm going to fuck him at the same time."

She wasn't sure if it would work since she was no expert at threesomes. Hell, she was no expert at sex at all. But she wanted to try it and she was sure the men would let her try anything she wanted.

"Facing me or Grant?" Eli asked, his question a bit strained.

After a second of playing her idea out in her head, she said, "Him. Grab a condom."

Eli's arms were long enough to be able to reach the box that sat opened on the nearby nightstand. He snagged one, ripped it open and rolled it onto Grant. "I assume this is okay with you, *mon amour*."

Grant's body shook beneath them as he chuckled. "I was just waiting to see if you remembered I was here."

"Hard to forget that, *mon amour*," Eli replied with amusement. "Especially with my cock in your ass. In French, *ma chérie*, that's... *surtout avec ma bite dans ton cul*. Though you will never have to use that saying."

Liv laughed softly. "No, I won't."

She carefully moved to turn around so she no longer straddled Grant's face but instead, his waist and she leaned over him, her hands planted on his chest.

"*Ma chérie*," Eli groaned. "You are tempting me greatly. I can see both *ta chatte rose et lise et ta rosette serrée*. Grant may be getting one, but I may take the other."

Liv shuddered at his words. On a breath, she said, "Guide him inside me," while shifting backwards until the head of Grant's cock brushed against her sensitive, swollen flesh.

The urge to impale herself on him swept through her and when

Eli gripped her hip and held Grant's hard length in place, she did just that. A long hiss escaped her as he filled her deeply and she felt the rush of being in control of the pace. When she moved to sit up, Eli pressed a hand to her back and pushed her back down. "Stay down, *ma chérie*, I have plans, too."

Grant lifted his head to study their position, Eli still deep in his ass, Liv riding his cock. "Have I died and gone to heaven?"

Eli chuckled. "I think we have."

"I agree," Liv gasped as she rocked back and forth, taking his whole length then releasing him until just the tip remained inside her.

Eli tapped her hip. "Stop... only for a moment."

She stilled and turned her head to watch him grab the lube which was still on the bed, pop the cap open and squirt a generous amount down between her ass cheeks. The cool gel ran down her crease, but Eli quickly collected it and spread it around her anus, poking the tip of his finger inside. Just that little touch felt amazing and she shifted back, encouraging him to do more.

He tapped her hip again. "Now ride him as you'd like."

Liv began to move again, taking all of Grant's cock and she knew exactly when Eli began to move again, too. Grant's eyes rolled back in his head and he let out a long, low curse.

"No, not heaven. Complete euphoria," he groaned. "Baby... fuck... you have no idea."

"I plan to," Eli answered, his finger starting to dip deeper into her tight hole farther and farther. "Relax, *ma chérie*. Let me please you."

As much as she tried, she couldn't, but Eli pushed on anyway, and finally... finally, he worked her at the same pace he fucked Grant. The sensations spiraled around her, through her, the energy gathering in her core. She squeezed both of them tightly deep inside her.

Grant's gaze met hers, and when she dropped her head and bit his nipple, his body arched beneath her as his fingers dug into her hair, pulling hard. She gasped which released her grip on his flesh, but she moved over to his other nipple and did the same thing, leaving a mark in his skin.

Then she shoved her face into his neck and bit him there, too.

"Fuck, honey. Fuck!"

His reaction drove her to do more and she grabbed his neck like he had done to her and squeezed hard.

He gasped and bucked beneath her wildly.

"*Mon amour*," Eli murmured. "Easy."

"Faster, baby. Fuck me harder. *Please*," he groaned. "Kiss me, Liv."

She did what he demanded as did Eli, with her taking his mouth and rocking her hips faster and Eli pounding him harder, their flesh slapping together.

Liv barely lifted her mouth from his. "Tell me if I squeeze too tightly."

Grant said nothing, so she did just that, put pressure around his throat. And she swore his cock got harder. She brushed her lips against his as she pinched his nipple hard. His mouth opened, and she swept her tongue inside. When he groaned, she stole it from him, swallowing it.

With Grant's cock and Eli's finger inside her working her to a frenzy, with her taking Grant's mouth and pinching his nipple, she was at her limit. She teetered on that edge, ready to fall over. But if there was time, she wanted to climb back up and fall once more.

However, the men were at their limits, too. Which became obvious when Eli slipped his finger from her, grabbed her hips tightly and began to fuck Grant so hard, she almost felt as though he was fucking her at the same time. The pounding was jarring, and Grant broke the kiss to encourage his husband on.

Grant wedged a hand between them, finding her clit and pinching it as hard as she had pinched his nipple. Gasping, she twitched, her pussy throbbing around him, her fingers tightening on his throat even more.

His eyes met hers when he groaned, "I'm coming."

His words made her orgasm hit her hard. She tried to say, "Me, too," but the words failed her. Instead she threw her head back and wailed as the climax rushed through her. Then Eli's fingers dug into the flesh at her hips even more and he thrust one last time, staying deep inside Grant and she could only imagine he was spilling inside his lover, his mate, his husband.

Then his damp forehead pressed to her back and she could feel the rapid rise and fall of his chest, the thunderous beat of his heart. With a satisfied sigh, she rested more of her weight over Grant's chest, his breathing also rapid and rough. He combed fingers through her tangled hair and brushed a thumb along her bottom lip. Then he tilted his head up and snagged her lip gently with his teeth. On a sigh, he released her, and his head flopped back to the pillow.

"I could stay like this all night. You on my cock, Eli in my ass. Like I said, complete euphoria."

"Mmm. Next time we do this position, I'm on the bottom," Eli murmured against the skin of her back.

"How about if we put it into regular rotation," Grant said, his eyes crinkling at the corners.

Regular rotation. They would need a third for that. She wasn't going to be here long enough for it to be her. She wondered if now that they've added a third to their sex life, they'd want it to continue.

"I can attest to whoever you find that it's a worthwhile position, especially for the woman."

Eli lifted his cheek and his weight from her back, his fingers flexing along her waist. "Whoever we find, Olivia? What do you mean?"

"Well, I can't imagine this mess I'm embroiled in will go on for any length of time, will it? Please tell me it won't."

"I hope not," Eli murmured. "We're doing what we can."

"So once that's all settled, I'll head back to my apartment, my job, my... life, so to speak. Will you look for someone to join you?"

"No," Eli said sharply. "*Absolument pas.* Absolutely not."

"Well, Grant mentioned a regular rotation. I don't plan on being here that long, so he can't mean me.'

"*Ma chérie...* he means you."

Liv tried to climb off Grant, but he grabbed her wrists and pulled her down onto his chest. His deep voice vibrated against her. "I meant you, honey."

She closed her eyes for a moment and tried to wrap her head around what they just said. "So, even after I leave, you want the sex to continue?"

"Olivia... you think this is just sex?"

Grant stared over her shoulder and she turned her head enough to catch a glimpse of Eli. Both their faces were way too serious for just having explosive, mind-blowing sex.

After a moment, Eli said softly, "Why don't you go clean up, we'll follow in a second."

Eli helped Olivia climb off Grant and watched as she padded to the master bathroom, closing the door behind her. His eyes slid back to Grant, then he slipped from his husband.

"*Mon amour,*" he began.

"*Eli.*"

"Let's let this go for now, yes? We have other things to worry about, to deal with at the moment. Once things settle down, we can revisit it."

"Eli," Grant repeated.

"It's sudden for all of us. And... Shit! I fucked up."

"What do you mean?"

"Gryff knows."

Grant groaned. "Fuck. Was he pissed?"

"He wasn't happy. But for now, we both have our jobs and I don't have a broken jaw, so that's a good sign."

"He tried to hit you?"

Eli shook his head. "No, but..." He released a loud breath. "He wants to keep this from Trey for now."

"Trey might fucking flip."

"Right. So, we keep this from him until we see what this is. I know and you know it's not just sex. But what is it? That's the million-dollar question."

"Do we let her continue to believe it is?"

"*Mon amour*, I just told her it wasn't."

"But we didn't get into any details."

"Do you want to try to explain it, Grant? Because I can't. Can you?"

Grant was quiet for a moment. "No. Honestly, I can't."

Eli nodded. "Let's just let this ride for now. Okay?"

Before Grant could answer, the bathroom door opened, and Olivia paused, her eyes on the bed.

"Are you having a serious conversation? Should I go back to my room to give you two privacy?"

Eli smiled. "No, *ma chérie*. Not at all." He patted the bed. "Come, get comfortable while we clean up."

A small smile tugged at her lips and, as she moved toward the bed, Grant and he rolled off it and headed toward the bathroom.

They washed up in silence, their eyes meeting occasionally, fingers brushing along ribs, a hip, the indentation of each other's spine.

Eli loved the man who stood next to him at the sink so much he thought his heart would burst. He never thought his love could grow stronger, but it did. Which was odd, since someone else was now in their life. But Olivia seemed to strengthen the bond that he and Grant had.

Eli moved behind him, wrapped his arms around Grant's waist and settled his chin on his husband's shoulder. He stared at the two of them in the mirror.

"What are you going to do to get the target off her back?" Grant asked softly.

Eli took a deep breath and then released it. "First, I'm going to make a backup of the evidence she has and lock up a copy in Gryff's safe tomorrow. Then I'm going to start digging around and see if I can find someone not in Dean's pocket to give a copy to."

"You're going to hand it over directly?"

"I don't know. I don't think so. I'm going to see who can be approached with the information, but I might anonymously give it to them. Then I'll sit back and see if the info comes to light. If it does, I'll know the person's trustworthy and isn't afraid to do their job."

"You could be putting that person in danger, too."

"Maybe," Eli murmured. "But we need to do something. I'd like to hand it over to the DA..."

"I could talk to her, baby. See if I get a sense she's not in Dean's pocket. Just strike up a conversation next time I run into her. I don't want to search her out as she might get suspicious."

"I don't want you to put yourself in harm's way, *mon amour.*"

Grant patted Eli's arm. "I won't. It'll be casual conversation, that's all."

"Are there any ADA's that you trust?"

Grant stared at him through the mirror as he hesitated. "I don't know. I've never dealt with any cases involving powerful politicians to get any kind of read on them in that regard."

Eli pressed his cheek to Grant's. "We just need to be cautious."

"I agree."

"I don't think Trey should come over here. They might be watching him."

"Again, I agree." Grant reached up and laid his hand along the side of Eli's face that wasn't pressed to his. "Before we go back out there, I need to say this..."

The seriousness in Grant's eyes made Eli's heart skip a beat. "What?"

"I didn't think I'd ever want to share you."

Eli watched in the mirror as Grant's Adam's apple bobbed when he swallowed hard.

"And I can't believe I'm saying this, but I don't mind sharing you with Liv. It should bother me, but it doesn't."

Eli gave him a small smile. "You must remember I'm sharing you, too."

Grant smiled back. "Yes, you are. And you can share me like you just did anytime you want. That was," he shook his head, "fucking incredible."

"Mmm. Now I'm tempted to go back out there and do it again but with me in your place."

"Next time."

Eli released him and laid a kiss on his shoulder. "Yes, next time. Let's not make her wonder what we're doing in here."

Grant opened the door and they saw Olivia curled up under the covers, facing the bathroom, her eyes shut, her breathing steady.

Eli shot Grant a glance as they approached. They split off to either side of the bed and carefully climbed in, trying not to wake her.

But when both their heavy weight settled onto the mattress, her eyes opened, and she rolled to her back.

"I fell asleep," she murmured sleepily.

"You can go back to sleep if you want."

"I can go back to my room. I don't want to crowd you two."

"Olivia, you're not going to crowd us. Sleep here."

She rolled to her side to face Eli. "I want to curl up with you, but I want to curl up with Grant, too."

Grant shifted closer. "I can spoon you." He sandwiched her between him and Eli, curling an arm over her waist and planting a hand on Eli's belly.

"That's nice," she murmured, her eyelids drooping.

"Yes, it is," Grant murmured back.

Eli covered Grant's hand with his left and with his right, he brushed fingers through Olivia's long tresses then combed them through Grant's shorter hair.

He laid there for the next hour, watching them sleep.

CHAPTER 12

Eli leaned back against the headboard and took a sip of his coffee. Grant had gotten up early and made them an extensive breakfast, bringing it all upstairs so they could eat in bed.

Not Eli's preference, as he'd rather not have crumbs in his sheets, but Grant put a lot of work into it, so he wasn't going to complain. Plus, Olivia was enjoying it, smiling between bites of toast with strawberry preserves and sips of Chai tea.

"You were never served breakfast in bed before?" Grant asked her after swallowing a mouthful of his fluffy scrambled eggs.

"No, but these are the best eggs! What do you put in them?" Olivia asked.

Eli loved his husband's scrambled eggs. Somehow he made something so simple taste gourmet. And the man could brew a cup of coffee like no other. Though, Eli had splurged on getting him an outrageously expensive coffee maker last Christmas. One that made espresso and other fancy coffees, actually ground the beans, and it also wiped Grant's ass. Or so it should, for the price. Coming from humble beginnings, Eli had to force himself to lay out that much money for something that made coffee. But it made Grant happy.

And if he was happy, so was Eli.

Grant was definitely enjoying their lazy Saturday morning in bed, even if he did do all the work.

"It's a secret," Eli said. "He won't tell anyone."

"He's correct. I don't tell anyone, but," Grant winked at Olivia, "I will show you."

"I love to cook," she said softly.

"Your lemon chicken was very good last night. Maybe you can share that recipe with me," Grant said.

"I found it on the internet, so I'd be glad to share. It's not like it's a family secret."

Eli was sure her and Trey's mother didn't bother to ever cook for her children. The only meal the woman had been worried about was a liquid one.

"How did you learn to cook?" Eli asked her.

"Just by trial and error." She licked some strawberry preserves off the tip of her finger and immediately Eli's cock twitched and thickened.

It must have affected Grant also, since he pointed to her lips and said, "You've got some right there." He leaned over, kissing away a spot of jam off the corner of her mouth. He didn't pull back, but instead deepened the kiss for a moment. Watching that didn't help Eli with his erection. It was expanding by the second and would soon be knocking on the wooden tray that had been placed over his lap with his meal.

"Mmm. I love strawberries," Grant said with a smile. He straightened back up to take another bite of sausage.

"Me, too," Olivia murmured, running a finger enticingly over her bottom lip.

"Stop, Olivia," Eli warned. "Or I'm going to toss these trays onto the floor and take you before you've had a chance to finish your breakfast."

"Stop what?" she asked, her eyes sparkling.

Grant chuckled. "I don't think she's even aware of how much she gets our *blood flowing.*"

"I'm aware," she said, popping the last bite of jam covered toast into her mouth. She wiped her finger through a spot of the sticky preserves on her plate and dabbed it onto her bottom lip. "Who's going to help me with the mess I just made?"

Eli laughed but lunged quickly before Grant could and licked away the sweet fruit from her mouth.

"Mmm. I like this breakfast in bed concept," she laughed.

"Me, too," Grant said with amusement.

"*Je suis tenté à recouvrir tout ton corps avec ces confitures et de te lécher jusqu'à que tu sois toute propre.*"

Grant laughed again. "Count me in on that."

Olivia's head spun from Eli to Grant. "What did he say?"

"*Ma chérie*, I said that I'm tempted to spread those preserves all over your body and lick you clean. Would you like that?"

A grin lit up her face. "Yes, I think I would."

A noise came from the back of Grant's throat, then he said huskily, "I'll add a few more jars to the grocery list."

"Good idea."

Olivia sipped at her tea and turned to study Eli. "So, why are you fluent in French? You haven't said."

No, he hadn't. Neither he nor Grant had talked much about themselves. And because of previous background investigation on Trey, he knew more than he probably should about her upbringing. So, it was only fair she learn a little bit about his own.

"I'm originally from Martinique, so I grew up speaking both English and French."

"Oh! Are your parents still around?"

"Unfortunately, my *maman* died over a year ago. My father..." Eli took a deep inhale. "He was an American who came to our island on vacation. He knocked up my *maman* and left at the end of his trip not having a clue that he created me. Not that he would have cared. My *maman* struggled to raise me, so I did my best to help her put food on the table and pay the bills by working odd jobs and sometimes even begging. We were very poor."

Olivia reached under the tray and squeezed his thigh. He covered her hand with his and returned the gesture.

"Like you, I wanted to leave at sixteen. But for me it was to come to the States to find my father. My mother convinced me to stay and obtain my *baccalauréat* from *lycée* first. Here in the States it's the same as your high school diploma. Anyway... I had this fantasy that he'd be thrilled to find out he had a son. Honestly, I didn't know much about him since I only had a name along with a picture of him and my *maman* together.

"Well, needless to say, I found him, and I was dead wrong. He was horrified that I tracked him down and wanted nothing to do with me."

Her fingers tightened on his thigh. "Why? Why would someone turn away their own flesh and blood?"

"He was married when he had his vacation fling with my *maman*. He not only had a wife, but had three kids already." Eli tucked a finger under her chin closing her gaping mouth. He smiled softly. "He actually threatened to kill me if I ratted him out, ever showed up again at his house, or even contacted my half-siblings."

Liv gasped. "That's horrible!"

"Since I had no ties to the man, other than him being a sperm donor, I walked away. But one thing good did come out of it."

"What was that?"

"By finding him, I realized what I was good at. I could put pieces of information together like a puzzle. I could read body language and pick up things from simply a tone of voice. I was good at recognizing patterns. I realized I had a natural instinct to do investigative work. See? Fate had a plan for me.

"However, I came to the States with nothing but a few dollars in my pocket and the clothes on my back. So I went to work for a P.I. for free in what he called an 'internship.' Though, I was no more than slave labor, it did get my foot in the door and gave me some good experience. I learned surveillance, tracking, research. Since the job paid nothing, I worked odd jobs like I did when I was a kid. I scraped together enough to buy a piece of shit, rusted-out Corolla. I ended up living in it for a year since I couldn't afford rent and the asshole I 'interned' for wouldn't let me stay in his back room which he only used for storage. But, again, I learned, honed my skills, built up my contacts and got enough experience under my belt to become a certified investigator.

"Then when I demanded my so-called mentor to start paying me for my time, he refused. So, again, I simply walked away. And, again, I had nothing but the clothes that I purchased in a second-hand shop, my car and a quarter tank of gas.

"But, like you, Olivia, I was determined to make it. Make something of myself. I, too, wanted no hand-outs or hand-ups. I wanted to only rely on myself. Did I do things that I'm not proud of to get me through the tough spots? Yes. So did your brother with that coach, as I'm sure you did, too. We all have our burdens to bear."

Olivia was quiet for a few moments while she seemed to process everything he'd just told her. She wrapped her hands around her tea and as she lifted it to her lips she asked, "So, tell me about this coach. What happened?"

"That's Trey's story to tell, Olivia, you must ask him. My point is this... I now have this house, a man I love and respect greatly, an amazing job with people I highly respect and admire, and now... Now we have you."

"Me?"

"You've come into our lives to make it even better. More special."

She shook her head slightly with a frown. "No, I'm a nobody."

He took her mug from her and placed it on her tray, then traced his fingers over her cheek and along her jaw. "No, Olivia, you're not a nobody. You care about people. You're willing to give when you don't even have anything for yourself. That's not a nobody. That's a somebody. You helped a prostitute get off the street, find a place to live, and get a job. How many people can say that?"

"She got killed," Liv whispered.

"Not your fault."

"I wanted her to be safe. And she wasn't safe enough. I should've done more."

"Like what?"

"I don't know."

"You did what you could. That's more than most."

Grant reached out and hooked his fingers under her chin, turning her to face him. "Liv, Eli's right. You're not a nobody. You're a somebody to a lot of people. And you're definitely someone special to us."

"Very special," Eli agreed. "Now..." Eli slipped the spaghetti strap of her nightgown over her shoulder until the silky fabric fell away exposing her left breast. "Even though breakfast was *magnifique*, I'm still hungry and ready for dessert." He swiped his finger through the preserves that remained on his own plate, then brushed it over Olivia's peaked nipple. He removed his tray off his lap, placing it onto the floor, grabbed hers and did the same. His mouth watered as he saw the strawberry jam clinging to the tip of her breast.

Grant moved his tray to the floor on his side of the bed, but not before getting a glob of preserves on his finger. He slipped the right side of her gown down and dabbed the jam on that nipple.

With a quick eye flick to each other and a smile, they both dipped their heads and sucked in a nipple.

Olivia arched her back on a gasp, her hands wrapping around both their heads, holding them to her. Not that there was any chance that he or Grant were going anywhere anytime soon.

Then he felt Grant's warm breath against his ear. "Kiss me."

Eli released her nipple and said, *"Vraiment délicieux."* He took Grant's mouth, their tongues tangling, the taste of the preserves making the kiss even sweeter.

"Very delicious," Olivia translated.

When they separated, Grant said, "Agreed."

Again, they each took one of Olivia's nipples into their mouths, making her cry out. Eli dragged the bedcovers down her legs and pushed up her long nightgown. Finding her damp heat, he slipped his middle finger inside her. She was wet and ready.

He was ready, too. And he could imagine so was Grant. He didn't need to see the evidence. Adding a second finger, Olivia's hips bucked upward as he thrust in and out of her. Grant's hand brushed his as he circled and teased her clit.

Eli only lifted his head long enough to groan, "Tell us when you're going to come." Then he scraped his teeth over the hard tip of her nipple and then sucked it deep once more.

"I..." Then she moaned loudly as her body convulsed against them. Eli could feel the strong contractions around his fingers and once they subsided, he slipped them from her. Both men sat up, and Eli wrapped his hand around the back of Grant's neck and pulled him close again, pressing his slick fingers to his husband's lips. Grant licked along his digits and then sucked them into his mouth with a groan.

When he was done savoring her juices, Grant kissed Olivia, who now leaned against the headboard like a ragdoll, loose and relaxed.

"Did I say I liked this breakfast in bed concept?" she asked once Grant released her mouth. "I was wrong. I *love* it."

"Me, too, but breakfast isn't over yet," Grant said with what he was sure was a big, dumb grin on his face. It probably mirrored the one Eli wore.

He still had this crazy notion that this whole thing wasn't real. He had a difficult time wrapping his head around the fact that he and Eli had a woman sleeping in their bed. Not just sleeping, either. And not just in their bed but between them. Never in his wildest dreams would he have thought that his relationship with his husband would take this turn.

He'd watched Rayne, Trey and Gryff's relationship for the past year or so in fascination as it developed and bloomed. Well, once Gryff stopped wanting to pound Trey into the ground. But now they were happy and completely in love. Same with Gryff's brother Grae with Paige and Conner. Another very unconventional relationship that worked and thrived.

And they weren't the only committed threesomes he knew. Paige's brother, Logan, was in one, too. Was polyamory becoming more accepted in general?

Grant didn't know. Nor did he care. If that was something that he and Eli wanted to partake in, then they would. The people who judged them could go jump off a cliff. Love was love.

Not that it was love in this case. At least, not yet. He loved Eli completely, but Liv... this was still all very new. But he could see himself, and even Eli, falling in love with her. Wanting her to remain a permanent part of their lives.

Again, it was crazy, and the idea made his head spin. But he certainly was open-minded about it. As long as nothing jeopardized his marriage, then he'd be good with it.

However, right now, he needed to stop worrying about how unbelievable all of this was and just enjoy what, or who, literally landed right into their lap.

This morning, he was in the mood to take control, so he tossed the covers back from all of them. "Nightgown off, Liv."

Since it was gathered around her hips and waist, it didn't take much for her to shimmy out of it and toss it aside. A flush rushed up from her chest into her cheeks and her eyes gleamed. He could only hope from anticipation.

"Seems like *mon cher mari* is taking control this morning, hmm?"

"Taking control as well as taking you," Grant informed him matter-of-factly as he climbed off the bed. "You want her facing you or from behind?"

"From behind, *mon amour*, since I have a feeling that's how you'll be taking me."

"Yes, I will," Grant confirmed. "Everyone off the bed. Liv, come to me."

After crawling off the bed, she came to stand in front of Grant, blinking up at him with parted lips, her breath panting just slightly from between them. He placed his hand at her throat, feeling her pulse beat quick and strong.

"Do you want this?"

"Yes," she hissed, her eyes unfocused and hooded, her nipples puckered tight.

"Do you want Eli to fuck you?"

"Yes." Her hands came up to cup her breasts and squeeze them.

"Are you wet for him?"

"I am," she breathed.

"Show me."

She slipped a hand between her legs as Eli approached from behind, pressing his chest into her back and snaking an arm around her waist.

She brought her hand back up, her fingers as slick as Eli's had been earlier after her first orgasm of the morning.

Grant hoped they'd give her many more.

He took her fingers into his mouth and did exactly what he'd done with Eli's. He licked and sucked them clean, savoring her taste. "Again," he demanded. "For Eli."

She repeated what she had just done, inserting her fingers deep inside herself, her face softening as she did so, then held her hand over her shoulder as Eli wrapped his mouth around her fingers.

Grant didn't have to touch her to notice her body quivered.

"Mmm, *ma chérie, merci pour le partage.* Thank you for sharing."

"I should be thanking you two," she murmured.

Grant grabbed her hips, and spun her around while Eli moved away. "Put your hands flat on the mattress. Yes, that's it, honey. Ass in the air. Like that. So beautiful." He peeked a glance at Eli. "Tempting, right?"

"Very," Eli agreed as he moved away to grab a condom and the lube and quickly returned.

Eli handed the lube to him, then rolled a condom down his own dark, thick length. He stepped behind Liv, sliding the tip of his latex covered cock up and down her pink, swollen folds. Grant didn't miss the tremor in her arms and legs.

"She wants you badly, big man." Grant ran a hand down Eli's spine. "Just as much as I want you."

"Then take me, *mon cher mari*," Eli whispered as he lined himself up and thrusted forward, sinking deep into Liv.

Her gasp and Eli's grunt made Grant close his eyes and stroke his cock. Eli didn't hold back, instead he thrusted hard and deep into Liv. With Grant's eyes closed, just listening to the two of them, along with the slap of their flesh made the precum gather at the head of his cock. Opening his eyes, he swirled it around, spreading it with his thumb, then moved behind Eli, watching the play of his muscles along his back, his ass, and his thighs as he took Liv over and over. His husband pulled at Liv's nipples, not being gentle at all, and none of the sounds escaping her made it seem that she didn't enjoy any of it. Grant appreciated a little rough play. And if Liv kept showing signs that she enjoyed it, too, it made this situation so much better.

He popped the cap on the lube and coated his length with a generous amount. After closing it, he tossed it onto the bed and shuffled forward to press the crown of his cock in between Eli's muscular ass cheeks. He pressed a hand to Eli's back. "Bend over, baby."

Eli leaned over, covering Liv completely, grinding his hips against her ass. Grabbing Eli's cheeks, he separated them, lined himself up and powered forward. "That's it, baby. Take all of me." Eli released a long, low groan as Grant filled him completely. "That ass is mine, baby. Mine."

Eli had stilled when Grant entered him, but now he started to move slightly, getting the feel of the position and all three of them in a line. This was a position that made the middle person set the pace, but it gave Grant an opportunity to watch Eli fuck Liv, to feel the clenching and releasing of his husband's muscles which made him lose his breath at the sudden tightness.

Grant leaned forward to reach around Eli, grabbing Liv's hair and tugging it back roughly, making her neck arch until it couldn't bend any further. "Like that, honey? Does that feel good? Do you like me pulling your hair?"

"Yes," she gasped.

"Fuck, *mon amour*, she's squeezing me so tightly."

Eli's ass was just as tight, and Grant's eyes rolled back for a moment as he tried to gather himself. "Just like you're doing to me... Hold still for a minute, baby," Grant panted.

When he did, with one hand on Eli's hip and the other wrapped in Liv's hair, Grant began to pound Eli's ass. He was not gentle at all. Instead, he took his husband hard and fast until he had to make himself slow down, or he'd come. Circling his hips, he ground against Eli, then leaned over and bit him where his neck and shoulder met.

Eli jerked beneath him, making Liv cry out with the movement.

"Fuck me, please," she begged, and Eli turned his head to glance at Grant.

He straightened and smacked Eli's ass. "Do your thing, I will enjoy the ride," he jerked the fistful of Liv's hair he held, "and holding onto the reins."

"Don't be afraid to tell him if he's too rough, *ma chérie*."

"I like it," she breathed.

With a smile, Grant trailed his tongue up Eli's spine, making the man shudder. He traced the outer shell of Eli's ear with the tip of his tongue before pressing his mouth close. "Fuck her good, baby. Make her come. I want to hear her whimper as she takes that big cock of yours. I want to hear you as I give you mine."

"Donne-moi tout ce que t'as."

Give me everything you have.

Eli groaned as he slammed back against Grant, then pushed forward, slamming into Liv. Eli took over, controlling the pace. Every once in a while, his body would hiccup when Grant would do something like reach around and squeeze his sac or twist his nipple hard. He would almost lose it every time Eli's muscles flexed and his slick canal would clench his cock tight.

He had no idea how Eli was keeping himself together for so long. He knew how difficult it was when Eli and Liv both rode him last night. It might not have been a marathon session, but it was sure worth the fast, intense orgasms that they all had.

Their sex life had never been lacking and they enjoyed it quite often, but Grant had a feeling they would be fucking more than ever with Liv involved.

And he wasn't going to complain about that.

"Tell me," Grant demanded as Eli tensed.

"Fuck... she just came."

It was hard to miss since Liv had cried out that she was, but he liked to hear Eli tell him anyway. "Make her come again, baby. And when she does, I'm going to come in your ass." Grant trailed fingers over Eli's sleek dark skin, feeling his muscles working hard. "Do you want that, Elliott? Do you want me to come deep inside you? Do you want me to fill you up?"

"Yes, *mon amour.*"

"Then make her come." He wanted to add "quickly" to that because he was hanging by a thread. Being deep inside his husband while watching the man make Liv squirm and cry out beneath him was a dangerous thing.

Dangerous for his control. Or lack thereof.

Suddenly, Eli reared back, slamming Grant in the chest. Grant released her hair as Eli twisted Liv around and jerked her legs up. With another jerk he sank into her once more with a grunt. Grant reached around and helped hold her legs up since only the top of her shoulders and her head now remained on the mattress. Grant slid in and out of Eli as he pounded Liv at a pace that was now frenzied. Leaning over, Eli sank his teeth into Liv's breast and her body bowed as she cried out. She raked her nails over Eli's shoulders and screamed that she was coming.

Breath rushed out of Grant in relief. He was just about to blow as it was.

"Come inside me," Eli told him as he curled his body over Liv and took her mouth, capturing her whimper.

Eli didn't have to tell him twice. As Eli stiffened, Grant reached around and circled the very root of him with his fingers, feeling the strong pulses as he came deep inside Liv, and with a groan, Grant let himself go, his cum releasing in intense spurts deep inside Eli.

Once again, he'd marked Eli as his. His husband, his lover, his partner for life.

As Grant disengaged from him, he brushed a kiss over the scratches Liv left behind on Eli's shoulder.

Then it hit him. His husband, his lover, his partner for life was no longer only his.

CHAPTER 13

Liv groaned. With a full belly of Grant's delicious breakfast and now completely sated sexually, a distant buzz was disturbing their cozy nap. Three sets of entangled limbs were partially covered with sheets half on the bed and half on the floor.

The satisfaction level of being sandwiched between two amazing men was off the charts. As long as they were both willing, she planned on staying in their bed for the remainder of her stay instead of moving back into the spare bedroom.

Being in bed was so much more satisfying when you had two hot, virile men in it.

"Who could that be?" Grant grumbled, lifting his head from her breast he was using as a pillow.

"I was wondering the same thing, *mon amour*." Eli's voice was thick with sleep. With an irritated sigh, he sat up after unwrapping his legs from Liv's. He picked up his cellphone and hit the power button. "It's eleven."

"Don't care if it's three in the afternoon, tell whoever it is to go away," Grant grumbled again, snuggling deeper against Liv. She silently agreed with him, as she trailed her fingers up and down his back.

"Apparently this is going to be Bossy Saturday for *mon amour*."

Liv turned her face away from Eli to hide her giggle.

With another sigh, Eli climbed from the bed as the buzz sounded again. He yanked on a pair of long, loose shorts he snagged from the floor and left the room.

Grant tipped his eyes up to her. "Do you think I'm too bossy?"

Liv widened her eyes and dragged her fingers through his dark hair and then over his barely-there beard. "Mmm."

"That's not an answer."

"I know."

The arm Grant had thrown over her waist squeezed her tighter. "You don't like it."

"I like it, but there's a time and place for it."

"Eli has his moments, too."

"Yes, he does," she agreed. She'd been on the receiving end of some of his demands.

"Always feel free to tell us if you don't like something. Eli and I are a partnership. We want you to feel the same, that we're all equal."

"I will." Though she said it, she wasn't sure if it really mattered. Hopefully, Randall Dean would get caught soon and she'd be free to go back to living her life. Even if it meant some extra people in it.

Her "new" family consisted of a lot more than just her brother now. She definitely needed to sit down with him, have some long discussions and take the time to rebuild that bond that was broken when she left him behind.

Her heart squeezed with guilt every time she thought about it.

"How long can it take to tell someone to get lost?" Grant murmured against her skin as he placed a kiss between her breasts.

His answer was Eli appearing in the doorway.

"Finally," came from Grant.

"Get dressed and come downstairs. You, too, Olivia. In something other than that nightgown. Gryff's here with Rayne. And though I know she picked that out for you, I'd prefer that our boss doesn't get an eyeful of you in it."

"Mmm. Agreed," Grant said. His head twisted to look up at her. "See? He's bossy, too."

"That he is," she said with a smile.

Ignoring them, Eli moved into the room, grabbed a T-shirt from the dresser drawer and pulled it over his head.

With a soft groan, Grant rolled from the bed to find something to wear.

"Do you want me to grab something from the spare bedroom?"

Liv noticed that Eli didn't say "your room." That could mean he wanted her to stay in their room for the duration, also.

Or maybe she's just reading too much into it.

"Baby, do that. There's no point in her getting dressed twice. And then this way whatever you pick out will be acceptable in your eyes," Grant informed him with a smirk.

"There's not much to choose from," Liv told them both.

"What you wore to the firm will be fine. We'll get you more clothes soon. That's probably why Rayne is here." Then he was gone and back with the jeans and shirt she had worn the day she arrived at the law firm.

She took the clothes from him and got dressed. As soon as they were all decent, she and Grant filed down the stairs on Eli's heels. He led them into the family room, where her brother's lovers waited. But there was no sign of Trey.

Gryff's dark eyes landed on her immediately and he studied her carefully. "Everything good here, Olivia?"

"Liv, please. And yes, everything's fine. Why?"

Gryff's eyes flicked to Eli and then back to her. "Just wondering since we tried to call and text all three of you and only received silence as an answer. So we decided to drive over."

Rayne made a noise and hooked an arm around Gryff's waist, patting his stomach with her hand. "We know you're fine. Don't we, Boss? We just wanted to give you a heads up that we were dropping off some gift cards for online clothing stores. I was supposed to give them to Eli yesterday, but I got waylaid with a difficult client. However, we wanted to make sure you shopped 'til you drop today even if it's online." She approached Liv, holding out a small gift bag.

Liv accepted it and pulled out a couple of the cards. One had a $500 credit on it. Another $1000. And the bag was full of them in different denominations. "This is too much."

Rayne waved a hand. "Nonsense. If you need assistance in picking things out, I'd be glad to help."

"I... uh..."

"I could've sent them electronically, but I wasn't sure if you had your new laptop set up or even had access to your email yet. Not that I had your email address, either."

"That reminds me, maybe she should change her email. At least temporarily," Gryff suggested.

"Will that screw up your login for your courses, Olivia?"

She didn't know why she didn't correct Eli when he called her Olivia. She automatically did it to everyone else. But hearing her full name on his lips affected her similarly to when he spoke French. It sounded lyrical, especially with his barely-there accent.

"I... I don't know. I doubt it," she murmured, dragging her gaze from the insane amount of money in that little bag to Eli. "I should be able to do that. Why? Is that necessary?"

"I know it's not convenient, but we can't be too careful," Gryff said.

"Where's Trey?" she asked.

"He's out shooting an energy drink commercial."

"Does he need to do that?" Liv couldn't imagine her brother needed the money.

Rayne laughed. "No, but he enjoys the attention."

"Can you tell him to stop over here? I'd love to spend some time with him."

"That's not a good idea," Gryff said.

"No, he needs to stay away," Eli agreed.

Her eyebrows shot up her forehead. "Why?"

"We don't know if Dean has anyone tailing him, so they can find you," Eli explained.

"And we don't need him finding out what's going on under this roof. At least not right now."

"Wait. What's going on under this roof?" Rayne asked Gryff, her eyebrows raised, too.

"Like you didn't plan this," Gryff answered her.

"Plan what?"

Gryff planted his hands on his hips. "The nightgown?"

"The nightgown?" Rayne repeated, clearly confused. Then her mouth formed an *O* and her eyebrows furrowed in anger. "You think I bought her the nightgown so she could seduce them? Are you serious?"

Gryff's face became a dark, blank mask. "This is Trey's sister, Rayne."

"I'm well aware of that, *Boss*. And?"

"And we're supposed to be looking out for her."

"As opposed to throwing her to the wolves? Which is what you're indicating in your tone. Like Eli and Grant can't control themselves around a beautiful woman, be it Trey's sister or not?"

"Well, apparently, they couldn't."

Rayne's brows popped up. "Oh?" Her gaze bounced from Grant, to Eli and finally landed on Liv. "Did something happen?"

"We're three consenting adults, Gryff," Eli said in a low tone.

"Did something happen?" Rayne asked again, her voice now higher and a little more excited. It looked like she was biting back a smile.

"See? I knew you were scheming!" Gryff barked. "If Trey finds out..."

"What are you talking about? Of course, he's going to find out. Why—"

"Rayne," Gryff said in a low warning. "*We*," he waved a finger back and forth between him and her, "are not going to tell him."

"But, Boss, if he finds out we knew and didn't tell him..."

"He'll get over it," Gryff said firmly.

"No, it'll break his trust of us. We can't not tell him. He trusts us to be completely honest and open with him." Rayne shook her head. "I can't do it. Maybe you don't mind when he doesn't talk to you for a week when he's angry, but I do. It kills me. And it makes for a difficult time at work."

"Rayne."

"If you do keep this from him and he finds out, I'm going to join him in the spare bedroom. You can sleep by yourself for as long as he's pissed."

"Rayne," he warned again.

"Boss, be smart about this."

"I am, that's why I'm making this decision."

She threw her hands up and made a noise. "What the fuck, Gryff?" She shook her head. "Maybe I should move into the spare bedroom and when Trey joins me there and asks why we've both moved out of the master bedroom, I'll tell him to ask you why."

"Not even funny."

"I don't hear anyone laughing. Do you, Liv?"

When Rayne's snapping green eyes landed on her, Liv pressed a hand to her throat. "Uh... no."

"How about we girls go into the kitchen and talk? I can tell you both the good points and the bad points of a triad. One good point is if you're mad at one, you still have one more you can cuddle up with. It's nice having a spare." With that she stomped toward the kitchen.

She glanced at both Eli and Grant who both stood frozen in place, almost appearing as if afraid to move, while Gryff stood still also, his body completely solid, a thunderous look on his face.

With a grimace, Liv followed Rayne.

When she entered the kitchen, the other woman was leaning against the counter, her long strawberry blonde hair gathered up in her hands and held on top of her head.

"Are you okay?" Liv asked.

"Yep. Perfectly fine."

"I didn't mean to cause such a mess."

"You didn't. It's not you. But is what Gryff said true? Are you sleeping with them?"

Liv felt the heat rush up from her throat to her face. "I—"

Rayne raised a palm. "You don't even have to answer; your face says it all. Honestly, that wasn't my intent by buying that nightgown. So those pigheaded men are wrong. I just thought you deserved something sexy and pretty other than wearing a man's T-shirt to bed."

"I love it."

Rayne gave her a broad smile. "I'm sure it looks really hot on you. You have the body for it." She tilted her head to the gift bag that Liv still held in her hand. "Now you can buy one in every color available. Or buy some sexy teddies. Who cares? As long as it's something you want, Liv. Like being with Grant and Eli. Great, great guys and, truthfully, I couldn't be happier. But I also love Trey to death and he's family so that means you are, too. And I don't want anything to hurt you. Even pigheaded men."

"They've been nothing but good and kind."

"And by good, I hope you mean good in bed."

"Very generous in all aspects of hospitality," Liv quickly said.

"You can have anything you put your mind to, Liv," Rayne said softly.

Liv thought that her words had a much deeper meaning than what was at the surface. "Are you talking about Eli and Grant?"

"Only partially. Look how far your brother has come. He's a great example."

That was true, but still... "Rayne, I'm thirty-two. I don't need a pep talk like I'm a teenager."

Rayne laughed and shook her head. "I know. Sorry. I'm just so very proud of him."

"I am, too. Believe it or not, I've followed him and his career. I've kept up with everything he's done. That's how I knew where to find him."

"Why didn't you come back to him sooner?"

Liv took a deep breath. She had an answer but not a great one. Not one somebody on the outside might consider an acceptable one. "Trey and I were always treated as a burden to our mother. She dragged us to bars just so she could get drunk and she didn't have money to pay a sitter. Hell, if she had, we probably never would have seen her... which may have been for the best. But my whole youth, I felt as if I was a problem that had to be dealt with. When I left... when I *escaped*, I vowed to never feel that way again. I was determined to make it on my own. I didn't want to ask anybody for anything. I had some very bad days." She shook her head. "No, bad weeks, months, years. Sometimes there were long stretches of just trying to make it. But you know what? I did it. I survived, and I believe it made me a stronger person."

"So you thought coming back to Trey when he had so much and you had so little would be like being a burden on him?"

"Yes. Is that stupid? Maybe. But not to me. I figured when... one day... when I was successful, we could become close again on equal footing. I never wanted to ask Trey for anything and I knew if he saw how I was struggling, how I was living, he'd step in. And you know what? That's exactly what's happening now." She swept her arm around the kitchen. "With all this. I'm being taken care of. I don't want that, Rayne. I don't." She held the gift bag out to Rayne. "I can't accept this. I don't want it."

"Liv..."

Liv shook her head. "I don't. Again, I know it probably doesn't make sense to you, but—"

"You have a sense of pride," Rayne stated.

"Yes."

"You can have pride and still accept help when you need it."

"Maybe so. But I'm not used to such generosity."

"Why not accept it and be happy you have people in your life now that can do that for you? Who *want* to do that for you."

"I've been on my own for so long…" Liv whispered.

Rayne moved closer and threw an arm around her shoulder, giving her a squeeze. "I know. But you're not now and we won't let you pull away, either." She laughed. "You're stuck with all of us now, I'm sorry to say. So, please… you'll make us extremely happy if you take what we're willing to give."

"Baby," came a deep voice from the kitchen entranceway.

Both women looked up to see Gryff there, a worried look on his face.

"We need to go. Eli's going to follow us back to the house."

"Why?"

"Trey just called. He got home and found the house broken into. The police are on their way due to the alarm system activation, but still, we need to be there. We don't know if this is related to the Dean thing or not."

Eli pushed past Gryff and came to Liv, gathering her in his arms. He pressed his lips to her temple and murmured, "I'm going to check it out. Grant's staying here with you. He's going to arm the alarm when we leave. Just stay inside and do what he says, please."

Liv nodded woodenly. It felt as though all the blood had drained from her face. "I'm sorry if this is because of me," she whispered to Gryff and Rayne.

Gryff looked surprised and opened his mouth but before he could say anything, Rayne was there, taking his arm and dragging him out of the kitchen. "We'll speak again soon, Liv," she tossed over her shoulder.

"I have to go. This is not your fault, so don't even think that. I'm just glad you weren't staying with them. I had a feeling they'd look for you there."

He pressed another kiss to her temple and then Grant was there, taking her from his arms and holding her close. The two men shared a kiss goodbye, then Eli was gone.

CHAPTER 14

Eli's chest was tight as he surveyed the damage to the rear French doors to Gryff's house. The glass was shattered on one side, and the house had been gone through in a rush. Nothing was missing, not much even broken, the major issue only the door itself. Whoever had broken in had been looking for something specific... or more like someone specific.

Olivia.

As soon as the three of them had arrived at the house, Trey met them on the front steps, a worried expression on his face. "They were looking for Liv," he announced as Eli climbed out of his Land Rover.

That's what Eli had suspected, that Dean would send some goons over looking for her.

Now they stood on the back deck in the shade, trying to avoid the heat of the afternoon sun, as the police walked through the interior of the house, writing up a report. Before law enforcement had arrived, the four of them discussed not mentioning Olivia at all and what was happening with her situation.

They still didn't know who to trust. Any of the cops who arrived on scene could be corrupt, so it wasn't worth the risk. He just knew, come Monday, he and Grant needed to start putting feelers out quickly to try to find someone to leak the evidence to.

Or a few people. Maybe if they picked a few, at least one of them would step up and do the right thing.

Though that was no guarantee, either, but he had to do something.

"Do you think you're being followed?" Eli asked in a quiet voice, keeping an eye out for the police.

Trey shot him a surprised look. "I don't know. If I am, it's not obvious."

"Well, someone has eyes on the house obviously, even if Trey isn't being followed," Gryff said, keeping his voice down, as well. "They knew we were all gone. If they thought we were hiding Liv, they just found out they were wrong."

Eli ran a hand over his chin, his fingers brushing against the morning growth of beard. "I can't imagine they'll pull whoever's sitting watch on the house, though. So we need to keep her where she is."

"Agreed," Gryff said.

"I want to see her," Trey insisted.

Eli shook his head. "It's not smart. You shouldn't come to the house in case you're being followed. Likewise, they might have eyes on the firm, so I don't want to bring her there."

"Fuck," Trey barked, shoving a hand through his dark blond hair. "My sister's finally back in my life but she's really not."

Rayne leaned into him and Trey snaked an arm around her waist, pulling her close. She rested her head on his shoulder and grabbed a fistful of his shirt to hang on to. "As soon as this is over, you can spend lots of time with her," she said.

Trey frowned but said nothing.

Rayne continued, "How about you just video conference with her? You guys can talk and get caught up in the meantime."

Trey's head twisted toward Eli. "Do you think she knows how to Skype?"

"If she doesn't, I'll show her."

Trey nodded. "Tonight. Tell her we'll video chat."

"Not too late, though, *mon ami*, yes?"

Trey's frown deepened. "Why? Does she go to bed early? It's Saturday."

All eyes turned to him and Eli swallowed uncomfortably. "You two probably have a lot to say to each other and you really haven't had the chance. So, I can imagine your conversation will take a while."

"Okay, and?"

Rayne patted his stomach. "Trey, you can video chat right after dinner. Eli, tell her around seven."

Eli nodded and sent a look of thanks in Rayne's direction.

Gryff only scowled and shook his head as he stared at a spot on the deck boards.

Finally, the two police officers exited through the unbroken side of the French doors, notepads in hand.

"Find anything?" Gryff asked.

"Nothing. Just looks like a typical burglary. And you said you didn't notice anything missing, so there's nothing much we can do about it besides file a report for your insurance company."

"You're not going to check for fingerprints?" Eli asked.

One of the cops shook his head. "Sorry, we're not calling our forensic unit for this amount of damage. It's minimal and they're in the middle of a major murder investigation. The damage will probably be less than a thousand dollars."

Right. Eli didn't believe anything coming out of the man's mouth. Maybe there wasn't anything to go on, but it would've been nice if they'd at least checked for prints.

Eli studied the two cops carefully as they handed Gryff their cards and told him to call if they discovered anything further.

So that was that.

Their house gets broken into by who knows who and "Here's my card. Sorry for your problem, but we couldn't care less."

Once the cops left, Rayne asked, "Do you think the major murder investigation was Liv's friend?"

"No. The cops finding a dead former hooker in her apartment wouldn't be considered anything major," Eli murmured. "I'm heading home if you don't need me here."

Gryff whacked him on the back. "Thanks for coming out and thanks for keeping *an eye* on Trey's sister."

Eli ignored Gryff's sarcastic tone as Trey shook his hand, who luckily hadn't picked up on that tone. "Yes, thanks. I appreciate you keeping her safe. Tell her I'll call later and to have her computer set up."

"Will do."

"Talk to the DA on Monday. Drop some nuggets and see if she jumps on them." Eli told Grant.

The district attorney might be a great starting point, though Grant had only dealt with her a couple of times since she'd been elected into that position. He usually dealt with the assistant DA's when it came to the criminal defense cases he handled. "Since the new DA's a woman, she might not be the biggest fan of Randall Dean."

"A powerful, independent woman at that, too," Eli added.

"She could be our way in to get him investigated for the murder."

Eli sighed and pinched the bridge of his nose. "Doesn't mean there won't be a cover up."

"I don't know, I heard she's like a pit bull."

"Still..." Eli began.

"We slip her that bone and she might not let it go."

"That would be too easy."

"Tell me about."

Eli grabbed Grant's arm and pulled him into his arms. "How was she after I left earlier?"

"Fine. Though, I shouldn't be surprised. She wears an armored shell, Eli. I don't know if I'd be so calm if I knew someone was out to get me for something I witnessed."

"She was nervous that first day," his husband reminded him.

"Well, that's understandable. Not only was she on the run with nowhere to go but she knew she would be dealing with her brother who might not be so happy to see her. And—and this is a big *and*—she was coming to him to ask for help. Something she's not used to doing."

"She doesn't want to be a burden," Eli reminded him unnecessarily.

"Right. She says that, but she doesn't realize she's not. She doesn't realize that family, for the most part, should step in and help each other. That's not her normal. You might have had a shit upbringing, but you had your *maman*. She loved you and would do anything for you."

"And you had your family... At least growing up."

"True. Until I came out as bisexual." Grant didn't want to think about being shunned by his own family. It happened after he came out and he'd moved past it. There was no point in trying to repair a relationship with such close-minded people, even if they were his own flesh and blood. "If they can't accept me for who I am, then that's their problem, not mine."

"I'm glad you look at it like that, *mon amour.*"

"No other way to look at it, baby. I love you. I'm with you. And there was no way I was going to hide my relationship with you like I hid all the rest of them. I knew you were here to stay. That wouldn't be fair to you or to me. So if they can't accept me loving a man, then..." Grant shrugged.

"Their loss, *mon cher mari.*"

"Their loss," Grant repeated with a nod.

He'd never forget that night he came out to his parents and his brother. Even though he had been an adult at the time and living on his own for a few years, it was still an unpleasant task. But after meeting Eli and knowing he was "the one" for him, there was no way he'd come to holiday dinners and family gatherings without his future husband and the love of his life by his side.

Too bad that his blood didn't feel the same way. By the time he'd left their house that night, he knew his relationship with his family was irrevocably shattered.

Eli tried to shoulder some of the blame. But it wasn't his fault and Grant couldn't make that clear enough. The problem wasn't Eli. No, the problem was Grant was bisexual and coming from a conservative family, they insisted that his sexuality was a choice. One he could change. They would never admit that they had produced a child who enjoyed and had no hang-ups about being with both genders.

Grant had no regrets since his "big man" ended up being his *everything*.

He nuzzled his nose into Eli's neck and inhaled his husband's familiar scent. One that always tended to calm him. "Do you think it's safe for her to remain here?"

"Where else can she go?"

Grant sighed. "I just worry that Dean's goons might put two and two together."

"Hopefully, they only think our connection with Trey, Rayne and Gryff has to do with work, not Olivia."

"They might not leave any stone unturned, baby. We should keep that in mind."

"Where could she go to be completely safe?"

"Grae and Gryff's parents in Arizona? Maybe Paige's brother's farm? Ty and Logan could look after her," Grant suggested.

"Let's hope it doesn't get to that. Let's see what we can figure out on Monday, try to get the info to a couple of people by Monday night and then hope something comes to light."

"And if it doesn't? Or doesn't immediately?"

"Then we'll consider sending her out to Logan and Ty's place for a little while. However, I know their hands are full with the kids and the business."

"It wouldn't hurt for Gryff to talk to Paige, so she can give her brother a head's up."

"Right."

Grant released a long sigh. "I know you don't want her to be apart from us. Not now. And I feel the same way. But it may be for the best. At least until Dean's in custody."

"Not just in custody, *mon amour*. He needs to be charged and held without bail. Then I might breathe a little easier."

"Understood." Grant brushed a knuckle over Eli's cheek, then let his hand slide down his chest and to the waistband of his loose shorts. Tucking a finger into the elastic he pulled it away from Eli's stomach and peered inside. "What do you have for me, big man?"

Eli grabbed his hand and shoved it down his shorts, wrapping Grant's fingers around his growing erection. "Find out for yourself."

Grant chuckled into Eli's throat. "Hard to miss that." He stroked Eli's hard, hot length slowly.

"I wonder how much longer Olivia will be video chatting with Trey?"

"Mmm. Is someone getting impatient? We could start without her."

"That we could, but, *mon amour*, I think we need to set some ground rules."

Grant slipped his fingers down to cup Eli's sac and squeeze gently. "Ground rules? Like what?"

"Like who and when."

Grant frowned. "Explain."

Eli pulled away from him, breaking Grant's hold. He pulled his hand from Eli's shorts and stepped back. "What are you talking about?"

"First, we need to decide whether this thing is temporary with Olivia. Is this just a 'thing' because it's new and exciting for us? Or are we serious about adding her to our lives?"

"Like permanently?"

"Yes, that's exactly what I mean."

Grant studied Eli, but his expression gave him nothing. "Should we be having this conversation without her?"

"We need to know what we want before we can ask her what she wants. I need to know what you want. *Tu es mon cher mari et mon amour. Tu es tout pour moi.*"

Grant's heart thumped hard in his chest. "You are my everything, too, baby. Do we have to decide this right now?"

"No. But we should soon. If we can get her issue solved shortly, she'll want to go back to her apartment and her job, if both are still available. If they're not, then she'll want to get her own place and find another job."

"But that doesn't mean we won't be able to see her, Eli. She's not going to go a world away. What are you worried about?" A look crossed Eli's face. One Grant didn't recognize. "You want this to be permanent," he said softly. He shouldn't be surprised, but he was. And he wasn't quite sure how he felt about it.

"I think I do. Does that bother you?"

Grant swallowed hard. "I don't know. I mean, I'm enjoying what we have right now. Do I want this for the rest of our lives? Our *married* lives? When we got married we vowed that there would just be the two of us. I'm open-minded, you know that. And I'm not against threesome or triads. But is this something I want forever? I do love having you to myself. And then, like you said, there will need to be ground rules."

"Which comes back to why I began this line of conversation. The ground rules. We know there can't be jealousy. We've been around enough triads to know that doesn't work at all. Will it disturb you if I'm with Olivia when you aren't around? Will it bother me to know you and Olivia are making love without me?" Eli shook his dark head, his eyes worried. "I don't know. Our relationship's strong, but is it strong enough?"

"On the other hand, will it bother her when we're together

without her? I don't want to give up my alone time with you. Not ever, baby. If I can't have you to myself at least every once in a while..." Grant shook his head. "It's something we all need to think about. But I understand that we need to figure out what we want first and then approach her and lay it all out. See if she's on board."

"If she's not, then we don't have to worry about it."

Grant had a feeling if Liv wasn't interested in continuing a relationship with them, Eli would be very disappointed. He had a connection with the woman. But then, so did Grant. Just not as strong as one Eli had. Not yet, anyhow.

The sex was great, yes. But, in the end, becoming a threesome meant he had to share his husband with someone else. And not just every once in a while.

He had to do some serious thinking about it. But first and foremost, they had to get her safe. Solve the first problem then move on to the next.

But when Liv walked into the family room and announced, "Well, Trey and I had a great talk but I... uh... I accidently let it slip. He's not very... happy."

Eli and Grant gave each other an *oh-shit* look, knowing what *it* was. Another problem might have just leapt into the number one spot.

Liv sat at the kitchen table, her Marriage and Family textbook open to the left of her new laptop, her spiral notebook to the right. After scribbling down some notes, she picked up her highlighter to mark a passage in the chapter she was reading.

After running the highlighter over an important sentence she thought might be on the next test, she threw it onto the table, leaned back in the chair and sighed.

She didn't hate schoolwork, but she didn't enjoy it, either. She saw it as a necessary evil. She wasn't going to get anywhere without a degree. Her brother not only finished his Bachelor's before being drafted into the NFL, he went on to get his law degree and pass the bar after winning the freaking Super Bowl.

And here Liv only had a third of the course credits she needed to finish her Bachelor's degree in Social Work. She had a long way to go, especially only taking one online class a semester.

When her and Trey had their long, deep, and somewhat emotional conversation Saturday night, he stated he would pay for her education. But once again, someone was trying to step in to take care of her. She told her brother that he didn't have to do that, but he'd insisted.

That was even after he blew his lid when he found out she was sleeping with both Eli and Grant. Luckily, Rayne had popped up from who knows where and calmed Trey down by reminding him of their own relationship and how it came to be.

Even though Rayne didn't give too many details, it was enough to calm Trey down and stop his rant about beating Eli and Grant's ass. Not to mention firing them.

Which made Rayne roll her eyes hard enough that Liv actually had to fight back a giggle.

It was obvious that the woman had those two men wrapped around her pinky. And she was a magician when it came to calming their tempers.

After Rayne had wandered off screen again, Trey had given her the details of what happened to him after Liv left. Her heart broke when he told her the story about what he'd done with his high school football coach. Though, Trey blew it off like it was nothing more than someone looking out for him and helping him get ahead.

She never hated her mother more than after hearing Trey's story. And when she told Trey that, he'd said, "Family isn't always blood."

Which was true. He'd risen above their upbringing to become not only a successful man, but he had landed in a loving family made up of Gryff and Rayne and their respective families.

Now, Liv had Trey back in her life. And she'd been thinking long and hard all day about Grant and Eli, too.

She wasn't sure what the men wanted from her after Dean was hopefully arrested. They hadn't said anything concrete yet. She did hope their relationship would continue. She could see moving back to her own place, and then the three of them getting together often.

She really hoped they wanted that, too. But if not, she'd move on. She always did.

However, the sex with them was the best she'd ever had, and she wasn't sure she could give that up so easily—

A crash came from her left and she jumped. When the security alarm's high-pitched wail sounded, her heart raced, and she leapt to her feet.

She heard a male voice grumble and saw movement from the direction of the family room, which was right off the kitchen.

Holy shit!

Grabbing her cellphone, she took off through the house, her heart trying to beat right out of her neck, her breath constricted with fear. Her mind spun as she tried to quickly figure out where to go.

He had to know she was there. She hadn't been quiet; in fact, her chair had fallen backwards to the floor when she'd quickly rushed to her feet. Her laptop had been left on, too.

She wasn't sure if she should run out the front door. Someone might be waiting for her out there.

Shit! Shit! Shit!

She had to think and do it quickly.

She had no idea where to go. Her hands shook as she hit the power button on the burner phone. She tried to type a text as she rushed through the first floor of the house, but she couldn't do it. It was nothing but a jumble of letters and numbers.

Frustrated, she quietly opened the door to the basement. Stepping through the door, she shut it just as quietly and wished there was a lock on the knob. She carefully moved down the steps, trying to make the least noise as possible. But she couldn't hear anything but her own pounding heartbeat in her ears.

"Fuck," she whispered, her voice shaking. When she got to the bottom of the steps she glanced around. It was hard to see anything in the dark, of course, so she held up her lit cellphone and spotted a pile of boxes in a corner. Maybe she could hide behind them. As she used her phone as a flashlight, she moved closer and found one big enough to hide in. She pulled it out of the pile and opened it to find it full of linens and towels. She tossed the stuff, hiding it behind another box and climbed in, trying to control her breathing, but it was impossible. Pulling the flaps down, she waited.

She lifted her phone, hit the power button again to light it up once more and finally was able to text a semi-logical message to both Eli and Grant at the same time.

Intruder. Male. Hiding in basement.

She held the volume button down on her phone until it went into silent mode and did it just in time since she received two texts almost simultaneously.

Stay put from Eli.

On our way from Grant.

Then *Stay quiet. Keep calm* from Eli.

Right!

She tried to slow her breathing by sucking air in through the nose and out through the mouth. In through the nose, out through the mouth. But it wasn't working. She tilted her head to listen and heard heavy footsteps above her, which didn't help her breathing at all.

Squeezing her eyes shut, she told herself to stay calm. *Stay put. Stay quiet. Keep calm.*

The footsteps moved on and she didn't hear anything for the longest time. She was tempted to dial 911 but knew that could be dangerous. Maybe she should text her brother to say goodbye and tell him she loved him, just in case something happened to her.

She started to do just that when she heard the footsteps again making the floor joists squeak above her. Then the knob turned at the top of the steps.

Oh fuck!

She froze, her muscles tight and held her breath as the wooden stairs creaked with each heavy footstep.

Fuck. Fuck. Fuck.

She wished she could peer out and see where the man was, what he looked like, so she could text that information to someone. Eli, Grant, whoever just in case she was gone by the time they got to the house. It might give them a clue who to look for.

But no, the flaps were at the top of the box and for her to poke her head out would be stupid.

She curled herself into a tight ball and closed her eyes again as the footsteps came closer to her and the boxes. Then she jerked when he kicked one across the room with a loud curse.

"Where are you, bitch?" came the low, soft question. "You have to be in this house somewhere." Then he yelled, "I'm not leaving until I find you!"

Holy fucking shit!

She couldn't hold her breath anymore and let it out as slowly as possible. She gripped the phone so hard in her fingers they locked up, but she wasn't moving. Not until he did.

She tried not to touch the sides of the cardboard box more than she had to since she was trembling, and she didn't want him to notice the box moving.

This was freaking crazy! Why couldn't her life be simple and easy and quiet and...

A tear slipped down her cheek. She pressed the back of her hand to her mouth, so she wouldn't start blubbering.

"Make this easy on yourself and come out from wherever you're hiding. I'm not going to hurt you."

Oh, right. Like she believed that.

"We just want to talk to you."

Another lie. Liv pressed her lips together and closed her eyes again.

"Fuck," he muttered and then she heard what sounded like him tossing a box across the room.

Shit, if he kept kicking or moving boxes, he would find her.

Oh, please, please, please... move on.

Then she almost whimpered in relief when she heard him climb back up the stairs. She carefully lifted one of the flaps and peeked out, catching a glimpse of his handgun as he moved out of view.

With trembling fingers, she typed in *GUN!* and hit Send.

Jesus Christ, Eli and Grant were going to walk into a situation where they could be killed.

She jumped as she heard a few male voices shouting and then a gunshot. Then another one. A scuffle, then another gunshot, one that went through the floor and the stray bullet hit something nearby.

She wrapped a hand around her mouth to make sure her screaming stayed in her head and didn't escape.

She had no idea who was shooting. If it was the intruder or if it was the police because of the alarm activation.

Or maybe even Grant or Eli.

Fuck. They could be hurt or dead.

She wanted to move, to check, but she remained frozen in place.

Then her cell lit up and she looked at it quickly.

Remain in place. U OK?

Yes, she quickly typed back to Eli with shaky fingers.

Cops here. Shot intruder. Where r u?

Oh, God. What if it wasn't Eli? What if someone got his phone and was trying to figure out where she was?

Tell me what u call Grant in French, she typed rapidly.

There was a long hesitation then, *Mon amour.*

Liv sighed in relief and another tear streaked down her cheek.

A box in basement.

Stay there. We'll get u when it's clear.

OK.

She remained where she was for what seemed like hours. Her muscles cramping, her bladder in pain, her mind in a constant spin.

But she didn't move. She heard the voices, then the cops sweep the house. One even came down to the basement, moving close to where she hid. But finally, he yelled up the steps that the basement was clear and went back upstairs.

Then what seemed like another hour went by and everything got quiet.

The seconds felt like hours, the minutes like days, until the front door slammed, and two sets of feet hurried down the steps.

"Olivia!"

"Liv!"

She closed her eyes for a second, breathed and then stood up, her muscles complaining and shaking as she pushed through the cardboard flaps.

"Oh, thank fuck," Grant shouted when he saw her.

"Mon Dieu," Eli muttered as they rushed over to her and helped her out of the box and into their arms.

They crushed her between them and then she seriously started to cry.

At first, she thought it was from relief... And maybe some of it was, but then she realized it was because she was being held by these two men and she'd never felt so loved or secure before.

Crazy, but true.

"I'm sorry," she blubbered, trying to swipe the tears off her face.

"T'as pas à t'excuser, t'as rien fait de mal," Eli murmured into her hair.

"He's right, honey. Nothing to be sorry for. We're just glad your safe."

"Only for the moment," she whispered. "You two aren't safe with me here."

Neither said a word as they helped her upstairs.

"There's blood in the foyer," Grant warned her. "Cops got him in the chest, so there was a lot of blood."

"Is he dead?"

"I don't know. I hope so," Grant said as they reached the first floor.

"I don't. He needs to be questioned." Eli helped her over the threshold and guided her away from the foyer.

Glancing that direction, she said, "I'll help you clean up."

Grant shook his head. "No, we have more important things to do right now. We'll get it later."

"We're packing the little stuff you have and taking you out to Paige's brother's farm," Eli informed her.

"What?"

"Yes, actually, we're not taking you in case we're being watched, but someone else will pick you up nearby," Eli clarified. "We'll sneak you out the back of the house and over a block where Ren and Cole are going to pick you up and take you there."

"Who's Ren and Cole?"

"They're safe and can protect you. Get your stuff together. It's going to take them about an hour to get here with the traffic."

"I don't want to drag more people into this," she whispered.

"Honey," Grant said softly, "we all just want to keep you safe. Please let us do that for you."

Her gaze met his and held. Worry showed in his eyes. She nodded. "Just for a little while?"

Grant tucked a strand of her long hair behind her ear. "Yes. Just a little while. Eli and I plan to leak some information out there and see what happens."

"I don't want to leave."

"We don't want you to leave, either, *ma chérie*. But you must, just for now."

"Are you coming out to this farm, too? It's not safe for you here, either."

She didn't miss the look that Eli and Grant gave each other.

"I don't know," Eli finally said. "We need to make sure this information gets into the right hands. I'm not sure if we can do it from there."

"Do you know how long?"

Eli shook his head. "No. As long as it takes to get you safe and that bastard locked up."

"I need you two to be safe, too."

"We will. Now let's get your things. Think of this as a vacation in the country."

She sniffled and then let out a thick laugh. "Right. A vacation."

"Quinn and the kids will love you," Grant assured her.

Unfortunately, she had no idea who Quinn was.

CHAPTER 15

Liv sat soaking in the warmth of the late afternoon sun on a large back deck. The sprawling log home it was attached to overlooked a whole lot of nothing. Just grass. Lots and lots of grass.

No, it wasn't grass. It was sod she was told. Sod used for sport stadiums, arenas and such.

Ty, Logan and their wife, Quinn, had been the perfect hosts. Funny and kind, they clearly all loved each other and their kids, of course.

The kids, Preston and Cayden, were active little hellions but actually a joy to be around.

It was easy to see who the biological father was for each one. Logan for their son, Preston, and Ty for their daughter, Cayden. But to watch the men, there was no distinction and both men answered to "Daddy."

It was sweet. But the house could get a bit crazy at times. Especially when Paige, Grae and Connor were there, too. And Paige was around *a lot* since she helped out with the sod business which was based on the property.

Logan's sister was also an emotional mess, which did not help the chaos at the house, since she'd just found out she was carrying twins. Whose twins, Paige didn't know. Or care. She just cared that her body would be stretched beyond belief with two babies growing inside her. So the woman tended to walk around the house crying, stuffing cookies in her mouth, and carrying a container of cocoa butter while asking Grae or Connor to rub the stuff onto her belly every hour on the hour. It got to the point that everyone, including the kids, would sigh in relief when the three would finally leave to go home.

In fact, Logan and Ty both threatened to put Paige on early maternity leave and have Liv stay to take her place as their "Girl Friday" until the twins were born. It seemed that both men couldn't take anymore of Paige's out of control hormones.

Liv wanted to take them seriously because she could use the work, but she knew their farm was too far out from the city and she didn't have a car to commute that long distance.

But it was a nice offer anyway. Though, she'd been enjoying the time she'd spent with the Reed-White family, she was ready to get back. She was definitely ready for all of this to be over.

She was tired of relying on others to keep her safe.

Besides, she missed Grant and Eli.

So very, very much.

She talked to her brother almost every night by Skype, as well as Grant and Eli.

How could she miss the two men so much when she'd only spent a few days with them? A few nights, too. But even so...

And now she'd been there a week. A whole five days and nothing had changed as far as she knew. Randall Dean was still as free as a dirty bird while she still remained in hiding.

But the only good thing was Grant and Eli were on their way out to the farm since it was Friday and they planned on spending the weekend. Logan, Ty and Quinn decided to take the kids camping before the weather turned cold. Which left the men and her to have the house to themselves.

The rear sliding glass door opened, and Liv turned her head, hoping to see Eli or Grant or even both of them.

"They're only twenty minutes out," Quinn assured her as she stepped out onto the deck and shut the slider behind her.

The easy-going woman had long wavy dark blond hair, was a natural beauty, and had a great sense of humor. She could see why Ty and Logan were so in love with her. And, though they'd been together for years, the relationship between the three still appeared fresh, even after having two kids.

"I appreciate everything you've done for me."

Quinn smiled and sat in the Adirondack chair next to Liv, turning to face her. "And you for me. Believe me, I know our kids are active and even though we have three sets of hands raising them, it's nice having a fourth set to give us a break. You're good with them. You'll make a great mother."

"I doubt that's in the cards."

Quinn tilted her head to study Liv. "You don't know that."

"You're right, I don't. But it's not something I've thought about."

"Maybe soon."

Liv blew out a breath. "Maybe."

"Do you want to talk about it while my hubbies are wrangling up the kids? We have a few minutes to speak privately."

"Talk about what?"

"You. Eli. Grant."

"Do you know them?"

"Yes, I've met them. *We've* met them a couple times at some gatherings. But I don't know them all that well."

"Right. Because your sister-in-law lives with Grae, whose brother is Gryff, who Eli and Grant both work for."

"Yes, simple, right?"

Liv laughed. "Very."

"I know it's a bit bizarre."

It was Liv's turn to study the other woman carefully. "What is?"

"These," Quinn waved her hand around in the air, "unconventional relationships."

Liv didn't say anything. While it wasn't the norm, she didn't have a problem with it. Everyone were adults and could make their own decisions. What worked for them might not work for anyone else and vice versa.

Quinn continued, "If you want to talk about it or if you have questions... Please, you can ask me just about anything." She leaned closer to Liv and whispered loudly, "Just don't ask Paige, she's not in her right mind right now."

"Because of the twins."

"Because of being pregnant at all. I don't think it was planned. Hell, I know it wasn't planned since she's been very adamant about not having kids anytime soon."

"Oh boy." If that was true, the poor woman was going from not wanting kids to popping out two at the same time. At least she also had two capable men to help out.

"Right, so she's a little miffed with her men since someone's little strong swimmer is making her 'fat' and hormonal."

"But she loves them both."

Quinn smiled softly. "Yes, she does. It's just her crazy hormonal changes speaking right now. Once the babies are born, she'll be fine."

Either that or even more crazy being saddled with two infants.

"So—" Quinn stopped speaking as soon as the glass sliders opened again.

When Liv turned her head to see who it was, her eyes widened, and she leapt out of her chair to rush forward and right into Grant's arms, since he was the first out the door.

"Hi, honey, we've missed you," he murmured into her hair.

Liv wrapped her arms around his waist and squeezed as hard as she could. Her eyes closed as she shoved her face into his chest and inhaled his scent deeply.

A deep, gruff "Olivia" came from over his shoulder and she opened her eyes to see Eli standing there with a smile.

She quickly released Grant and went to Eli, who wrapped her tightly in his arms, pressing a kiss to her lips. He deepened it for a moment then released her mouth. " *C'est tellement bon de te voir mais surtout te toucher, chérie,*" he whispered.

"And that means?" she whispered back.

"It's good to not only see you, since we've been Skyping, but to touch you, *ma chérie.*"

"Oh, a man who speaks French! *Très sexy,*" Quinn said from behind them.

Eli glanced in her direction. *"Est-ce que tu parles français?"*

Quinn laughed. "No. Not really. I remember some from high school, that's all."

Eli nodded and stared down into Liv's face. "Are you well?"

"Yes, now that you and Grant are here. Very well. But they've been very generous hosts."

"And we were just talking about the kids. How she's been very helpful with them." Quinn began to move past them to go into the house. "Good practice, maybe?" Then she patted Grant on the shoulder as she stepped into the house. "We'll get out of your hair. I can't wait to go camping!" The slider then closed.

"Sounds like she's being sarcastic," Grant said.

"Apparently, Logan and Ty love to camp with the kids. Her? Not so much."

"But she goes anyway?"

Liv lifted one shoulder. "She sees it as a worthwhile sacrifice."

"Logan and Ty were packing up the SUV when we drove up, so they should be gone shortly," Eli announced.

"And that means?" Liv asked, wiggling her eyebrows at him.

Eli smiled at Grant, then down at her. "Whatever you would like, *ma chérie.*"

Grant then announced, "Logan said they changed the sheets in their room, so we could have the big bed."

"Yes, they have a huge bed that was custom made. It's quite impressive," she added, smiling in anticipation of making use of that bed and soon.

"Then I can't wait to see it," Eli said.

"Me neither," Grant added with a smile.

~

L iv gasped as Grant's fingers dug deep into the flesh at her hips as he pumped in and out of her. She whimpered when Eli sucked her clit hard.

She was on her hands and knees in the center of the biggest bed she'd ever seen with Grant behind her and Eli laying on his back underneath her. His mouth worked wonders on her pussy and Grant's balls. Every time Eli took his husband's sac into his mouth, she got the benefit, too, because Grant would grind himself harder against her, driving his cock as deep as possible.

Eli's cock was long, hard, and twitching, the precum leaking onto his lower belly as he not only worked them with his mouth, but he had snagged both of her nipples between his fingers and tweaked them until her core clenched around Grant.

"Baby, whatever you're doing, keep doing it," Grant panted behind her.

Wrapping her fingers around Eli, she dropped her head enough to lick him clean and suck the crown into her mouth, circling the edge with her tongue.

She wasn't surprised that Eli didn't answer Grant. She wasn't capable of having a conversation at the moment, either.

And when Grant's hand came cracking down on her ass cheek, she gasped again and tried to avoid biting down on Eli.

Eli finally pulled his mouth away. "*Mon amour*, are you trying to have me neutered?"

"No, sorry. But... I... I have to," he groaned.

Liv quickly let Eli slip from her lips just in time for Grant to spank her again. She squeaked and jerked forward.

"*Ma chérie*, tell him to stop if you don't want him to do that." Then his mouth found her clit again, his tongue flicking and making circles, which made her want to collapse into a puddle.

"No, I... I like it. Do it again." She turned her head to glance back at Grant who wore a tight smile and his eyes appeared dark as he watched her.

When he lifted his hand again she braced because she knew what came next. The crack of his palm against her flesh made her gasp but she held still, trying not to dislodge Eli from his wicked machinations.

"Again," she groaned.

He grabbed a handful of her hair with one hand and with the other struck her ass so hard that she yelped because of the sharp sting. She closed her eyes and let the burn roll through her, making her wetter than she already was from what the two men were doing to her.

Eli shifted beneath her. "Enough," he said, his voice tight. He moved from under her. "I can't take anymore."

His dark eyes were heated as he watched Grant continue to fuck her from behind.

"Does that excite you, too, big man?"

"You know it does," Eli answered, reaching out to grab a condom. Tearing it open, he then rolled it down his length. He also grabbed the lube and Liv wondered what his plan was.

She found out soon enough when he laid on his back, reaching out a hand to her. "Come to me, *ma chérie*. On top. Grant release her."

Once Grant let her go, she moved over to straddle Eli. With his hand on his own cock, he guided himself inside her as she sank her weight down on him. "That's it, *ma chérie*. That's it. Lay your chest against mine. Like that. Yes."

Eli's eyes flicked to Grant and he gave the other man a small nod.

Then Liv felt Grant move behind her again, his knees between Eli's legs.

Eli offered him the lube and Liv heard the cap pop open and felt the cool gel drip over her heated skin and down her crease.

She quivered at the thought of what was about to happen. And she wasn't quite sure it would. It seemed impossible that she could take two men at once. Especially two that weren't on the smaller side.

"Are you ready, honey?" Grant asked, his voice low, husky as he slid the head of his cock up and down her crease and over her tight hole, spreading the lube.

"I... I don't know," she answered truthfully.

"We'll go slow," Grant said as he pressed forward. The pressure against her anus was immense. It wasn't like it was just a finger, it wasn't. It was much more than that.

Eli held her still as Grant pushed forward. "Tell him to stop if it gets to be too much, *ma chérie*. I remember my first time."

Liv bit her bottom lip and nodded. Just when she thought she wasn't going to be able to bear it, Grant slipped past her tight ring. She gasped, as she now had two men inside her at once.

No one moved for a moment, and slowly Liv relaxed all the muscles she didn't realize she had locked.

"We're going to go very slow," Grant said again. "Very slow. *Fuck*."

"*Mon amour*, I should be jealous that you are the first."

"I'm smaller than you," he answered back, his voice tight.

"Not by much," Liv added, still trying to decide if she liked having them both inside her at the same time. She was afraid to move. Her insides were stretched beyond what she could ever imagine as they both filled her tightly. "Okay, now what?"

Eli chuckled beneath her. "How about we let you decide what to do from here?"

She tentatively began to rock her hips, small movements to test how far she could go without it being uncomfortable.

"Even those little movements, honey, are going to drive me crazy," Grant groaned. "You would be tight normally, but with big man in there also, it's... *Fuck*. I need to move. Sorry."

Grant began to slide in and out of her, going deeper with each slow thrust of his hips. Every time Grant pushed forward, Eli would tilt his hips, pulling almost all the way out to give him room inside her.

Once she got a hang of the rhythm, she relaxed even more, letting the sensations of having the two men at once rush over her. Though intimidating, it felt amazing at the same time. Grant curled over her as he began to thrust a little faster.

He pressed his mouth to her ear. "So tight, honey. So fucking tight." He slipped his hand around the front of her throat and put slight pressure to it.

"Grant," Eli's warned in a low tone.

"She's fine, baby."

She met Eli's gaze. "I'm fine. I like it." Then she dropped her head even more to kiss him. Eli made a noise at the back of his throat and she captured it in her mouth, her tongue brushing with his. He slipped his fingers into her hair and held her to him as he deepened the kiss.

As Grant's fingers tightened on her neck, he grunted as he became more frenzied in his movements.

Eli broke their kiss. "Grant."

"Baby... I'm not going to... last... Sorry." With another grunt, Grant surged forward then stilled, his breathing harsh and rapid against her skin. Then he laid a line of kisses along her spine as he raised himself back up. "Sorry, honey. I didn't mean to lose it like that... You're just... *Damn*. I can't wait to try this again."

I can't wait to try this again.

Which, once again, sounded like they planned on continuing whatever they had together.

Grant slipped carefully from her. "I'm going to go get rid of this. I'll be right back."

As soon as the bathroom door closed, Eli flipped the two of them over, so he was on top. "Now, we take care of you, *ma chérie*."

He began by moving slowly, the movements of his hips in tune with hers. With each stroke he hit the spot that made her cry out and get even wetter. Dropping his head, he sucked one of her peaked nipples into his mouth, his teeth scraping her skin.

When he ground his pelvis against her clit, she squirmed and wrapped her legs around his hips, digging her heels into the back of his thighs.

They moved as one, pushing, pulling, Eli driving himself harder against her.

From a distance, she heard Grant come out from the bathroom, but her attention was quickly pulled back to Eli as he thrust over and over with a not-so-gentle, not-so-slow force that made her body jolt.

She encouraged him by raking her nails over his shoulders and down his back, then sinking them into his powerful ass cheeks as they flexed with his movements.

"*Ma chérie*, I cannot get enough of you. Not nearly enough."

"Me neither," she whispered, holding on even tighter.

She threw her head back and cried out as a climax ripped through her. Eli jackknifed his hips once more and ground against her as he came, his cock throbbing deep inside her, his breathing ragged as he shoved his face against her neck.

As Liv turned her head to invite Grant to join them in the afterglow, her heart stopped.

He was gone.

CHAPTER 16

Grant thought he was okay with it all, that he was fine with sharing Liv. And he *was* okay with sharing her. But maybe not so much when it came to sharing his husband.

Coming out of the bathroom to see Eli on top of Liv as they had sex without him... In one way it excited him, in another it scared the shit out of him. But it hit him hard that he could possibly lose his husband. Eli would no longer be his alone, that this wasn't a little "experiment" in their relationship. That Eli wanted to be with this woman.

The possibility of Liv becoming a permanent part of their life might mean that Eli and Liv would continue to have sex at times without Grant.

Eli had said they needed to lay down ground rules and working out those details would be absolutely necessary.

As Grant stood at the railing of the back deck, looking out over the vast fields of well-manicured sod, he sucked in air through his nostrils in an attempt to settle his confusion.

The glass slider opened behind him and he didn't need to turn around to know who it was.

He knew.

When Grant left the bedroom in a hurry, he only took the time to snag his jeans off the floor on his way out. Now, dark arms circled his bare waist and Eli pulled him against his chest. Normally, their skin to skin contact would be soothing. Right now, it wasn't.

"Mon amour," Eli murmured, his mouth against Grant's ear. *"Je suis désolé si j'ai fait quelque chose de mal."*

"You don't need to be sorry, Elliott. You've done nothing wrong. I... It... *Fuck.*" Grant raked his fingers through his hair. "I came out of the bathroom, saw you two and it just... it scared me."

"Je suis désolé."

I'm sorry.

"I am, too. I'm sorry I reacted like that. I think the reality of the two of you in that bed together, alone, without me... just..." He shook his head, then turned in Eli's arms to face him. "I don't know if I can do this."

Eli remained quiet. Grant knew his husband well enough to know the man was disappointed.

"You finished. I thought you wouldn't mind us finishing, *mon amour.* I should've waited until you joined us again. My mistake."

"When I first stepped out of the bathroom, I saw you two caught up in each other and it excited me, I have to admit. But then, the jealousy and the fear crept in, Eli. I'm sorry, but it did. Watching the two of you have sex—"

"Faire l'amour."

His gaze shot to Eli's and his mouth opened. "What?"

"Grant..."

"You don't make love to a stranger, Eli. You have sex with a stranger."

"Too harsh, *mon cher mari.* She's not a stranger."

Grant closed his eyes for a moment, trying to calm his out-of-control thoughts. "Right. You're right. She's not a stranger. I'm sorry."

"Don't be sorry. I want you to be completely honest with your feelings. I *need* you to be completely honest. If this is going to work—"

"This," Grant repeated, cutting him off. "Do you love her, Elliott?" His chest became tight, and his heart began to pound when Eli didn't answer him at first. "Elliott…"

"I don't know," Eli said softly. "I tried not to think about it because I know it's so soon. Can it be possible to love someone we've only just met not two weeks ago?"

"We fell in love almost immediately," Grant reminded him.

"We did. You're right."

"It wasn't instant, but it was quick. We knew, Eli. We *knew*."

"Yes, we did."

"So, for you, is it the same with her as it was with me? Do you know?" Grant laid his palm over Eli's heart, not missing that it pounded furiously. "Do you know in here?"

Eli covered Grant's hand with his own. "You know I'd never want to hurt you. I never want anyone or anything to come between us. My vow to you was to be with you forever. Don't ever think anything differently. You're my husband and I'll love you forever."

Grant waited for the "but."

Eli's fingers tightened over his, and his hand along Grant's back moved slowly up and down his bare skin.

Eli finally continued, "But I do think that love is there. It's blooming and becoming stronger by the day. However, I will heed your wishes. I won't risk anything and everything we have. I want you to love her, too. I want her to love us. I want us to become as one and don't want her to leave us once she's safe. I don't want the three of us to be over when that happens. But if you say no, that isn't what you want, I will listen. If you simply need more time, I'll give you that, just say the word."

Grant pulled his hand from under Eli's and cupped his jaw. "I love you, Elliott. You're my husband. I've loved you like no one else before you and if anything happened to you, I'd never find anyone to love just as completely. You're my everything. You said we needed to figure out what we want before we even approach Liv. But... I'm not sure of what that is. Do I like having sex with Liv? Yes. I more than like it. Do I love the three of us having sex? Absolutely. But, again, I'm afraid. I'm afraid that one day you might love her more. Is that a reasonable fear? I think so."

"I understand your fear, but, *mon amour*, my heart's big enough for both of you. And just like having children, do you love one more than the other? Or both just as much?"

"Some parents love one of their kids more than the others. They just don't admit it," Grant said, a smile curling his lips.

Eli chuckled. "You're probably right. But I also want to say that your heart," Eli pressed his index finger over Grant's heart, "is big enough for both Olivia and me, also. Again, if you'll feel better that it's only the three of us together when we make love, then I have no problem with that. At least in the beginning, until you're more comfortable."

"What if I'm never comfortable with it just being you and her when I'm not around?"

"Then you aren't, and we'll respect your wishes."

"You're speaking for her now? Do you even know what she wants?"

Eli shook his head. "No, I don't. So this whole conversation may be moot."

Grant brushed his thumb over Eli's full, dark lips and Eli kissed it. "I'll tell you what, let's get through this weekend. I think I want to watch the two of you together again—"

Eli's brows shot up. "Without you?"

"Well, I can join in afterward, but I'd like to sit back and watch and figure out what I'm feeling when I do see the two of you together alone."

"Okay, and what else?"

"And then I'll see how I feel after Sunday, then once we know this mess is all cleaned up, we can approach Liv and see how she feels. You never know, she may be sick of us after this long weekend locked up in this house together."

Eli chuckled again. "Very true, *mon amour*. Dealing with two very bossy males may very well make her run for the hills."

"Or a faraway sod field."

"Hmm. We might have to explore the farm somewhat this weekend."

"I actually heard that they have a St. Andrews Cross in the basement."

Eli cocked an eyebrow toward him. "Really."

Grant smiled. "Really. I doubt they'd mind if we knocked the dust off the thing this weekend."

"Are you volunteering to be strapped to it?"

Grant laughed. "Not me, no." Then he sobered quickly when he wondered if Liv waited in bed for them confused by his quick departure. "We should get back to Liv."

Eli dropped his lips to his and kissed him briefly. "Yes, we should."

"I have an idea... How about we go back in there and you sit in the corner of the bedroom and watch Liv and me? This way we figure out if being one on one with her is okay with both of us."

Eli pressed his lips to Grant's ear again, his voice low and husky. "That's a wicked idea, *mon amour*. I think I'll enjoy watching the two of you together. I'll struggle to sit in a seat and do nothing."

"Who said you had to do nothing?"

Eli straightened and laughed. "Very true."

"And how hot will that be if we watch you pleasuring yourself as we have sex."

"That could be very hot."

"Then what are we waiting for?"

"Lead the way, *mon amour*. Olivia's probably waiting for us impatiently. We shouldn't keep her waiting any longer."

～

L iv sat in the large bed, chewing on her bottom lip. Eli had rushed out after Grant as soon as they noticed he was gone. And now she wondered what was going on between the two. But she wanted to give them some privacy. They were married, for crissake, she didn't need to be in the middle of their business.

Dread gnawed at her insides. She wondered if Grant had considered her and Eli having sex without him as cheating. Even if it was only for a few minutes and they were in no way hiding it? They were only finishing what they'd started.

She didn't want to be the reason for turmoil in their relationship. It was bad enough that the whole Dean mess was causing a hassle for all of them.

She would never want to be considered the "other woman," because she wasn't like that. She would never knowingly do something so hurtful to someone. And she appreciated everything that they'd done for her so far. Especially when, prior to moving into the bedroom, Eli and Grant had given her an update on the Dean situation...

"There's some good news, the DA doesn't appear to be on the take. So we slipped the information to her anonymously and also leaked it to a female detective in the precinct where Peggy lived. We can only hope that the women have a serious dislike of Dean like most women do."

"So now what?" she'd asked Eli.

His answer had been simply, "We wait."

"This waiting's killing me," she'd replied.

Eli had shaken his head. "No, what will kill you is Dean. Waiting is just inconvenient, *ma chérie.*"

He was right.

But now as she waited for them to return, or at least Eli, she wondered if she should go back to the room she'd been staying in since arriving at the farm. Maybe it would be best to give the two men alone time to work out whatever was going on with Grant.

Or maybe they'd decide to leave the farm and head back home. Grant might no longer want to be with her. Or, possibly, no longer wanted Eli to be with her.

Suddenly her chest tightened and her stomach churned.

If that was true...

Never in her life had she needed anyone. She was used to being by herself, doing things on her own. But now...

Damn. Things had changed. The thought of not spending another minute, another second with both Eli and Grant, of not seeing their faces, not hearing their voices, of not touching them, was...

Devastating.

So, she had to make whatever was wrong with Grant right. She needed to make him see that she wouldn't destroy their marriage or hinder the men's relationship.

That was never the intent.

She didn't even want either one of them more than the other. She looked at Eli and Grant as two halves of a whole. She...

Holy shit.

She loved them equally.

Her mind spun as she dug deep to see if that was true, if that was what she really felt.

How could it be love?

Impossible.

The only other person she'd ever loved was her brother. And even that had been screwed up after she left him so long ago.

So maybe she didn't understand how she felt. Maybe what she thought was love was actually more like lust.

That had to be it.

Because it was impossible to fall in love with one man in such a short amount of time, but two?

Never.

As Eli came back into the bedroom, his face not revealing

anything, her heart skipped a beat. Then a rush of relief went through her as Grant followed closely behind.

Eli didn't approach the bed, but Grant did. He sat on the edge of the mattress wearing only a pair of jeans, the top button unfastened. She let her gaze roam over his muscular, but lean chest, the light dusting of hair over his pecs, his broad shoulders, then she raised her gaze to his face and waited.

"I'm sorry, Liv."

Her heart flipped due to panic once more. He was about to give her bad news. They were over. He couldn't take the three of them being together. He didn't want her touching his husband...

"I shouldn't have left. I just needed some air and to figure out what I was feeling."

He wasn't the only one. "I understand. While you both were gone I did a little thinking, too."

A noise came from where Eli sat in the chair tucked into a corner of the room. She wondered why he remained so far away. Was it possible that he didn't agree with what Grant wanted? Which was to possibly break things off?

"And what did you come up with?" Grant asked softly.

"Maybe I should hear what you have to say first."

Grant shook his head. "I know what Eli wants. I need to hear what you want of out this. Out of us."

"Maybe not the same as you," she began but hesitated when he frowned, studying her face.

"So you don't want to take this any further?" he asked softly.

Liv's gaze hit his, then slid to Eli's, whose face remained a blank mask. "What?"

Grant reached out and grabbed her hands, sandwiching them between his warm, much larger ones. "Honey, what do you want from us?"

"Grant," came the low warning from the corner of the room.

His head twisted toward Eli and they shared a look. "I know I'm not doing this in the order you wanted, baby, but I need to hear it from her."

"What do you need to hear from me?" she asked. Because at this point, she was willing to tell him almost anything to keep them in her life.

Which surprised the hell out of her.

"I guess I need to hear that you want us both. That you don't just want to be with Eli."

She raised her eyebrows. "Did it seem like I did? If so, I'm sorry."

Grant shook his head and squeezed her fingers reassuringly. "No, you never gave any indication of that. Please, just humor me because I need to hear it."

Liv moved onto her knees and closer to Grant. When he released her hands, she reached out to trace her fingers over his cheek. She let them fall to his chest, flattening out her palms. "Of course, I want you, Grant. Just as much as Eli. I want both of you. I was just thinking how the two of you are two halves of a whole. And I'm the lucky one to get the complete package. That's..."

"What?" he prodded.

"That's as long as you two want me, also. I mean, I know you want me sexually, but the rest..."

"The rest?" Eli asked from across the room.

Shit. She didn't know how to broach the subject.

She swept a hand between them all. "The rest. More than sex."

"A relationship?"

"Yes," she answered softly.

"Commitment?"

"Yes, that too."

"Love?"

"Possibly. If you two could open your hearts to me, I think I would like that."

Grant ran his fingers through her hair and swept it over her bare shoulder. "I think we can open our hearts, honey. I just don't know what would come of it. I can't make any promises. Eli and I have been together a long time... Just the two of us."

She nodded. "I understand that. I would understand if you don't want to add me to your relationship. I'd be a third wheel."

Eli made a noise from the corner. "*Mon amour*, she's making it very difficult for me not to approach the bed to assure her otherwise."

"Why can't you approach the bed?" Liv's eyebrows furrowed as she stared at Eli.

"I'm going to sit here and watch Grant and you together... if that's okay with you, of course."

She shook her head in confusion. "Why?"

"To see if I'm okay with you making love with my husband without me being directly involved. And then, you and I will do the same, while he watches. Is that okay with you?"

The thought of having each man by himself while the other watched made her quiver. Her nipples beaded and her breathing shallowed. "I don't have a problem with it. But just so you two are aware, I do enjoy having both of you together. I never want you to think otherwise."

Eli chuckled. "Yes, we know you do. As we enjoy having you at the same time, also. But there may be times that we aren't all together and we need to know what works and what doesn't. What's acceptable for Grant, for me, and for you, too, Olivia."

She nodded. Sliding a hand over Grant's broad shoulders, she moved on her knees until her hard nipples pressed to his back and she wrapped her arms around his neck, running her hands down his chest, appreciating the short, wiry hairs that tickled her palms. Pressing her lips to his neck, she lightly scraped her teeth along his skin.

Grant reached up and grabbed her wrists, dragging one of her hands down to his cock, which was rock solid beneath his jeans.

"Do you want me?" Liv whispered in his ear.

"Do I leave you any doubt?" he whispered back.

"No, none."

With a nod of his head, he twisted his neck to look at her. "Then you're okay with this?"

"Yes, absolutely," she answered, her voice breaking with excitement. "Whatever you want..." She hesitated for a moment. "I need my own pet name for you. You call me honey. Eli calls me *ma chérie.* You call Eli baby or big man. So I guess I need one for both of you."

"Hmm," Grant answered, pushing from his seated position to a stand. "You can call me whatever comes natural. Now... take my jeans off, honey."

With a smile, she followed him off the bed and came around to his front, reaching for his zipper. She slowly slid it down, not breaking his eye contact. He wore no boxer briefs, so the lower the zipper went, the more his cock was exposed until it fell completely free of the pants. She stroked it twice before tucking her thumbs into the waistband and peeling his jeans down his legs. On her way down, she quickly licked the drop of precum that beaded on the crown. When she pushed the denim all the way to his ankles, he stepped back and before she could finish rising to her feet, he hooked her under her arms and tossed her back onto the bed.

She squealed then laughed as she landed with a bounce. But his mouth captured the last of her laughter as he kissed her hard, his tongue swirling against hers. When she moaned, he captured that, too.

He pulled away slightly. "Do you know what a St. Andrews Cross is, Liv?"

She shook her head.

"Do you want to find out?"

"Now?"

"No. Not right now. Right now is just for us. Then for you and Eli. By the time we're done with you, we expect you to be fully satisfied and ready to sleep. I'm sure we'll be, too. Maybe tomorrow we'll explore that option when we're fresher."

"Whatever you want, baby," she murmured and loved that his eyes lit up with that admission.

But it was true, she had decided earlier she'd do whatever she'd need to do to make everything right with Grant. And it wasn't a sacrifice at all. She would benefit by everything they did to her and everything they asked in return. She trusted them to never do anything she wouldn't want to do or to do something that would hurt her.

"How much do you want me?" Grant growled into her ear, his cock pressing against her thigh, his silky precum leaking onto her skin.

She snagged his hand cupping her breast and tweaking her nipple, and shoved it down between them. She pushed it between her thighs and with her fingers on top of his, she slipped both of their middle fingers inside of her. "Feel that?"

"I might have to investigate further," he murmured as he took small bites along her shoulder and down her chest, nipping one breast then the other. He nibbled down her belly and finally he sucked at her clit and their middle fingers worked in and out of her simultaneously.

He ate her like a starved man, his lips and tongue making her hips jump. She cried out his name, her back arching as he continued to fuck her with not only his finger but hers since he wouldn't let it go. When he sank his teeth into the tender flesh of her inner thigh, she jerked and then came with a rush of wetness.

"That's it, honey, give me everything you have. Show me how wet you can get," he murmured against her skin. Then he was up and over her, his large body covering her completely, taking her hard and fast, ramming himself deep.

A fleeting thought of him not using a condom swept through her but it was quickly forgotten as he circled her neck with his fingers and kissed her completely, thoroughly. The harder he squeezed, the wetter she got. Once again, he didn't take it far enough to hurt her, but just enough to make it exciting, to send that now familiar thrill shuddering through her.

He knew how to take it to the very edge, but not push past it. When he changed the angle of his thrusts, it only took moments for the buildup once more, the rush to the end, and when he pounded her as hard as he could, she fell... Her body rippling intensely around his, squeezing his cock. She gasped as his fingers flexed tighter and he broke the kiss, pressing his forehead to hers, their eyes locked.

"I'm going to come now, Liv... Tell me to come inside you."

"Come inside me, baby."

"Tell me again. Use my name."

"Come inside me, Grant. *Please.*"

With a grunt, his body arched over hers and he thrusted one more time before becoming still, his cock throbbing as he spilled deep inside her.

It was a few long moments before he broke eye contact and smiled down at her. "I made you mine. Eli will make you his next. Then, tomorrow we'll make you both of ours once again." He pressed his lips to hers lightly.

She wrapped her fingers around the back of his neck and whispered, "You didn't use a condom."

"No. You said you haven't had sex with anyone in twelve years and we get tested regularly. "

That was all well and good, but... "Grant, I'm not on any kind of birth control."

His eyes widened and he pulled back a bit. "*Fuck.* I shouldn't have assumed."

Eli's deep voice came from nearby. "But you did, *mon amour.* So now it's my turn. Tomorrow we'll go back to taking care until she's protected."

She and Grant both turned their heads to look at Eli, who now stood next to the bed, his hard length jutting straight out from his body.

"And if…" Liv started but then let it hang out there because she didn't hate the idea of having their child. Not at all. Maybe it wouldn't be optimal timing, maybe it wouldn't be planned. But being around Preston and Cayden this last week had brought out some mothering instincts she didn't realize she even had.

After having a mother who never acted like one, she never considered being one herself. She had no idea what being a loving mother was like. But watching Quinn in this short week showed her how naturally it should come.

But that was neither here nor there right now…

"Then we'll just deal with the consequences if something comes out of this." Eli offered his hand to Grant. "Now, *mon amour*, it's time for you to go sit in the hot seat and watch us."

"Do you want me to go clean up?" Liv asked, starting to rise as Grant slipped from her and climbed off the bed.

"*Absolument pas.* Absolutely not, *ma chérie.*"

Liv hesitated and considered what that meant. Eli wanted to spill his seed inside her along with Grant's. The thought was…

Hot.

Her heart started to race with the anticipation of Eli making love to her next.

She settled back onto the bed, watching as Grant took Eli's place in the chair, his cock still semi-erect. Then her eyes slid to Eli as the mattress sank beneath his weight.

"How do you want me, *mon coeur*?"

His dark eyes shot to hers and a broad smile spread across his face. "I didn't teach you that."

She returned the smile. "No. I've been taking a free online course while I've been here. But I plan on taking French 101 next semester, too. Would you like that?"

"I would love that, *ma chérie.* Now… *à genoux face à Grant, afin qu'il puisse te regarder quand je te ferai jouir.*"

She laughed because she had no idea what he just said. "Eli…"

He laughed, too, as he pulled her to her knees and with hands on her hips, turned her to face where Grant sat. "Hand and knees, *ma chérie.* Let *mon cher mari* watch me make you come."

Liv smiled at Grant as he settled more deeply into the chair, giving her a wink.

Then Eli easily made her come.

Twice.

CHAPTER 17

Eli groaned as he peeled himself away from Olivia's back. It had to be the middle of the night and he'd ended up spooning her while she curled against Grant's side.

He blinked as his phone vibrated again on the nightstand. The room was dark and for a moment he forgot they were still at the Reed-White's farm, sleeping in their big bed.

He rolled and sat up, snagging the phone, and looked at the time. Midnight. He guessed it wasn't that late after all, but even so, why was Gryff calling now?

With another groan, he got to his feet and hurried out of the bedroom, hitting the Answer button after shutting the door quietly behind him.

"Boss," he greeted.

"Sorry, Eli, if I'm *interrupting* anything. But I figured you'd want to know right away."

"You're not interrupting. We were sleeping."

"Then I apologize for waking you, but there's breaking news that can't wait."

Eli moved farther away from the bedroom so he didn't have to whisper. But his heart began to beat like a drum from the tone of Gryff's voice. "What is it?"

"Dean was just arrested about two hours ago. He's already been arraigned and is being held without bail."

Eli sucked in a breath and then let it out slowly, letting that news sink into his fuzzy brain. "Okay."

"Since it's for murder, he's being held without bail until his preliminary hearing."

"Right."

"Eli, that's good news."

"Of course it is."

"Why don't you sound more enthused? This is what we were waiting for. Now Liv can come back to the city and, hopefully, will be safe."

"He'll plead not guilty," Eli murmured.

"To be expected. But he's a flight risk no matter what, so they won't let him go."

"He's got power behind him."

"It's first degree murder, Eli," Gryff reminded him.

"Still..."

"She'll be safe, and we'll follow it closely. If, for some reason, they release him until his trial, which I can't imagine even he'd have that much pull for, we'll deal with it then. You can bring her home. In fact, Trey wants her here at the house until he finds her a better apartment."

Eli fought to keep his voice steady and neutral. "I see."

His boss's voice got low and grumbly. "You don't sound relieved, Elliott. What's going on?"

"Nothing."

"No, it's more than nothing..."

Silence hung between him.

"Fuck," Gryff murmured. "It's only been two weeks, my man. Not enough time for anyone to fall hard enough."

"Not true."

"Fuck," his boss repeated, louder this time. "So, you want her to go back to your place? Is that what she wants? You might get some flack about that from Trey. He really wants to spend time with his sister and not with you two sitting around holding her hands as he does so... Just a warning."

"Right."

Gryff let out a long, loud sigh. "For fuck's sake, why do I have the feeling I'm going to have to run interference on this one?"

Eli decided it was best to not answer that.

Gryff continued, sounding like he was talking to himself more than Eli, "Fuck. Maybe Rayne can do it. He's more agreeable to getting bad news from her."

As Eli opened his mouth to respond, Gryff cut him off. "Okay, well, I'll let Trey talk to his sister and she can tell him what she wants to do. Then we'll deal with the fallout. If I hear anything else on Dean, I'll call. Otherwise, see you on Monday."

The phone went dead.

Eli pulled it away from his ear and stared at the dark screen, then he glanced toward the closed bedroom door.

He wasn't going to wake them up to tell them the news. It could wait until morning and if it was up to him, he'd wait until at least Sunday night. He wanted nothing more than for them to finish spending their time together at the farm. He wanted to make sure everything was settled between the three of them before they headed back.

The last thing he wanted was Olivia to go back to her shitty apartment and job. And she may do that if she thought she was safe and those options were still available.

He needed to convince her before Sunday to move in with them.

So maybe he'd let Grant in on the news and just hold off on telling her.

Grant raked his hand through his hair as he jogged slowly next to Eli along one of the dirt roads bordering a sod field. Eli had just dropped the news of Dean's arrest and also his future plans. "You want her to move in right away?"

"Do you think we should wait?" Eli asked, skirting a loose rock in their path.

He cursed silently, then blew out a breath. "I don't know. We need to tell her."

"Not yet, *mon amour.*"

"Why?"

"I'd like to finish our weekend here. I'd prefer for us to spend time together without anyone else butting in."

"Anyone... Like Trey."

Out of the corner of his eye, Grant saw Eli nod. "That whole triad, yes. I want just the three of us for right now. Last night was a start. I had no problem watching the two of you together. You seemed to be fine with watching us."

Grant admitted it really turned him on once he faced his own fears. "Yes, there's still a little worry niggling at me. But, honestly, I think with time that will lessen."

"That's good news, *mon amour,* and if you're as sure about moving this relationship forward as I am, then we shouldn't wait. What do you think?"

Grant came to a stop in the middle of the dirt road. "Why are you in such a rush?"

Eli stopped a little ahead, turned and shook his head. "I don't know."

"You don't think we should give this more time? If Trey wants her to stay with them, why not have her do that? Simply a week, maybe more. However long they need to reconnect. Baby, they just found each other again. We don't want to deny them that time, right?"

"They don't need to be living in the same house for that," Eli insisted.

"No, but—"

"She could come work for the firm. She could work with Trey... As well as Rayne and Gryff. Get to know them all. We won't interfere with them spending time together."

"I know that. But do you want to piss off Trey?"

"No. But if we suggest they give her a job..."

"Doing what?"

Eli planted his hands on his hips and turned away, walking in a slow circle. "I don't know. It's a thought."

"But you didn't run this past Gryff."

"No. But I could suggest it."

"She wants to be a social worker. She wants to help people."

"I understand that, *mon amour*. She can finish her degree while working with us."

Grant sucked in a sharp breath. "Holy shit, Elliott, do you hear yourself? You can't control every aspect of her life. She's been independent for almost her whole life. At least until this Dean mess. Now you want to do everything for her. She's not going to accept that."

Eli walked away from him and Grant slowly followed, shaking his head.

"Maybe not."

"No maybes about it, Eli."

"Can we agree to not tell her until tomorrow evening before we leave? Can we at least have this weekend?"

Grant wasn't sure that was a good idea, but he understood what Eli wanted or even needed. After last night, he actually looked forward to the rest of the weekend, as well, to cultivate their relationship and enjoy each other without worrying about anyone else intruding on just the three of them.

Plus, he couldn't wait to try that St. Andrews Cross later. He eyeballed Eli walking ahead of him, wearing long, loose nylon shorts and a snug T-shirt that clung to his muscles. The man's ass still did it for him. He jogged to catch up. When he did, he reached out, grabbing Eli's arm to halt his forward progress. "Hold up, big man."

Eli stopped, his eyebrows raised. "What's the matter?"

"Nothing," Grant answered, turning his husband toward him. "I have to say, after all these years, I still appreciate that fucking ass of yours."

A slow smile crept over Eli's face, his eyes crinkling at the corners. "Yes?"

Grant answered with a wicked smile of his own. His voice sounded husky even to his own ears. "Oh, yes. Would it be wrong of us to share a private moment out here among these romantic fields of green grass?"

Eli glanced beyond him to the vast field with a cocked eyebrow. "You think these sod fields are romantic?"

Grant laughed. "No, but it sounded good."

Eli tilted his head as he studied Grant. "Is this a negotiation, counselor?"

"You mean do I get to top you if I agree to wait to tell her until tomorrow evening? No, but... now that you mentioned it..."

"*Do* you agree?"

Grant sighed. If this is what Eli wanted... "Yes, I'll agree. But if she gets pissed that you held back that information, I'm placing the blame all on you."

Eli laughed. "I accept that."

"Do you accept me topping you out here," Grant swept an arm around, "in the midst of all this nature?"

"Out in the open?" Eli jerked his chin toward a line of trees that separated one field from the next. "Or can we go amongst that batch of trees over there?"

Grant slid a hand over his throbbing erection, showing his husband what he had coming to him. "Hmm. Fucking you against a tree... I like the sound of that."

Eli suddenly took off at a jog toward the trees. "Then hurry up, *mon amour*, I'll be waiting," he tossed over his shoulder.

As Grant watched his husband get farther away, he realized with disappointment that they had no lube, so fucking would be out of the question. But that still didn't mean he wouldn't get to come. With a smile, Grant chased Eli down.

Liv wiped her hands on the dishtowel and then hung it to dry. She was a little sad that Grant and Eli would be leaving soon to head back to the city. At least they'd enjoyed a last meal together before they left.

The Reed-White family was due to return soon anyway. So it wasn't like the house would be quiet for long. She only wished she was going back home with her men.

Her men.

She had to admit, even though the reason she was hiding out on the farm wasn't a good one, she had enjoyed this time with them. Most of the weekend had been spent either naked or barely clothed, just talking or being intimate.

Hell, she had even enjoyed being strapped to the St. Andrews Cross in the basement yesterday while Grant and Eli had their way with her, trying things that she never knew existed and definitely didn't think she'd ever enjoy.

But she did. Very much so.

Grant even discussed getting one for their own house. Eli had agreed readily and if they asked her, she'd give that a big thumb's up. She never thought she'd be into the kinkier side of sex but it was fun and exciting and, though she wouldn't want to do it all the time, she could see the three of them doing it once in a while to mix things up.

She could see the three of them doing it once in a while.

Like they were going to be a permanent thing. Which hadn't

been discussed.

Though she'd like it to be.

Maybe she should bring it up before they left. In fact, maybe she should head into the living room right now where they cuddled on the couch, watching some police drama, waiting for her to finish cleaning up in the kitchen.

Grant had cooked, Eli had set the table and helped with the prep of the meal, and Liv had agreed to clean up the dishes. They were a great team.

Her burner phone rang nearby and she picked it up to see who was calling.

Her brother.

She hit the Answer button. "Hey, Trey."

"Hey, sis. How are you?"

She moved over to the kitchen sink to peer out over the back deck. The sun was just starting to lower. "Great."

"So, we need to discuss what you're doing when you get back tonight."

Liv turned and leaned back against the counter. "What do you mean?"

"When they bring you home tonight, I'd like you to come stay with us for a while. At least until I can find you a nicer apartment."

What was Trey talking about? "I'm not coming back with them tonight, Trey."

"Sure you are... Unless you want to stay at the farm? Not sure why you'd want that."

Liv shook her head. "I'm confused."

"They haven't talked about where you'd go when you got back?"

"Grant and Eli?"

Trey let out a hiss. "Yes, of course, Grant and Eli. Who else would I be talking about?"

"Is it safe for me to come home?"

"For now, yes. They didn't tell you?"

Liv pushed away from the counter, the blood rushing into her head. "Tell me what?"

"That Dean was arrested and is being held until his prelim."

Liv looked toward the kitchen entranceway. "No, somehow they forgot to tell me."

Trey whistled softly on the other end of the phone. "Another good reason for you to come stay with us for a while then."

"When did they know?"

"I just know Gryff told Eli Friday night."

Liv's mind spun. Eli said nothing to her Friday night. Nor Saturday. Nor all day today. "They should've told me," she whispered, more to herself than her brother.

Trey sighed. "Look, I love those guys like brothers, but they shouldn't have kept this from you."

She frowned. "No, they shouldn't have."

"So, my suggestion is what I told Gryff to tell Eli, that you get dropped off here. We can grab the rest of your clothes from their house tomorrow."

"What about my apartment?"

"I paid the remaining balance on your rent and broke your lease."

"Why would you do that?"

"Because that place was horrible and unsafe, that's why."

"Trey, I—"

"Liv, I'm your older brother, it's time I start helping you. We can help each other, okay? Like siblings should. Please, don't fight this. Come stay with us. Then I'll get you settled in a new place and we'll find you a job that not only pays better but will let you concentrate on finishing your degree. Isn't that what you want?"

Of course it was. She'd wanted to finish her degree for a long time, but... "Yes, but, Trey—"

"But nothing. You've been on your own for long enough. Did I agree with it? Honestly, no. Do I understand why? Yes. So let's put that all behind us and move forward. Please?"

Liv closed her eyes and nodded her head even though Trey couldn't see it.

"I'm your big brother, Liv. Let me be that for once." He sounded dejected and that made her heart squeeze. She didn't want him to be sad. She wanted him to be happy. He deserved it.

And so did she.

"Okay."

"So you'll come back here?"

Her eyes flicked back to the open entryway to the kitchen. "Yes. For just a little while."

"That's all I wanted. I'll see you soon. Love ya, sis."

"Love you, too, Trey. See you soon."

The call dropped and Liv stared at the phone for a moment before stepping forward to place it on the nearby rustic wooden table.

Eli knew that Dean had been in custody since Friday and said nothing to her. Grant knew, too. Both of them kept that important information from her.

She did not like that. At all.

As she stepped into the large great room of the log home, she hesitated just inside the entranceway. Eli and Grant were on the couch with Grant leaning into the darker man, Eli's arm thrown around his shoulders.

Suddenly a pain shot through her at the thought of not being with either one of them. If it was true and it was safe for her to go back, did she really want to go stay with her brother? Or did she want to go home with Eli and Grant? Now that it was safe, would they want her to remain in their house? Or would they expect her to go back to her apartment?

So many questions, so many decisions. And she needed answers.

But first, she needed to know why they'd kept Dean's arrest from her.

When Eli's head turned to look over his shoulder, he spotted her and sat up straighter, taking Grant with him. Grant turned to look at her, too.

"Are you two heading out soon?" she asked.

"Can you come sit with us for a moment? We need to talk to you," Eli said, uncurling his arm from around Grant's shoulders.

Liv moved farther into the expansive room and came around the couch to face them.

"Liv, sit, please?" Grant asked, indicating the space between the two men as they slid apart.

She nodded and suddenly felt as if in a fog like the first time she ever saw Eli in the lobby of the law firm. Though, it was only a little over two weeks ago, it felt like a lifetime.

They both watched her carefully as she sat between them, their thighs touching, their warmth seeping into her bones. The safeness and caring she felt sitting in between them rolled over her and filled her heart and mind.

But she still wanted to know why she wasn't told about Dean. That bothered her.

"Do you have something to tell me?" she asked carefully.

"We have something to ask you," Eli clarified.

She turned toward him to study his dark features. His bald head that fit him so well, his black eyebrows, his dark brown eyes, his wide nose, his deep dark brown tones of his skin, his full, smooth lips which had brought her to pleasure numerous times. His long fingers with the neatly manicured fingernails as he reached out to tuck a strand of her hair behind her ear...

In a very loving way. His expression was soft and because of that, she had a hard time holding on to any resentment she felt from him keeping Dean's arrest a secret.

"What do you need to ask me?"

Grants hand brushed down her back and she glanced over at him next. His dark hair which was currently a ruffled mess, his glasses which made him look so smart and emphasized his beautiful and expressive hazel eyes, his tightly-trimmed shadow of a beard, his corded neck she liked to sink her teeth into. Both men had broad chests and their bodies were absolutely beautiful. She appreciated everything about the two men. Including their intelligence.

And sitting in between the two felt right. It felt like home, like she belonged there.

For once, she belonged somewhere.

She felt included. Wanted. Needed. Appreciated.

Her heart swelled.

"Olivia, we'd like you to move in with us."

She blinked and before she could stop them, her words spilled out. "Trey wants me to stay with them."

"You spoke to Trey?"

She nodded and met Eli's gaze. "Yes, just a few minutes ago."

She didn't miss when Eli's eyes slide to Grant before quickly coming back to her. "What did he say?"

"What you forgot to tell me... Or didn't forget, just omitted. You want to explain why?" She needed to at least give them the opportunity to explain. She owed them that much. And it wasn't like she hadn't enjoyed every minute she'd spent with them over the weekend. Even if she knew Friday night, the possibility of staying at the farm for the weekend might have crossed her own mind.

"He told you about Dean's arrest," Grant said from behind her with a flat voice.

She peeked over her shoulder at him, but he was already moving off the couch and coming to kneel on the floor at Eli's feet so she could face them both at the same time.

She nodded. "Yes, he did. And like I said, he wants me to come stay with him. Why shouldn't I do that?" She wanted to hear it from them.

"First of all," Eli began. "It was my idea to withhold the information until this evening."

"Why?"

"So we could spend this time together. Just us. Are you angry with me?"

Liv studied Eli, who genuinely looked a bit worried about how she'd react. She reached out and traced her fingertips over his jawline. "I'm disappointed that you weren't honest with me. Not that you actually lied. But you should've told me and given me the choice to stay or go."

Both Eli and Grant nodded.

"You're right," Grant said, placing a hand on her knee and squeezing. "We should have. It's not just Eli's fault, Liv. It's mine, too. I agreed with this. I really think we needed this time together to figure out what we all meant to each other. Would you have wanted to stay if we'd told you?"

"Yes! That's the thing, I would have. This weekend was wonderful. It cemented what I was realizing."

"What were you realizing?" Eli repeated, his face appearing hopeful.

"That it feels good to have someone—or *someones*—there for you. It's nice to be able to lean on someone in troubled times. To feel loved."

"Yes, it does."

"So just because it's safe for me to find a new place to live, to go back to my job, doesn't mean I'd never see either of you again. I mean, we don't live a state away. Hell, we don't even live in two different cities. I'd be close."

"But you'd be closer if you moved in with us permanently," Eli suggested.

"As much as I love being with you two, you can't keep supporting me."

"Liv, we can afford to while you go to school, finish your degree. Find your dream job."

Dream job. She had no idea what her actual dream job would be. "Right now, I just want to find something that will pay enough so I'm not always struggling."

"I can understand that. But now you can figure out what your career path should be, whether it's social work or not, and not be forced into taking a shit job. And you'll never be struggling if you're living with us. That I can promise," Grant insisted.

"You could always come work for the firm," Eli offered.

Liv shot him a surprised look. "To do what? Clean the toilets? I don't have any skillsets for the firm."

"Gryff could find you something."

"And he's in agreement with that?"

She didn't get an answer. So she figured Gryff may not know anything about what Eli suggested.

"Let's not worry about that right now. What do you think about what Eli proposed?" Grant rose up on his knees and leaned into her legs, capturing her hands. He pressed them to his mouth and kissed her knuckles.

She stared down at him at her feet. "You're completely okay with this?"

"Yes, I am, honey. I honestly am. Never in my wildest imagination would I think that my husband and I would be inviting a woman to come live with us, to become a part of *us*. But I am. He is. We are."

Relief flooded through Liv. She wanted this, too. She couldn't be happier at the offer of her moving in with them. Losing some of her independence would take some getting used to, but she was sure all the good that would come from being in a relationship with two men she loved would be worth it.

"I have something to confess," she said.

Neither said a word, instead they just waited patiently as she gathered her courage.

"I know this is too soon, that things like this normally don't happen this quickly, but this weekend made me realize..." she hesitated. She was going to flay herself open by admitting what she was about to admit. She would be making herself vulnerable, but she wanted them to know. And if they didn't feel the same, that was fine. Maybe their feelings would grow to equal hers eventually.

"What?" Eli finally prodded, beginning to look anxious.

She cupped his cheek with one hand and Grant's with the other. "I'm pretty sure that I love you."

Both men jerked. Grant sat back on his heels, grabbing the hand at his cheek and sliding it to his mouth to place a kiss on her palm. Eli grabbed her other hand and squeezed her fingers.

"When you say that, do you mean both of us?" Grant asked.

"Yes," she gave him a small smile. "Both of you."

"You're *pretty sure?*" he asked, his lips twitching.

"Yes, pretty sure," she confirmed with a sharp nod of her head, fighting back a giggle.

"What would make you very sure?" Grant teased.

"Time," she said honestly.

"That we can give you," Eli said. "We're pretty sure we love you, too, Olivia."

She rolled her lips in for a second, then asked, "You're *pretty sure?*"

Eli's lips curled at the ends. "Yes, pretty sure."

"What would make you very sure?" she teased back.

"Like you, time. I think time's needed to make this something solid. We're willing to give it that and it sounds like you are, too. That makes me very happy, *ma chérie,* as I'm sure it does *mon cher mari,* too."

"Are you willing to give up your apartment, honey?"

"Trey already broke the lease, so I have no choice. Are you sure you two don't want me to stay with Trey for a week or two as we explore this further?"

Grant and Eli's gaze met and held for a moment before they both looked back at her.

"Only if that's what you want or need, *ma chérie,* otherwise, we'd prefer you to be with us."

Liv thought about it for only a moment before saying, "I want to come home with you two."

"You can always stay with Trey if you need a break from us bossy men," Eli said.

"That's true."

"I was only kidding, *ma chérie*," he laughed. "I hope you never need a break from us."

Liv pushed to her feet, breaking their contact. She headed for the spare bedroom where her stuff was being kept.

"Where are you going?" Grant called out.

"To get my things. I'm ready to go home now," she called back.

She smiled as she walked down the hall. Her heart was full. She was going to make a home with these two men and she couldn't be happier.

Even coming from rough beginnings, her brother had found his place with people he loved.

And now she had done the same.

Finally, after all these years, she was going *home*.

EPILOGUE

"You did perfect, honey," Grant said, carrying a bottle of wine into the study along with three glasses. "I was impressed. I'm normally not rooting for the DA, but in this case, I was, and you were the perfect witness. If I were Dean's attorney, I would have seen my case going down the shitter as soon as you started answering questions."

Eli moved away from the stereo, music now playing softly through the hidden surround-sound speakers. "Yes, I'm proud that you didn't let his attorney get to you. You kept your calm and held your own. *Très impressionnant, ma chérie.*"

"When's his sentencing?"

"We'll find out soon, but you won't need to attend," Grant assured her, setting the glasses on the nearby table and filling them.

"No, I want to. If you two don't want to come along, then I'm sure Trey won't mind."

Grant and Eli exchanged glances.

"*Ma chérie*, we're all in this together. If you want to be there, we'll be by your side. Trey can come along, too, if he'd like."

Grant added, "They would've been here today, as well, but they didn't want to make you nervous with all of us there."

"I wasn't nervous."

Eli smiled. "We know. You were quite fierce with that defense attorney."

"Very," Grant agreed, turning from the side table with a glass in hand. "It made my balls shrink up at the thought of ever having to cross-examine you."

Liv laughed, sinking into the comfy couch that sat in front of the cozy fireplace. Eli had started a fire as soon as they got home since winter was not being kind to the Northeast. "That'll never happen."

"No, it won't. But it was very hot to see you like that," Grant murmured, handing the glass to Eli as he moved close.

Liv's lips twitched. "Mmm, was it?"

"Yes, I think I got hard watching you on the stand being so ferocious," Grant confessed as he approached with the two remaining glasses of red wine. He handed one to her.

Eli settled on the couch to her right, laughing. "He's not the only one."

"I have to admit it, even though I had to sit on the witness stand and face that monster, it was a good day. Dean will hopefully find a boyfriend to change his diapers in prison and I have the love of two good men who are about to make me forget what I just said about Dean."

Both Eli and Grant barked out a laugh.

"I think we all need brain bleach for that one," Grant agreed, settling to her left.

"I agree, *mon amour*." Eli lifted his glass. "The wine should help since we are celebrating."

Grant and Liv lifted their glasses, too.

"Here's to putting all of this behind us and moving forward together," Eli said, his voice low and gruff, relief clear in his expression. He lifted his glass up toward the ceiling. "Home." He held it out toward the fireplace. "Hearth." Then he made a circle motion encompassing the three of them. "And love."

"Agreed," Grant answered as they clinked their glasses together.

Both men took a long sip. Instead of joining them, Liv leaned forward to set her glass on the table.

Both sets of eyes landed on her untouched glass.

"No wine for you, honey?" Grant asked in surprise.

"Mmm," Liv murmured. "I'm going to pass on that."

Both men put their glasses on the coffee table and turned toward her.

"What? You? Turn down wine? Unheard of!" Grant boomed.

"Is your stomach still upset from the stress of today, Olivia?" Eli asked, his face a mask of concern. "You did throw up this morning."

Not that she needed that reminder, she remembered it way too clearly. Eli had rushed into their master bathroom to hold her hair back. "No, that's not it." She gave him a small smile.

Eli frowned. "Then what?" His face running through a gamut of emotions. "You threw up yesterday morning, too," he announced suddenly as if she hadn't been there for that memorable experience, either.

A pensive look crossed Grant's face. "And you went to the doctor yesterday," he whispered. "I thought it was because you weren't feeling well... Holy shit, does that mean we have something else to celebrate?"

Her smile widened. "Uh huh."

Both men glanced at each other then back at her in shock.

"Are you sure?" Eli asked, his eyebrows furrowed. "You went on the pill six months ago."

"Pretty sure," she teased.

Eli gripping her shoulders as he stared at her, his eyes bouncing back and forth from Grant to her. "And what would make you very sure?"

"I'm very sure." She smiled up at him. She slipped from the couch to her knees on the floor, so she could face them both. She placed a hand on each of their thighs which they both quickly covered with their own. She inhaled deeply before saying, "I know this wasn't planned and I guess I'm in the small percentage of people where the pill fails... When the doctor confirmed I was pregnant... I must admit that I was happy. But I want you two to be, also. It's unexpected, I know. We hadn't discussed this and I'm sorry if it's too soon... and..."

"Honey," Grant whispered, pulling her from the floor into his lap. Eli slid over and wrapped his arms tightly around them. It felt great to be part of their man sandwich. She couldn't imagine being anywhere else, with anyone other than the two men she had fallen in love with so deeply. She couldn't be more pleased at the thought of carrying their child. Of making a future with them. Of creating a family of their own.

Eli slid his hand down to her belly as he blinked more rapidly than normal, which made her do the same.

"So, you're happy?" she asked softly, trying not to bawl.

"Tellement heureux. Tu n'imagines pas comment, ma chérie."

"Mon coeur, I haven't learned that much French yet," she reminded him.

"He said you have no idea how happy you've made us. And I agree."

"Well, I'm glad because it's not like you had a choice in the matter," she giggled through her unshed tears.

Grant reached a hand between them and placed it along her belly with Eli's. "So that's our kid in there," he whispered with awe.

"Yep. The doctor thinks I'm only a little over five weeks, so it'll be a while until you can feel the baby bump."

Eli laughed. "I know, *ma chérie.* But I'm sorry, I can't wait until you are heavy with our child."

"Yes, something to look forward to, being fat," she joked, thinking about Paige and her meltdown over being pregnant. Now, late in her pregnancy, the woman had a hard time moving around with two active babies in her extended belly. Liv didn't know how she did it.

"We'll love you no matter what. And we'll love our child no

matter what, also. I'm glad you finally accepted the job Gryff offered you since now we won't miss a minute of this pregnancy."

"Mmm, yes, I am, too, but I'm sure not every minute will be so joyous. Like more morning sickness and swollen feet. And the actual birth," she reminded Eli.

He made a noise. "That's just all a part of the making of a life. One that will be a part of all of us."

"I'll remind you of that in the birthing room when I want to kill you both."

Grant snorted, and Eli laughed.

"Why didn't you tell us yesterday when you found out?" Grant asked.

"I was hoping today would go as we planned and this whole Dean thing would be behind us, so we could move away from that ugly past and into a future full of hope. Plus, it just gave us one more thing to celebrate today."

"You might not be able to enjoy the wine, but we can celebrate in plenty of other ways," Eli promised, brushing a kiss along her temple.

"And I look forward to each and every one of them," she admitted with a smirk.

"Mmm, me, too. Have you told Trey he's going to be an uncle?" Grant asked.

"Absolutely not, you two are the first to know, of course."

Grant's eyes crinkled at the corners and he smirked. "I want to be there when you tell him."

"Me, too," Eli agreed.

"Why?" she asked. "Do you think he'll get out the shotgun?"

"Well, he'll definitely flip." Eli added, "But I imagine in a good way. I think all three of them will love having a niece or nephew."

Grant shook his head, smiling. "That's going to be one spoiled kid."

"That he will."

"*She*." Liv corrected Eli.

"Whether a he or she, *he* will be very loved."

"Yes, *she* will. Just like her momma."

"*Comme nous tous.*"

Like all of us, Liv translated in her head.

She couldn't agree more.

Sign up for Jeanne's newsletter to learn about her upcoming releases, sales and more! http://www.jeannestjames.com/ newslettersignup

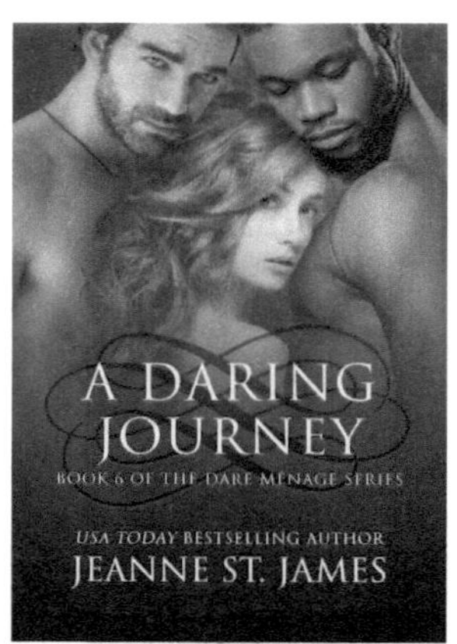

Two paths: one new, one familiar. And a burning desire to choose them both...

When Damon spots a stunning redhead on his plane, the pilot's determined to get to know her better. It's been a long time since he's experienced an instant connection with anyone. The last time was with his former lover, who left without an explanation over five years ago, devastating him. Though now cautious when it comes to relationships, MacKenzie just might be everything he's looking for and more.

Not expecting to meet the tall, dark and handsome captain on her flight home, Mac finds Damon's domineering persistence a turn-on. She decides to take a chance on him, which, in the end, might be a mistake when a person from his past returns. A man Damon loved and still does.

The last five years had been dark journey for Trevor, and he's now ready to return to the light. He's back in Boston to not only ask for forgiveness but to reconnect with Damon, since he still loves the man. However, there's a complication. Damon is seeing someone else and Trevor might be too late.

Turn the page to read a sneak peek of Book 6 of The Dare Menage Series: A Daring Journey

A DARING JOURNEY - SNEAK PEEK

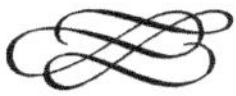

CHAPTER 1

Mac sighed softly and leaned her head back against her seat. Closing her eyes, she let her best friend and former college roommate's rambling words go in one ear and out the other.

She loved Gia to death, but sometimes the woman talked too damn much.

Not sometimes.

Most of the time.

And now, after spending the last week with her at her home in Arizona, she was ready for some peace and quiet. Which wouldn't happen anytime soon.

No. Because she was stuck on a plane with the woman sitting right next to her.

She loved Gia to death.

I love Gia to death.

But right now, she wanted to "kiss" her with a club.

Unfortunately, since they were on a plane flying to Boston, she didn't have a club handy. And, truth be told, the TSA frowned on carrying weapons in the cabin of an airplane.

Even if it *was* in first class. Which was where their asses were currently planted.

Maybe she should order another drink. They were free, after all, and it would soothe her frayed nerves.

She was never a huge fan of flying and was glad to have a companion with her, but still...

She was sorely tempted to get a third martini.

The only reason Gia was accompanying her back to Boston was because one of her brothers recently had twins. For some reason, Gia had volunteered to come help out Grae's newly expanded family for a little while, which surprised the crap out of Mac.

Apparently, the mother of said twins was a little overwhelmed.

Twins would do that to you, she guessed.

"She didn't even want kids in the first place," Gia was saying.

Mac lifted one eyelid. "Who?"

"Paige. She was in no rush to pop out any kids and then when she got knocked up, she freaked when she found out she was having twins."

"Does it run in the family?"

"Whose?"

Mac opened her other eye and shrugged one shoulder as she looked at Gia. "Hers. Yours."

"Not in ours. I'm not sure about hers. But I'm also not sure about Connor's."

Mac shook her head. "Connor?"

"Yes, I *told* you. Both of my brothers are in polyamory relationships."

Oh, yes, that's right. How odd was that?

Both of Gia's older brothers, Grae and Gryff, were "married" to another couple. Or however that worked.

Was that even legal?

She didn't care. It wasn't her business.

"Remember? Grae's with Paige and Connor." Gia leaned into Mac and whispered. "Connor is a hot hunk of Australian white meat. *Phew.*" She lifted a well-manicured finger. "*And* he still has his accent. Every time I hear it, I want to break out my vibrator, since Grae won't share him with me."

Mac twisted her head and stared at her friend. "Why in the hell would your brother share his husband with his sister?" She wrinkled up her nose. "Ew!"

Gia grinned, her dark brown eyes sparkling. "It's not like I'm related to him."

"Do they have an open relationship?"

"No."

Mac threw up her hands and rolled her eyes. "Well then... I don't blame Grae for not letting you 'borrow' his husband. Wait. Are they officially married now?"

"They're married, but I don't think it's legally binding. Paige and Connor were already married when they met Grae."

"Wasn't that weird?"

Gia shrugged. "Not for them, I guess. Not for me, either. It works. Honestly, I'm so damn jealous. I want what they have. I want what Gryff has, too."

Ah yes. Gryff. When Mac had met both Grae and Gryff while in college, she had endless fantasies about both of Gia's brothers. But she never told Gia because those fantasies were so dirty, she'd end up getting herself off just by thinking about them. Sometimes she pretended she was with both of them at the same time.

Yes, she could understand Gia's fascination with threesomes. And her brothers were dark and mysterious, and so damn hot.

Both were also super-duper alpha males.

Yum.

However, those types were great for sex, but hard to live with as Mac had discovered.

Mac squeezed her thighs together and slowly let out a breath. Getting horny thirty thousand feet in the air wasn't going to do her any good. Especially since she couldn't do anything about it.

It turns out that Gryff and Grae were both bisexual, which made those fantasies even hotter. Not that she had any with the two of them recently.

Okay, she might have. But she wasn't confessing that to Gia.

While she never met Connor, she had seen Trey Holloway, Gryff's husband or boyfriend or lover—*whatever*—on the television many, many times. He was a Super Bowl Champion, after all. If she remembered correctly, Trey retired from football a few years back and now was an attorney at Gryff's high-profile law firm.

She wiped at the corner of her mouth.

Maybe she needed to add Trey to her fantasy harem, too...

Oh good lord, she needed to get laid. It had been too long. She needed to stop fantasizing about the men in Gia's family like a sex-starved addict.

Ugh. Honestly, she just needed to get laid to take off the edge.

She realized Gia was still talking.

Of course.

"One of these days, I'm going to find two good men and won't our parents freak out when I bring them home for Thanksgiving."

"Why?"

"Because, can you imagine, three out of your four children being in threesomes? You'd probably start wondering where you went wrong."

That could be a little odd, she supposed. But then, weren't threesomes odd in general? While she'd fantasized about them, she'd never been in one in reality. "Or what you did right," Mac suggested. "What about Gayle?"

"Gayle can't find one good man to put up with her *bougie* ass."

Mac bit back a snort. "And you can?"

Gia's dark, full lips flattened out. "I'm picky."

A sigh slipped past Mac's. "I have no room to talk. I mean, we went to our college reunion as each other's dates the other night. So, I'm in the same boat. Where *are* all the good ones?"

A set of eyeballs peering in between the two seats in front of them had Mac jerking back in surprise and pinning herself to her seat.

The blue eyes blinked. The mouth also related to the face grinned. "Hi, ladies. I couldn't help but overhear your conversation. If you're looking for a volunteer to be in your threesome…" He waggled his blond, bushy eyebrows. "Being with two women has always been a fantasy of mine."

Gia stared at the guy, turned to look at Mac, raised a sculpted dark eyebrow and then rolled her eyes.

"It's most men's fantasy. It just will never be their reality," Gia informed him.

Suddenly, the guy was perched on his knees and leaning over the back of the seat. The stranger lowered his voice to an almost Barry White low. "But you ladies can make it my reality." No, Mac was wrong, it was more like Barry Manilow.

Did he think that come-on was sexy and irresistible? Because if so, he was dead wrong.

Gia's chin snapped back, and she lifted one finger. Again. But this time it meant something totally different.

Oh shit. Mac knew exactly what that meant. Gia was about to get real. And most sane people didn't want to be on the receiving end of that.

"Turn around and sit your ass down."

"I just want to offer my services."

"Did I stutter? Sit. Yo. Azz. Down."

"I am sitting," he huffed.

"If your ass ain't in that seat, you are not sitting." Gia circled that dangerous finger in the air. "Turn around, fool."

He frowned. "Well, if—"

"Bah bah bah!" Gia cut him off, close to shoving that finger against his lips. "Don't make me have the air marshal tase your ass. Turn. Around."

The man's lips flattened out and he flopped back into his seat with a grumble.

"Man thinks he can handle both of us. Puh-leese. And at the same time." She shook her head and tutted, "Uh uh uh."

Mac smothered a laugh with her hand.

Gia reached up and pressed the button for the flight attendant, who appeared by Mac's elbow so quickly that she jumped in surprise.

"Ma'am?"

Gia gave the woman a saccharin-sweet Gia smile. "We need two more dirty martinis and the man in front of me needs a tissue for his tears and a foam donut for his sore ass."

Mac didn't bother to stifle her laugh this time.

A few minutes later the attendant was back with their martinis and a travel-sized packet of tissues for the butt-hurt man.

Two hours later they were finally shuffling off the plane. She couldn't wait to exit and stretch her legs. While she had been in first class, she knew it was worse for the folks crammed into coach. And that's exactly where she would've been if Gia hadn't upgraded her ticket so they could sit next to each other.

As they got to the front of the plane where an attendant and one of the pilots stood thanking the passengers as they exited, Gia stopped short and Mac ran into the back of her with an *oof*.

Before Mac could scold her for stopping so suddenly, she heard, "Ooo. Look at that hunk of deliciously dark man meat," Gia purred.

Where?!?

Gia was tall. Mac was not. All Mac could see was the woman's back. And Gia quickly running a hand over her short bob to make sure her hair was perfect.

It was. Gia's hair was always perfectly coiffed. Unlike Mac's, whose red hair was always unruly and she had to use five thousand products and a flat iron, so she didn't look like an evil clown when it frizzed.

But it was all useless if the weather was even a little bit humid. *Poof.*

Her makeup was never on point like Gia's, either, because... whelp, she just didn't care. Or have that kind of skill.

She wasn't a sloppy person. She was neat and put together, but because she had to spend enough time on her hair every morning, she was too exhausted to do anything other than slap on some blush. And she only did that so she didn't look like death warmed over.

She spent most of her teenage years worried about covering her freckles with foundation. However, she was now past the point of caring. If someone didn't like her freckles, that was on them, not her.

People assumed she was from Irish descent because of her hair color and her blue eyes. Most of the time she didn't correct them. And—

Her thoughts were interrupted when Gia finally moved forward enough to see why the woman stopped short.

Oh yes.

Now she completely understood it.

Of course, it was because it was a man.

But not just any man.

A. MAN.

In uniform.

Tall. Dark. One with total panty-melting potential.

And the dark part wasn't just his hair. While that was black and trimmed neatly and tightly against his head, she was talking about his complexion. He was almost as dark as Gia.

Almost, but not quite.

He wore a pilot's uniform and a friendly smile surrounded by a neatly trimmed goatee as he thanked the passengers exiting. Gia was next in line.

Don't touch him, girl. Don't. I don't want to see you taken down by some air marshal and have to get Gryff to get you out of a jam.

Hands and feet to yourself. Tongue, too.

Please don't lick the pilot.

Wait. Was she warning Gia or herself?

Gia stopped in front of the man, doing a very obvious and thorough head-to-toe-and-back check. The pilot grinned, the corner of his dark brown eyes crinkled, and he gave her a deep and delicious, "Thank you for flying with us."

Gia actually visibly quivered in her very-inappropriate-for-flying high-heeled boots.

After a few seconds of Gia remaining in place, the pilot lifted his dark eyebrows and his grin slipped.

Mac could almost understand the look of fear the man was obviously trying to mask. Gia was probably looking at him like he was a chocolate lava cake and she was on a strict sugar-free diet.

"Gia," Mac warned her in a hiss.

Gia dismissed Mac with a wave of her hand over her shoulder.

However, Mac saying the woman's name had drawn the pilot's attention. *Oops.*

"I hope you fly with us again," the man said in a dismissing tone to Gia as he stared at Mac. His dark, full, very kissable lips widened into an open smile. It was big, seemed genuine and was so bright, Mac almost lifted a hand to shade her eyes.

Damn.

"Of course," Gia grumbled and violently yanked her rolling carry-on out of the plane and onto the ramp with a curse. "It's those damn freckles."

As Mac moved forward with her eyes glued to his, she watched in fascination as words began to spill from those luscious lips. "Thank you for—"

She gasped as she got slammed in the back and knocked forward. The pilot caught her before she accidently face-planted on him.

"Come on! I have a flight to catch," griped the man behind her.

With a hand to Mac's elbow and another on the handle of her

carry-on, the pilot tugged her to his side so the impatient man could pass. It was so tight in that spot that Mac felt the need to suck in her gut just to squeeze in.

"You okay?"

Holy moly, that voice. Deep, rich, smooth as blackstrap molasses. Now *that* could be compared to Barry White.

Heat spiraled through her...

"Want to see my cockpit?"

...then exploded from her center.

"Let's get out of the way," he suggested.

Mac's mouth gaped open and before she could respond, she and her bag were pulled into the cockpit. There wasn't much room in there, either. Especially after he closed the door behind her.

In fact, they were almost chest to chest. Except that wasn't exactly true since he was much taller than her. Much taller. Chest to stomach was more like it. And he was pretty damn broad shouldered to have to work in such a tight spot.

He cleared his throat and her gaze rose, landing just above his collar on his pronounced Adam's apple.

It bobbed when he said, "Let me introduce myself. I'm Damon Brooks."

Mac closed her mouth, swallowed, then told his sexy throat, "Mac."

"Mac?"

She closed her eyes for a second and shook her head, trying to knock some sense back into it. "MacKenzie Donovan."

She finally lifted her eyes, to see not only his grin, but amusement making his dark brown eyes twinkle.

"The name fits you," he murmured.

She tilted her head and grinned back. "So does yours."

His lips twitched. "Touché." He studied her for a long moment, then his brows pinned together. "You look familiar."

It didn't seem to be a pick-up line, he seemed serious.

"Maybe I have a doppelganger out there somewhere. You probably see thousands of people every year with your jet-setting ways." Though, she only hoped her doppelganger had much better hair.

"Hmm. No," he said slowly, concentrating even harder on her face which made her want to squirm. "No, I've seen you somewhere before. Not as a passenger. Do you live in Boston?"

Should she answer that? How many pilots were serial killers? She should ask Google, just to be safe. "In the area, yes. Do you?"

"I do. Maybe I've seen you in the city."

"I try to avoid the city." Which was true.

"Me, too. I prefer quiet when I'm not working." He put his hand on his jaw and tapped his finger against his enticing, broad, very suckable lips. Especially that bottom one.

Damn, she'd like to tug on that one with her teeth. After sucking on it, of course.

His head snapped up and his eyes widened. "Now I remember! I messaged you and never got a response back."

"Umm... You messaged me?" What was he talking about?

"You aren't on the Boston Singles app?"

Oh shit. Should she deny it? "I... umm..."

His delicious lips flattened out as he pulled something from his back pocket. Crap. His cell phone.

Mac's heart raced as she watched as his long, neatly manicured fingers tapped at the screen. A few swipes up, a few swipes right and *voila*! her own face was looking back at her. She was staring at her own profile pic on Boston Singles.

Busted.

At least that pic was taken on a good hair day. Though, every freckle across her face beamed like a melanin beacon.

"Umm..."

"That's you." His tone held a tinge of accusation.

"Umm..." *Shit.* "I didn't want to be on the app," she said quickly.

"My best friend forced me to. Don't take it personally, I haven't messaged anyone back, not just you."

"So, you remember my message."

Crap. She didn't. She hadn't wanted to join a singles app. Gia had forced her to over a year ago. After the last alpha-hole she was dating dumped her.

She had only joined to shut her up. While she had skimmed some of the messages—most were unbelievably inappropriate—she never responded to any of them. Even the hot guys who had a decent profile. She just didn't believe they were real. Otherwise, why would they need to be on a singles app? If their profile wasn't fake, wouldn't they have been snapped up by a woman already?

Of course, they would. Or so she told herself to push aside the guilt of ignoring all three hundred of her private messages. Or it had been three hundred the last she checked. Which was months ago.

A couple more swipes later, he held out his phone to her. She reluctantly took it and read his message.

It was well-written, polite and a dick pic wasn't attached to it. A rarity.

The grammar and spelling were on point. Another rarity.

Without looking at him, she clicked on his profile and scanned it quickly. Oh yeah. Another profile she felt was too good to be true.

I mean, c'mon, a hot pilot who was single? Pfsst.

She lifted her head and handed his phone back to him. His long fingers brushed against hers, causing a shiver to slide down her spine. "If it's any comfort, I did notice you. There are so many fake profiles..." *Lame.* "Then I noticed on your profile you were bi and open about it." She *did* remember that part. That had definitely stood out in his description.

He arched a brow. "You're against a man being open sexually?"

"No, but there are enough women out there I need to live up to, I don't need to add in the rest of the population. I'd go into any date with a bisexual man at a disadvantage, since you'd be comparing me to both sexes."

His mouth dropped open for a second, then he tipped his head back and laughed.

Mac licked her lips as she watched his throat arch and his wide shoulders shake with each deep, sexy chuckle. When he was done, he asked, "That's what you think?"

She shrugged and gave him a small smile. "That's what my neurosis thinks. Since I never dated someone who is bi, I can't confirm that notion."

"You never dated anyone who is bi *that you know of.*"

Good point. "True. You got me on that." She quickly took inventory of the men she had dated all the way back to junior high. Had any of them been bi? *Hmm.*

He glanced at his cell phone again. "Sorry to cut this enlightening conversation short, but I have another flight I need to prepare for soon." He tucked his phone back into his back pocket of his well-fitted uniform slacks. The ones that hugged what looked like very powerful thighs.

Thighs she'd never see, or feel, or ride. Damn it.

She went to turn but he grabbed her shoulder, holding her in place.

His fingers squeezed slightly. "I'd like to finish this conversation at a later time."

Not a question, but it sounded more like a demand. Even so, what was there to continue?

"Possibly over coffee." The corners of his eyes crinkled. "Or a dirty martini."

How had he known?

"When it comes to martinis, I normally prefer lemon drops. It's Gia who likes them dirty." Mac cringed on how that came out.

He dipped his head, still amused. "Lemon drops, then."

"I don't know. Maybe."

"I need your number."

Again, not a request, but a demand. However, she wanted to ask, why? Why was he interested in her? She was boring. And not nearly as gorgeous or exotic looking as Gia. Why had he focused his attention on her instead? Gia was the one always on the search for a man. Or *men*, to be truthful, since she was determined to find not only one, but two.

"You can send me a message on the app," she suggested.

"The app you don't respond to messages on," he said flatly.

Yes, that was the one. "I'll turn on the push notifications for your profile so I don't miss yours."

He clearly didn't believe her, which was confirmed when he asked, "Promise?"

No. "Yes, I promise."

His eyes slid to the closed door. "Your friend is probably worried about you."

Not worried, but waiting impatiently. Probably with her phone glued to her ear as she tapped the toe of her high-heeled leather boot with annoyance. Or Gia could be flirting with any handsome guy in her vicinity.

It could go either way with her.

Damon—it was nice to think of him as something other than "the pilot"—reached past her and unlatched the cockpit door, swinging it open.

The pull of his uniform shirt over what seemed to be some well-developed muscles caught her attention. Especially with the way the crisp white fabric emphasized the deep color of his skin. She lost her train of thought.

Until he smiled in amusement once again.

Damn.

She shook herself mentally. "It was nice meeting you. And thank you for landing the plane safely."

His lips twitched. "Anytime." He lifted a hand.

Mac stared at it stupidly as it hung there between them. What... *Oh.*

Good lord, she was losing it. She clasped his hand and his fingers curled warmly around hers. Those long, strong fingers. Instead of shaking hers, he gave her hand a firm squeeze.

Something deep inside her squeezed, too.

Then he went through his spiel, his deep voice washing over her, "Thank you for flying the friendly skies with us. It's been a pleasure to serve you and I hope to service you in the future," making her squeeze her thighs together and her nipples bead painfully.

Wait. "What?"

"I said I hope you fly with us again."

Before she melted in an embarrassing puddle at his feet, he released her hand and then raised it in invitation for her to exit the cockpit.

She unstuck her feet and moved forward after grabbing her carry-on's handle. As she yanked her bag with her, he called out, "Hey, MacKenzie…"

The plane was now empty except for some cleaning staff who were collecting garbage and putting away blankets and pillows. She twisted her head to glance back at him.

"I really want to get to know you."

While that sounded sincere, she still wondered why. She could only nod in answer.

"And I want you to get to know me," he added.

Wasn't that how it worked?

"To facilitate that, I'll give you this little tidbit that isn't in my profile."

Oh, here it comes. He was going to tell her how many inches was packed into his pants. That's what most of the app's messages she had received included. Some of the men even held a ruler next to their erections in the photos they sent to prove they weren't lying.

"My favorite color is red."

Her hand automatically went up to her hair, but she dropped it quickly when she realized what she was doing. A wave of heat burst into her cheeks.

Damn.

She took one last look at him to add him to her memory bank for later.

Grae and Gryff, move the hell over.

Get A Daring Journey here: http://www.books2read.com/ ADaringJourney

Thank you for reading Dare to Surrender. If you enjoyed Eli, Grant and Olivia's story, please consider leaving a review at your favorite retailer and/or Goodreads to let other readers know. Reviews are always appreciated and just a few words can help an independent author like me tremendously!

Want to read a sample of my work? Download a sampler book here: BookHip.com/MTQQKK

The Selkie Prince's Fated Mate *

The Selkie Prince & His Omega Guard *

The Selkie Prince's Unexpected Omega *

The Selkie Prince's Forbidden Mate *

The Selkie Prince's Secret Baby *

ABOUT THE AUTHOR

JEANNE ST. JAMES is a USA Today bestselling romance author who loves an alpha male (or two). She was only thirteen when she started writing and her first paid published piece was an erotic story in Playgirl magazine. Her first romance novel, Banged Up, was published in 2009. She is happily owned by farting French bulldogs. She writes M/F, M/M, and M/M/F ménages.

Want to read a sample of her work? Download a sampler book here: BookHip.com/MTQQKK

To keep up with her busy release schedule check her website at www.jeannestjames.com or sign up for her newsletter: http://www.jeannestjames.com/newslettersignup

www.jeannestjames.com
jeanne@jeannestjames.com

Newsletter: http://www.jeannestjames.com/newslettersignup
Jeanne's Down & Dirty Book Crew: https://www.facebook.com/groups/JeannesReviewCrew/
TikTok: https://www.tiktok.com/@jeannestjames

facebook.com/JeanneStJamesAuthor
amazon.com/author/jeannestjames
instagram.com/JeanneStJames
bookbub.com/authors/jeanne-st-james
goodreads.com/JeanneStJames
pinterest.com/JeanneStJames

Get a FREE Sampler Book

This book contains the first chapter of a variety of my books. This will give you a taste of the type of books I write and if you enjoy the first chapter, I hope you'll be interested in reading the rest of the book.

Each book I list in the sampler will include the description of the book, the genre, and the first chapter, along with links to find out more. I hope you find a book you will enjoy curling up with!

Get it here: BookHip.com/MTQQKK

www.ingramcontent.com/pod-product-compliance
Lightning Source LLC
Chambersburg PA
CBHW051301210726
48287CB00002B/617